9-2023

## DATE DUE

PRINTED IN U.S.A.

**Hayner PLD/Large Print**
Overdues .10/day. Max fine cost of
item. Lost or damaged item: additional
$5 service charge.

# The Butterfly Effect

Center Point
Large Print

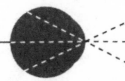

**This Large Print Book carries the
Seal of Approval of N.A.V.H.**

# The Butterfly Effect

Rachel Mans McKenny

CENTER POINT LARGE PRINT
THORNDIKE, MAINE

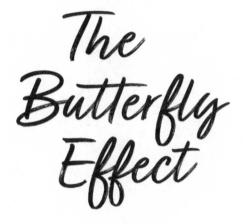

To my parents for their love and support
(and for not commenting on the
amount of swears in this book)
and in memory of my brother, Jesse

"It might help . . . to redefine the rules by which we coexist with the living world. Can love of insects make a difference? I am not sure. But I would like to believe that it does."

—Thomas Eisner, *For Love of Insects*

# PART ONE

## Winter

"By and large, most insects are solitary, indifferent to the company of others of their species except during mating and chance encounters."

—Rick Imes, *The Practical Entomologist*

# CHAPTER ONE

What was it to know the birthday of a woman you hated? While she was waiting at the airport terminal, the notification had appeared this morning on Greta's Facebook, with the nudge: *Wish Meg a Happy Birthday!* If Greta had known it was Meg's birthday, would she have scrounged up a little less antipathy last night when hearing her voice on the other end of the long-distance call? No, probably not. Meg shouldn't get credit for being born. She had been as responsible for that event as Greta was of flying this plane. This plane and the birth canal were both about delivering people somewhere they didn't want to be from someplace much warmer.

Meg's voice on the phone—*Happy early birthday, Meg,* Greta hadn't said—was a rocky sea, too wet and tumbling to get the full story. An aneurysm. Greta processed that much. Danny was alive and asleep. Meg said she would handle it.

It was a decision not to trust her, and Greta made that decision.

Greta stared out the window on the last leg of her journey. Twenty-four hours ago, she had been knee-deep in rain forest mud, watching butterflies circle above like a living mobile. Twenty-four hours ago, her mind was turning over the problem of how to keep their microscopic markers on butterfly wings in the humidity. It was nothing like tracking Monarchs back home in Iowa. Her research focused on the sex lives of glasswing butterflies or, rather, what their migratory patterns and reproduction said about global warming. Out of the one hundred and twenty thousand described species of Lepidoptera, she had fallen in love with the glasswing's clear scales and distinctive markings.

Bug sex had satisfyingly specific terms—partially why studying it fascinated Greta so much. "Lekking"—that term described the communal release of glasswing butterfly pheromones, one of the species' unique features. Butterflies were cheap dates, easy lays. A quick suck of nectar, a little body spray, and down to business. They settled down on a couch of leaves, their abdomens touching. "Butt to butt," Larry—Dr. Almond—had joked on their first day in the field. Butterfly mating didn't have the intense staring into the eyes that human romance required. Male butterflies also had specific body parts—valvae—which hooked the female during copulation. Luckily, also not comparable to human genitalia.

There were some direct comparisons to be made. Butterfly mating didn't take long. Like human mating, at least in Greta's limited experience. Insect peni were called "aedeagus," which combined the Greek words for "genitals" and "to lead," and hell if she hadn't met many men that led with those too. She thought about Meg and wondered if there was a female version of valvae that could trap someone in a relationship?

The glasswings' limited range made them a perfect test case for the changing climate. Or at least she hoped that would prove to be the case. Two weeks into her semester-long research trip, and now this airplane ride home. Two weeks was about enough time to collect one-twentieth of the data she needed for her dissertation.

Danny was sick, Meg had told her.

Greta took a drink of her Pepsi and returned it to the tray table.

Danny was hurt, Meg had said.

Another sip. The men in the seats next to her held hands on the armrest, the fingers of one lightly unclasping from the other while he fell more deeply asleep.

Danny was in the hospital, and Greta should come home if—in case—

Greta's hands shook, or maybe it was the plane. Probably turbulence, and her Pepsi sloshed a few sickly droplets onto the carpet.

Greta leaned over with a napkin to wipe up her mess, only to find two things. One, airplane carpet was disgusting. Its patterns must be designed to cover stains like what she was trying to rub out. Two, there was a caterpillar.

"Oh, hi," she whispered to it. Classically defined, it was a perfectly ordinary *Lophocampa modesta*, but current circumstances also identified it correctly as a "distraction."

Greta angled her boot to cage the spiny yellow caterpillar between the wall and the anchored seat ahead of her. Someday, this caterpillar would become a moth with small, dark patches spread over the veins of its tan wings. Unlike its butterfly brethren, moths fold their wings to hide their abdomen, something like the plane they were currently on. While his future dun color would be easy to pass over, now he was bright yellow against the dust-blue industrial carpet.

A plan formed in Greta's mind. First, she drank the remainder of her Pepsi. Both passengers next to her were now deeply asleep. She reached cautiously across the lap of the man in the center seat to take his cup of melting ice and tip its contents into the almost-empty cup of tomato juice on the aisle seat's tray table. Greta took the two empty cups and moved her foot slowly to uncage the caterpillar. It froze, but Greta didn't. She caught it between the cups and lifted.

When she pulled the two cups off the floor, she saw the caterpillar suspended on the lip of one, standing astride it like a tightrope walker. Now, the dilemma. Greta knew the airplane was beginning to lose altitude, from the changes in the view from her window, the pressure in her ears, and the roiling turn in her stomach. Now that she had it trapped, she wasn't sure how to keep it that way while exiting the airplane. Having gone to all this trouble, she wasn't going to leave it on the plane, like a pretzel wrapper. If nothing else, her friend Max would find it funny, and that was worth something. She needed someone to find something funny today. She arranged her hands so that one palm could "kiss" both cups together, and reached for the call button. Maybe the flight attendant had tape.

The caterpillar waited patiently with her by the baggage carousel. Its fuzzy head swiveled against the plastic cups, but it didn't seem to be in pain or distress. Whether insects got distressed was not really up for debate. Distress was mostly a human concern—humans had a million ways to be miserable. Generally, insects were either eating, fighting, flighting, or mating. After ten minutes, Greta's two maroon rolling bags appeared. Though technically old, they were nearly brand new. They had been high school graduation gifts from her father, but—surprise surprise—he hadn't lived long enough to see how little she had used them. Until now, she had never really gone anywhere besides a few weeklong research expeditions during undergrad. Those had been by car, with light packing emphasized. She had barely needed the items in these newish bags, and now she would unpack them.

Unpack them *somewhere*. Not her apartment, she realized, which had been sublet. Where she would stay should have been the first question on her mind, but it wasn't. The fact that her residency in Costa Rica had been paid for and her bank account was pretty much nonexistent only now occurred to her.

Fuck.

From Greta's spot by the car rentals, she watched the snow flutter past the window in lopsided flakes. She hadn't expected to return before June and had left her coat with the rest of her stuff in storage. Double fuck.

After a warning text, Max pulled alongside the curb. She saw his bare arms through the window. It figures he was too stubborn to put on a sweater since he didn't have to leave his car. His T-shirt was black with white lettering that just said, "No." Greta shouldered her backpack and trailed the rolling bags behind her. She ran as fast as she could, but the hatchback's trunk wasn't open to receive luggage. She tapped on it with an open palm, then a fist, and finally the latch released. By the end of the procedure, her ears were cold and her hair was wet with melting snow. Max unlocked the passenger door quickly for her, at least.

Max checked his mirrors and merged just as a

police officer seemed to get interested in them. No lingering at the terminal. "Flights okay?"

Max had, she noticed, gotten a trim so that the hair behind his ears was much shorter than the top, which stood suspended. His brown eyes tracked the falling snow from underneath his hair's dark, tamed wave. She was certain that Max spent more on hair products than she did.

"I found a *Lophocampa modesta* caterpillar on my last one and trapped it between two cups. The flight attendant got me tape to hold the cups together, and you should have seen her face when she saw what I needed it for—" Then Greta broke off, swearing. "I left it by the baggage carousel. God, I just had so much in my hands—"

"So you captured it?"

She felt a chide in his voice. "I thought I could bring it back to the lab. I wasn't going to let it run wild or anything."

"You joke, but maybe that's how Mothra really happened."

Coming off the airport road toward downtown Des Moines, the slush pounded against the sides of the car on the turn. "I thought it would be funny to bring home."

Max laughed. "I mean, it is, but don't you think it's funnier that you left it there by the arrivals gate?"

"Okay, you're right."

Max glanced quickly at her. "Whoa, whoa,

19

whoa. Wait. Do I get an award? I think that is the first time you've ever said I was right about something."

Rather than dignify that with a response, Greta watched Des Moines's skyline appear and disappear behind closer buildings. Even though she'd left behind brown grass only two weeks ago, the passing landscape now had a thick blanket of snow. "You know, Gary might have wanted to eat it. Apologize to him for me."

"I will, and you owe him one." Max said, keeping his tone fake-serious, but his eyebrow raise gave him away. Gary was a six-inch whip scorpion that Max kept as a pet.

"Oh, you bet. Next bug I get, it's his."

The traffic moved by them on both sides. Max always rode the middle lane when they drove on three-lane highways, and it drove her crazy.

They merged onto I-35 North and passed the first Ankeny exit. Max turned the radio to NPR, and the hourly news included a weather report. Breaking news: it sucked. Greta's stomach gave a loud rumble. She had forgotten to eat anything before she left the last airport, and had turned down the in-flight snack. Flying made her feel bad enough without adding food to the equation. The gurgle sounded again, and Greta wanted to hush herself, but then her stomach growled a third time, just as audibly.

"Want me to hit a drive-thru somewhere?" Max asked.

Greta shook her head and then remembered that Max's gaze focused on the road. "No, I'm okay."

Silence broken, Max asked, "What happened?"

Greta took a deep breath and was glad to not make eye contact. "Meg told me Danny was teaching band. One of the kids said that Danny's face drooped, and then the next moment he was on the floor."

"I'm so sorry," Max said. The windshield wipers collected and flicked off lines of wet snow. The rubber wiper treads made soft squeaks in the sudden silence. "Did you know?"

"What do you mean?"

He pressed his lips together, embarrassed. "I don't have a sibling, and I definitely don't have a twin, but did you feel like you knew before you, uh, knew?"

It was one of those moments where she seemed like a worse person telling the truth than she did constructing a lie. As it was, it felt like she and her twin didn't even hold one language in common anymore, let alone an emotional, cross-continental bond. When Danny had moved back to Ames after their dad's death, they ate Sunday dinner as a way of mourning. His apartment, then hers. A seesaw of traded grief. Then dinners were habit, less sad. He was suddenly just there, like the smell of home was always there, but not something she noticed until she had been away for a while. Maybe that was the closest to twin sense they'd ever gotten as adults. But then Meg happened, and it was like any chance of healing had vanished. No. She hadn't felt some extrasensory zap, some cosmic warning signal. "No. I felt the same, except better because I was there. And this is—"

"Iowa in winter?" he offered.

"Fucking Iowa in winter."

Max took the familiar sloping off-ramp to Ames, and the line of hotels on the highway welcomed her back. The radio was on, but she wasn't listening, not really. The mental wall she had built between the possibilities and life as it had been yesterday was crumbling the nearer they got to the hospital. They didn't say anything else until the car arrived in front of Mary Greeley. "Text me if you need anything," Max said. His shirt said "No," but his eyes said something else. His worried look made her feel even worse.

She tried to pay him for the ride. After some awkward fumbling, with "no" and "please," he accepted the rumpled twenty-dollar bill from her wallet.

The hospital glowered at her from its four-story height. Maybe it was judging her mud-caked boots or her smell. Between the airport dirt and the sweat from yesterday's research, Greta wished she could have showered before she saw her brother—too late for that. An hour after being picked up from the airport, she climbed into an elevator. Ten hours after jumping onto her first airplane, she checked in at hospital reception.

Greta hadn't seen Danny in over a year, let alone his girlfriend—fiancée now. She saw their relationship status change on the digital landscape of their lives: *"Hey guys, big news from us!"* A few weeks later she received a save-the-date postcard for October, as if the whole month was theirs. On the back, they clarified that only one Friday would be required—October 5. In the picture, Danny's head tilted toward Meg's like a magnet, but that wasn't the pull Greta had felt. Repulsion, in this case, wasn't because she and Meg were too similar. Greta had been surprised to get an invitation at all. The last time she and Danny had talked, she'd been drunk—and honest. Greta said it then, all out in the open, when he told her—he was also drunk—about the ring in his pocket saved for the right time. She'd asked how he could make vows with someone who entered the relationship as a cheater.

Greta should have called Danny sometime in the last year. She should have gone over for Christmas. She knew what she should have done, like getting the answers corrected on an exam.

That didn't make dealing with the aftereffects of her pride any easier.

The hospital was a sterile fantasy world of white coats and white walls and white-sneakered nurses. People walked with hurried steps past the white door to the probably white rooms.

Meg stood near the oval nursing station. She was unrecognizable from the posed and prettified version of herself on the save-the-date card or her filtered social media posts. She wore no makeup to cover the line of large freckles over the bridge of her nose. Meg's arms folded across her pink sweatshirt, and her blonde hair was wrapped on top of her head in a messy, damp knot. When she noticed Greta, Meg took a step forward, arms uncrossing and raising like an offer. Greta crossed her own arms in response. She didn't need a hug, especially not from Meg.

Meg's eyebrows creased as she stepped back again. "I just got here too. I was here during the surgery but had to run home to shower and send some e-mails and—"

"Why can't we see him?"

Maybe the doctor is in with him," Meg said. She gestured. "They've been so helpful. I know they'll let us know what to do."

The nurse in front of them cradled a phone to his ear and held up a finger.

"Excuse me," Greta said, tapping on the counter.

The nurse's eyebrows knit together as he

more emphatically waved the finger. He finally hung up, then spent a few seconds adjusting his paperwork before acknowledging them. "Yes?"

"Danny Oto."

The nurse pointed to a line of chairs against the nearest white wall. "If you'll just wait—"

Greta's jaw set as though in concrete. "Daniel Oto. Where is he?"

"You need to sit until they're ready for you," the nurse said calmly.

Meg moved toward the chairs, but Greta planted herself, elbows on the counter and gaze level. The nurse purposefully didn't look at her. He was close enough that she could smell the hand sanitizer on his desk. After a minute, a door down the hall opened, and a middle-aged female nurse peeked out. "Here to see Daniel?" she asked. After they nodded, she waved them inside.

"Cleaning him up a bit," she said cheerfully. "The doctor completed his hourly eval, and things seem stable."

The word "seem" hit Greta hard. "Seem" was slippery, poetic, metaphorical, and shifting. She liked certainty. The scientific method required testing a hypothesis with multiple trials, multiple scenarios to find consistency or, more often, not. But they were right. Danny didn't seem like Danny. He didn't look like he was sleeping, not at all. His unconsciousness masked his face, whitewashed it. The hospital had shaved his head as smooth as linoleum. Danny's features were misplaced without his hair—a map with the city names erased. His broken pieces were inside, but the wrongness reflected out from every part of him. Cords and tubes connected him to machines, machines that got closer to him than she could. In the movies, the machines beeped or printed out long slips of paper, but these flashed tiny lights like semaphore she didn't understand.

"You can get closer to him, if you'd like," the nurse said.

But Greta didn't want to. Now that she was here, she had lost her bravery. Meg must not have wanted to get closer either, because she stayed near the door, leaning on the jamb in a too-casual, print-model way.

Their father's dog tag lay on the metal table next to Danny's bed. Greta had found it in a box of belongings and given it to Danny on the day of the funeral. He usually wore it, and Greta wished he wore it now, like a magic amulet. As a child she remembered playing with the tag while they read bedtime stories. Leaning into that cove between their father's arms and chest, where the dog tag hung, had always made Greta feel safe. She tried to press hard enough to imprint the raised letters onto her skin to save for later. Now, she fingered the dog tag gently, then touched Danny's cheek. She willed some of their dad's strength to rub off on him.

After ten minutes, the doctor entered and shared some numbers that didn't mean anything to Greta. "The fact that he survived it is a good sign," the doctor concluded. It took most of Greta's self-control not to say, "Duh."

"Things will be touch-and-go for a while," the doctor said.

*Touch what and go where?* Abstractions didn't comfort.

The doctor pulled out a grayscale image of a brain. "Here's the MRI, and this part"—he gestured to a white portion, a blob half-hollow and half-defined—"this is the aneurysm. We stabilized and cauterized the area."

"And he'll be okay?" Meg asked. She was as pale as Danny.

"He should recover." The doctor closed the folder after tucking the MRI printout back inside. "There are no guaranteed outcomes, but the first responders got him to the hospital quickly, well within the golden hour. He might wake soon. In the meantime, check with the nurse on duty, Craig. We need some paperwork filled out to continue treatment."

Craig, of the glare and hand sanitizer, had the forms ready for them.

"Divide and conquer," Meg said, halving the stack and handing it to her. Some paperwork translated to half a tree. Hadn't Greta just been in an actual rain forest less than a day ago? She pictured the carcass of a mossy tree on her lap, her eyes moving over the words on the top page without really reading.

The stack of hospital forms didn't answer any questions—would Danny die? What would happen now? It only posed a hundred that Greta didn't know the answer to. Next of kin? She assumed herself, the only literal kin that Danny had. Insurance? Somehow, the thrilling world of health insurance hadn't come up in their dinners. Greta glanced over at Meg, whose pen danced across the pages. She wondered if Meg knew the name of Danny's primary care physician. Greta sure as hell didn't. She was positive that Meg didn't know the name of his pediatrician. They had both gone to Dr. DeVries, who gave out lollipops in exchange for shots and usually sucked on one himself during examinations. Dr. DeVries had died ten years ago. For all Greta knew, Danny hadn't been to a doctor in years. She hadn't. It wasn't that odd for a healthy twenty-something-year-old.

But if he hadn't been healthy.

If a check-up could have caught something.

Greta's head swam, and she stood. The hospital forms splashed onto the carpet, flying off in every direction. Meg peered up from her paperwork. "You okay?" Her gentle tone threw Greta off balance.

"Yeah," Greta said. She took a deep breath,

then knelt to collect the papers. After a minute, she had it together again—the paperwork, if not her thoughts.

Danny didn't wake before they left.

Meg dropped Greta off at the campus hotel, not exiting the car to help hoist her roller bags or backpack. Meg's car kicked up snow onto Greta's pants as it pulled away. Greta murmured a curse under her fogging breath.

In her room, she showered and changed into a fresh set of clothes from her bags. She wanted to wear her fluffy slippers down to the food court, but knew she'd have to walk through the wet slush from everyone else's boots. Instead, she slid on a clean pair of Nikes.

The Memorial Union hummed with dinner activity. Greta stood in the long line for brand-name Chinese and ordered too much. She brought it up the three flights of stairs into her hotel room for fear of being seen by a student or, worse, someone from her lab.

The food had cooled down by the time she got to her room, but still tasted salty and sweet. She ate every bite of it, dipping the egg rolls in the leftover General Tso's sauce. The cashier had tucked two fortune cookies in the bag, assuming charitably that Greta planned to share or that Greta needed more luck than usual. Greta ate both cookies too. When she finished, she lay back on the bed and eyed the clock. This time yesterday she had been on a night walk in the rain forest. The cloud forest: magical and distant and everything that wasn't central Iowa in January. She came back to find Meg's call waiting for her.

The hotel room smelled of a too-hot furnace, burning dust. As she settled under the thin comforter, she reimagined her small room back in Costa Rica. She could be back there in a matter of days once this was sorted out. The constant sweater of humid rain forest air was preferable to Iowa's winter chill. Even the word "Iowa" tugged her away from the mental picture of paradise. Ames, her city, sounded like an arrow shot left of its target. As she closed her eyes, the reality of this room's noises fell on her. No orchestra of insects and no birds conversing, only the sound of the furnace and the faraway voices of students accosted her. And now, now Danny was sick. Dying? Already dead since she saw him three hours ago?

Call Martha or not? That question hovered over everything else.

Meg wouldn't know to; Meg probably thought their mother was dead. Meg had been in the picture for only the last three years of their fifteen-year estrangement. Meg couldn't understand the missing part of an equation she'd never fully seen. Meg couldn't miss someone she never met, couldn't mourn the memory of Martha before. But also, Greta knew, Meg might understand Martha's leaving—the language of unfaithfulness—and that would be unbearable.

# CHAPTER TWO

Three days after the aneurysm, Danny regained consciousness. The nurse called, and Greta had to interrupt her strenuous schedule of sitting on the hotel bed staring at the wall and pretending she wasn't there.

Everything in her had wanted to return to Costa Rica now, but she'd made the wrong choice with Dad's heart attack five years ago. Danny, the good twin, left college in Ohio. Danny came home. Danny held Dad's hand. Danny missed his final exams, and Danny slept by his father's bedside. Danny found Dad dead the next morning. Greta? Greta was in the lab, only ten miles from the hospital, and assumed they had more time. She was sure she couldn't live now with another ghost at her shoulder, one with her birthday and who had half her childhood wrapped up in his brain. She couldn't lose Danny.

But thinking of Danny made her cringe. The problem was that she now had too much time to think of Danny. No job, no energy to call Max, and no desire to study, for once. Besides the physical baggage she had brought back from Costa Rica, which lay scattered around her hotel room, she pictured the emotional baggage flung there too. Fifteen years of it since their mother Martha left. Five years since their father died. Three years since Meg did whatever Meg did to Danny.

*Relationships—what a joke.*

A week, Greta had promised Larry Almond, her advisor. Then she could pack her real baggage and get back on the plane to resume her research. He had been all confidence and concern since Danny's hospitalization. Larry had even offered her some airline miles for her return trip.

But now, Danny was regaining consciousness, and Greta was here to see it. Crisis averted. The research could wait a week. It wasn't like the butterflies would miss her.

As she leaned against the back of the hospital elevator, Greta saw Meg enter the lobby. She made eye contact with Greta as she ran toward the door, its jaws already half closed. Meg tripped in her kitten heels but made it into the elevator in time to trigger the sensor. The door paused, then flew back again. Meg glared at Greta and punched the already-lit button for Danny's floor. "You could have hit the 'Open' button," she muttered.

"I could have." Greta refrained from mentioning that she hadn't hit the 'Close' button either.

Their rush had been in vain. By the time they got to Danny's hospital room, he was sleeping again.

"It takes a lot of effort to heal," the nurse said. Her reassuring tone failed to reassure. "But while you're both here, you should think about checking in with the social worker."

The last social worker Greta had met came after Martha left. That one had a clipboard and a clear sense of self-righteousness that stank as much as her raspberry body spray. "Your mother ran away?" the stranger had asked, sitting in their father's usual spot. He had been in bed since Martha left. "How does that make you feel?"

Danny had brought the social worker a plate of Oreos—a fourteen-year-old host at his finest. When the social worker left, she dropped a carbon copy of her report on the coffee table. "Continued assessment recommended."

Greta had crossed her arms then, and she did so now. "No thanks."

"Really, Nadine is great. She'll help get you set up with services." The nurse said the word "services" with relish, a prize car on a game show.

Meg checked the time on her phone. "I've still got half an hour of lunch," she said.

"Have fun," Greta said, walking toward the elevator.

"No," Meg said. "Come on. This is for Danny. We need to be a team."

Teaming up with Meg on anything was laughable. Perky Meg, whose voice sometimes had that rising, questioning inflection even when she wasn't asking something. Meg, who coached cheerleading. Meg, who used words like "squee" in her social media posts. And anyway, Greta did not do teams. She had faked her period to sit out of dodgeball in seventh grade and had asked to opt out of group projects in college. She worked alone or took the F, in the case of gym class. But she couldn't take an F for Danny, not when he was all she had left. "Fine."

Ten minutes later and two floors down, a woman with thin, dark glasses and a gray ponytail ushered Greta and Meg into a small room; it was little more than a closet with a desk inside. She offered her hand for both to shake. Meg took it, clutching like the woman was a handrail and she was falling. Greta did not shake hands; she was not a dog or a politician.

The social worker gestured at two chairs that sat so closely they were nearly stacked. After sitting, Greta scooted hers as far away as she could without ramming into the door.

"I'm Daniel's case worker, Nadine," the social worker said after they sat down. "The doctors already talked to you?"

Meg nodded. Greta crossed her arms.

"Well, I just like to talk to the family right away to ensure that we get records straight and that everyone understands patient rights."

Nadine pulled open a desk drawer. She flipped through paperwork, and a moment later she handed Meg another stack of pages and a few brochures from the plastic caddies mounted on the wall around her. The social worker lectured for the next ten minutes like they were about to be tested. Meg scribbled notes on a piece of paper while Greta stared at the woman's desk. Even with so little space in the room, she'd filled every inch of desk with football tchotchkes in the Iowa State college colors of cardinal and gold. Little quarterbacks, goal posts. Nadine droned on about insurance—what it covered and what it did not. Rehabilitation programs for brain injury. The Family Medical Leave Act.

Meg interrupted her spiel. "I can get leave from my job to take care of him?"

"There are some restrictions, of course. How long you've worked at your job, etcetera, but yes."

Greta's brain might as well have been a Jell-O mold at a picnic, the kind with little pieces of banana suspended in it. She had spent the past few days moping around the hotel that she couldn't afford, keeping out of the public eye and planning her return trip to Costa Rica. "How long will it take?" It was the first time Greta had spoken.

Nadine turned toward her. "Well, the time line is different for everyone. Once he's released in a week or two, he'll need some rehabilitation. We won't know the full scope until his neurologist, Dr. Traeger, can assess him. It will be a busy few months, though."

Greta should have figured brain injury wouldn't be like a windshield chip, repaired over a lunch break, but the time line of months caught her off guard. "I'm supposed to be out of the country. I'm supposed to be doing research for my dissertation."

Nadine leaned forward, her elbows denting the papers on her desk. She reached a hand across the desk, attempting to touch Greta.

Greta moved her hands out of reach.

Meg cleared her throat and looked sideways at Greta. "How do I apply? For FMLA?"

Nadine adjusted the paperwork and smiled at her. "Just submit a claim to your human resources, along with whatever documentation they require. For spouses—"

"Oh," Meg said. "I mean, we're engaged."

Nadine turned to her computer as if it had just become sentient. She tapped loudly on the keyboard. "I had it down that you were the wife?"

Greta snorted and Meg shook her head.

"You might be his emergency contact, but you wouldn't be allowed to file for FMLA."

"Then who is going to help me?" Meg's voice sounded as thin and reedy as she was.

Neither Nadine nor her computer had an answer for that.

Meg glanced at Greta, and in that look Greta sensed an entire rain forest receding into the mist.

The administrative wing of the hospital smelled less like ammonia than the floor Danny was on, replaced by a Pine Sol scent that reminded Greta of a retirement home. She and Meg left with brochures. Meg tucked them reverently into her purse and turned to Greta as soon as the door to Nadine's office closed. "So, what are we going to do?"

*"Nothing is certain until you're dead,"* Greta's dad had once told her. And then he'd died and left them, years before he was supposed to. And now what? If death wasn't a certainty here—and it wasn't, thank God—then Greta had responsibility for her twin. For all her preferences to be alone, that loneliness was better as a choice than a forced condition. That still didn't answer the question of what the hell she would do now for money, for data—

"I need a place to stay while I figure out what to do," Greta said.

"The hotel—"

Greta raised an eyebrow. "A *free* place."

Meg's mouth flattened and pulled in at the sides like a minus sign. The last time Danny had lent her money, maybe a year and a half ago, Meg had called. Greta never would have picked up if Meg hadn't called from Danny's phone. As it was, Meg got halfway into a lecture before Greta hung up. The long and short of it, in Meg's opinion, was that if Greta couldn't afford to be in her PhD program and if Greta couldn't afford to have an apartment alone, then Greta needed to make changes. Greta had wanted to hang up earlier, but she'd heard Danny as her advocate in the background. Meg turned away from the phone after he interjected something, but Greta could still hear her. "She should be an adult by now," Meg scolded him. "Let Greta grow up."

She couldn't meet Greta's eye now. "I don't know, Greta. Can't you ask one of your friends?"

Her assumption of the plural as concerned Greta's "friends" was incorrect. "Max lives with his parents. So, no. And I don't want this either," Greta said.

Meg laughed, short and humorless. "As if that makes it better. Tonight, okay? You can stay with me for tonight, but you need to sort it out. Find someplace else."

It only took ten minutes to gather her things from the hotel and check out, which left three hours until Meg would unlock the apartment for her. Meg had to rush back to school to teach her afternoon sections of pre-algebra and geometry and coach the middle-school cheer squad.

*Oh no—mustn't disappoint thirteen-year-old cheerleaders.*

But wasn't that just Meg in a nutshell? Jumping, waving, with tiny Barbie feet permanently pointed inside her pumps. The first time Greta met Meg, she'd had her pegged for a former cheerleader. Meg's arm around Danny's waist, Danny's arm around Meg's shoulder as they walked through the movie theater lobby. Greta walked ten paces behind them, unsure until he turned his head that it really was Danny. Danny with this petite, blonde stranger.

With a few hours to waste and an entire stretch of unplanned months in front of her, Greta loaded her things in the car and walked across campus. The snow from her arrival day had been shoveled into neat walls along the sidewalk. Greta reminded herself to go to her storage unit to retrieve better winter clothes.

The ATRB—Advanced Teaching and Research Building—loomed across from the campus stables. The ATRB was a windowed behemoth, as tall and creatively named as scientists could devise. Housed inside were the labs and offices of the entomology department and some other departments that Greta hadn't explored. A PhD program is a special kind of bubble. While the undergraduate students flitted from building to building across campus, graduate students holed up in a single hallway for six or seven years—educational pupa—and emerged as exhausted academics.

Her education was mostly funded by fieldwork for agricultural companies on pesticide testing, but her dissertation was supposed to be all hers. Now, not only would she lose out on a week—or maybe all—of the research she needed, she'd lost her funding that paid for that corner of heaven. If she was stuck in Ames this semester, she had no salary, and there was an actual laugh track that played in her head when she checked her savings account.

As she walked the hall, it occurred to Greta that she should have called or e-mailed first. Larry had assumed she was returning, and unless Max had blabbed, everyone in the department assumed that she was in Central America. The look on her department chair's face as she caught him by the copy machine said Max had been as good a secret keeper as he was an office mate. Tom Plank was a round man, shorter than Greta (though many men were shorter than Greta). His face appeared even rounder as his mouth gaped open, his eyes stretching from waning crescents to full moons in an instant. He ran her lab, had been the one who'd accepted her into the program all those years ago, and was the person who spread the budget to various projects. She wondered if his shock was worth anything, a pittance for his pity.

"Greta, what the hell are you doing here?"

Greta never could make small talk, so it was just as well he jumped to the main event. In science, there was a reassuringly exact vocabulary. Caterpillars were a good example of this. Caterpillar feces had its own artful term: "frass." Frass. When in the middle of a frassy situation herself, Greta struggled with a simple way to explain. She settled on the catchall: "Family emergency."

Plank's eyes lost their owlish wideness. "Oh, I'm sorry to hear that."

"And it looks like I'll be here for a few months."

The copy machine whirred in the silence of the elapsing minute. Like Larry, still in the rain forest hard at work, Tom had a stake in Greta's research. Only six PhD candidates were meant to defend their dissertations in the next thirty months, and Greta was supposed to be among them. The copy machine finished burping out exams, and Plank turned to Greta. "So what are you going to do?"

"I thought you might have some advice for that." In the optimistic corner of her brain (a very small corner, cordoned off from the rest), she hoped a late staffing issue might necessitate her picking up a class or lab section.

Plank removed the papers from the copier, moving to a counter to staple them into packets. Greta trailed him. "The copy machine can collate and staple for you."

Plank turned back to her, stapler in hand. "Really?"

"Trade you a lab section for the secret," she said. "Or if there's a research assistantship, you know—"

Plank raised an eyebrow and resumed stapling. "Quid pro quo, eh? It's three weeks into the semester. I'm sorry, Greta, but we don't have any classes for you." He straightened his pile of exams. "Plus, I bet Leslie can teach me how to do the copy-machine thingy."

Greta made some pretense about checking her office mailbox, and then turned to go. Plank stopped her before she left. "A piece of advice."

She turned, her hand full of mailers from the local pizza place. "Yeah?"

"Get your emergency sorted out. With the economy like it is, not so many grants coming down the pipe for your type of project. Stay on track."

The words echoed in Greta's head. The work she did was so different from the work of the other PhDs in her lab. It was easy to see the purpose of the PhD candidates' work around her: they would solve huge challenges with global food supply. Her questions were less easily quantified: one butterfly against the unstoppable tide of global climate change. While she studied butterflies, they studied bean beetles. She hatched pupa while they picked at aphids. She could admit that aphids were fascinating. Take reproduction, which was a research area of interest for her (God, how often Danny had riffed on that). Aphids reproduced by a process called parthenogenesis—no males involved in fertilization and all offspring genetically identical to the mother, who birthed them live, tiny clones released into the world.

Thank God that wasn't how humans worked.

Interesting reproductive cycles or not, she couldn't get fully excited about the agricultural applications of her field, even at one of the best agricultural programs in the country. She had fallen in love with butterflies at the same time she had fallen in love with her ex-boyfriend, Brandon, and sadly, an intense interest in butter-flies didn't break up with her when he did.

The ATRB had closed-door offices for the faculty and a series of cubicles for the grad students. She didn't think the layout was supposed to mimic a beehive, but it felt that way. She had two square feet to herself, and if it hadn't been Max in the cubicle next to her, she would have verbally stung whoever it was. The cubicles were quiet, but she knew Max was at his desk before she even turned the corner. He always wore Old Spice. She peeked her head over the top of his divide.

"What is it?" The voice was as grumpy as she remembered it from five days ago. He didn't look up from his laptop. He was streaming an episode of something that was obviously *Star Trek*, but she couldn't catch which series.

"I'm back."

She counted three beats from her greeting to his noticing her. "How's Danny?"

She sat down, rolling her chair close so she could talk to him. Her explanation to Max of the frassy situation included more detail, but by the end of it, she noticed the uncharacteristic appearance of wrinkles between Max's eyebrows.

"Don't pity me," she told him.

The lines disappeared. "Why would I pity you? You didn't have the aneurysm."

Words caught on her tongue. An argument, half formed, but she swallowed it. The muted *Star Trek* episode continued playing on the computer behind Max. She saw a glimpse of Captain Sisko. "You don't get it."

"No, I don't think you do. I hope things go okay for your brother. Can we do anything?"

"Thanks, but I honestly don't know what he needs."

"Just let us know."

It always surprised Greta that Max included his family in his offers. He lived with his parents and had even brought them to departmental picnics. His mother was a short, well-dressed woman who, Greta had noticed, was always smiling. She worked at a bank in town, and Greta assumed it must be part of the job, and mentally thanked God that centipedes never commented that she herself should smile more. Max's father had a more balanced range of facial expressions, in Greta's opinion. After moving from China to Iowa, he got into the business of buying and refinishing dilapidated barn wood to sell to city yuppies aiming to add "country charm" to their homes. While Greta hadn't seen the interior, she had told Max she was surprised to see his house was completely brick. "Brick lasts" was all Max had to say about that.

Max snapped his laptop closed. "I've got to get to the lab. See you around?"

"Maybe not, since I don't have funding."

He started to gather books on his desk, putting them into the canvas satchel he always carried. "You could always apply to Reiman, you know."

She rolled her eyes. "And you know Brandon's in charge over there now."

"It was just a suggestion," Max said, his voice even. "Did I ever tell you about the cockroach lab where I got my undergrad?"

"No. I bet he was a terrible grader."

Max laughed. "In my intro bio class, the professor refused to make us do the frog lab—

you know the one. The pithed frog lab, where they remove the frog's spine but it still reacts to stimuli."

"I remember that one."

"My professor swore that headless cockroaches were a more humane way of performing the experiment."

"Did she guillotine them in front of you?" Greta pictured a cockroach Marie Antoinette.

"No, no. Her TA did it the day before, I heard later." They both sat with that for a moment as current teaching assistants, then Max continued, "It worked as well as any frog could have. It scratched with the leg adjacent to the stimuli. I think it was one of the first times I really thought of an insect like that. Like it could teach you something."

"So?"

"The more I get to know Brandon, the more I think he might have been like that professor."

She didn't say anything, and he slipped by, leaving her with only her ruminations.

That night, she was still contemplating the pullout couch in Danny's apartment, unable to fall asleep. She kept thinking about aphids. Though in the early parts of the year they reproduce asexually, as the season draws to a close, they paired up, laying eggs with each other. Like half of her high school class. Like her parents. Like Danny. Like she and Brandon seemed like they were going to. Maybe. More of the pairing up, less of the offspring.

Damn it all. She had an e-mail to write to her ex-boyfriend and rewriting it thirty times in her head wouldn't get it sent.

# CHAPTER THREE

In the morning, Greta stopped at the hospital. It wasn't that she was creating distractions from the e-mail she needed to write—or at least it wasn't only that. Meg had disappeared by the time Greta woke, and they passed each other at the hospital entrance. "Tag team, I guess," Meg muttered on her way out. Dark circles ringed Meg's eyes, and her pink pencil skirt looked wrinkled. "See you after school."

The recliner next to Danny's bedside still felt warm from Meg's body. Greta stood up when she realized that. It gave her a sense of uncomfortable intimacy, like forced hugs at family reunions. So much about the hospital felt forced. The nurses encouraged them to talk to him. Meg probably had tearful blab sessions, but Greta couldn't do that. The nurses also said that bodily contact could help him gain more consciousness, but Greta couldn't do that either. She wouldn't have touched Danny if he were awake, so why would she now?

As she sat, his eyes fluttered open momentarily, then closed again. She had gotten used to this tease, this promise of awareness. In some ways, it reminded her of backyard campouts as kids, before they moved from their old house.

She had owned a Ranger Rick sleeping bag with a broken zipper; his was a Batman one. During their father's second deployment, she used to beg Martha to let them sleep out every night from May until October. Informal entomology lessons often came through camping. From the heart of firefly season through cicada chirps, Greta hunkered down in that sleeping bag, all the while scratching mosquito bites. In her mind, camping was as close as she could get to her father's lifestyle. Her mother usually acquiesced, at least when it wasn't rainy, and Danny would tag along.

One occasion particularly stood out. They were six years old, and she woke in the middle of the night. Heat lightning streaked the sky, and she'd wet the sleeping bag because of a nightmare. She flipped on the flashlight, and there was Danny. It was the first time she'd ever seen someone else sleep. His eyes roved back and forth behind his closed lids in REM sleep. The whole thing made her wonder what he saw in his dreams that she couldn't. It was the first of many times that Greta had wondered that.

But comas didn't really look like sleep. That was a lie from television. She'd felt like she was on solid scientific ground when the doctor had explained the coma scale to her. Danny's doctors measured his coma based on body movement, ability to open eyes to stimuli, and speech. Comas were measured on a continuum, not like a switch flicked on and off. If anything, Danny's condition reminded her of that episode of *The Next Generation* when a near-future Picard gets sent back in time and ends up on the *Enterprise*. When they bring him to Sick Bay, he flits in and out of consciousness. He moves erratically, can't speak, and can't focus. For future Picard, the cure was catching up with his own time. For Danny, who knew what it was?

As she watched, Danny's mouth twisted and untwisted, and his eyes opened again. They didn't have the focused expression that she was used to seeing in them. With his eyes open, though, she didn't feel as silly talking to him.

"Hey," she said.

He didn't turn to her. The nurse had warned her he wouldn't be able to make sense of sights and sounds, but that didn't stop her from trying again.

"Dan," she said, softly, "if you don't wake up, you'll never get to hear me apologize for being an asshole."

But he didn't stir.

On her way back to the apartment, she stopped by an ATM and checked her account balance. It spoke with all the subtly of a politician. Greta knew she couldn't leave with Danny in his current condition, but living with Meg wasn't a long-term solution. She couldn't put it off any longer. She needed a job, and she needed to complete research, and the only place to combine those interests was the only place in Ames that she didn't want to set foot in.

She had been able to shake the irony of studying Brandon's field of interest after Brandon lost interest in her. He hadn't hooked her with some sex organ, but he had impregnated her with his research interest and then promptly flitted away to a teaching post in New York for a year. Without Brandon, she might have been elbow deep in honeycomb. Research funding looked like the agricultural stalwarts of honeybees and mites, not butterflies. Was it his fault she was in this mess in the first place? They used to have sex with piles of undergraduate lab reports watching from his desk table, and she wondered once, after Brandon left the bed to shower, if there was hormonal transference airborne from their fucking. If a chemical trail was left such that when handed back, the reports would make the student's arm hair prickle.

She would not picture Brandon naked.

She would not mention that he had made her see Lepidoptera as intrinsic signs of an ecological order, not as decoration.

She would not write "Dear Brandon" or "Hey Brandon" or "Attention, Dr. Utz." Instead, she skipped any introduction and jumped right to the query.

The e-mail took her three hours to write. Brandon e-mailed back fifteen minutes later that they should talk in person. She took the bus from Danny's apartment and tramped the mile from the station toward the botanical gardens. Her path took her past the football stadium and the lines and lines of student commuter vehicles. As she got farther from the main traffic, her footsteps made a new path in the fresh snow. Each boot print looked like child's artwork on a fresh plaster cast.

The parking lot in front of the Reiman Gardens was almost empty at ten in the morning. Acres of outdoor plantings attracted visitors usually, but snow covered those beds now. In the spring and summer, Reiman Gardens grew formal tea roses and giant circles of peonies. The tulips drew a large crowd around Easter each year, the beds of school-spirit red and yellow so big they mimicked a stadium crowd. In the winter, Reiman only housed an indoor train exhibit as well as the only all-year, unchanging attraction: the butterflies.

The butterfly wing jutted out from the side Reiman Gardens like an open glass book. The butterfly wing's prestige came from being one of the only university-adjacent butterfly conservatories in the country. Most butterfly houses were run by museums or zoos, but Reiman offered opportunities for research, not just tourism, and thus could hire a PhD to be its head.

Dr. Brandon Utz leaned on the welcome desk in the front lobby, still as tall and thick as ever. She imagined Brandon formed from potter's clay, the incredible solidness of every part of him. Even his hair grew in thick, brown and wavy and longer than she liked it when they dated. He made her feel small. At several inches over six feet, he had always made her feel small, but that had been in an all-encompassing, bear-hug kind of way. Now she felt like a kid trick or treating after the lights had been shut off at a house. He waved her inside, past the gift shop and the fingerprint-covered window separating visitors from a display of pupa.

She wondered if they were too familiar for small talk. During their walk to his office, the conversation came out rehearsed and flat. When Midwestern people don't know what to talk about, they recruit the weather into service. Talking about snowfall and sleet with someone who had run his tongue over her breasts felt wrong.

They turned into the administration hallway, and Brandon opened a door. His office reminded her of his grad student office, except his new desk bore a taller stack of paperwork and no framed photo of them near his computer. She tried not to notice that there wasn't a photograph of anyone else either. She ordered her heart to beat slower, but it took orders about as well as she did. He motioned for her to sit across from him and placed his large hands on the desk. "Your brother okay?"

"Okay is a relative term. Better than a few days ago."

"But you lost your research, your former advisor, and your fieldwork funding."

Her stomach clenched. "Yep. Misplaced that funding along with those pesky single socks at the laundromat." She should be nicer. She should be kowtowing. She imagined her checking account like Dickensian orphan, kneeling at her feet. "Please, we want some more." After a deep breath, Greta wrangled her mouth into a smile.

"I mean, technically you've caught me at a good time. I've got funding for a research partner approved for half a year, through the summer. But we have already interviewed some potentially great hires."

"So potentially I'm shit out of luck."

He used the tone he took on with strangers at dinner parties. Cool, collected, impartial. "Listen, my main concern is professionalism. You're great at data collection, but—"

"My father called me prickly. Is that what you mean?"

"No, I mean our history." He said the word with as little enthusiasm as a kid studying the subject. "I'm the lead researcher here, and I need a team player who can be coached. With me as the coach."

*What's with everyone and teamwork these days?* "I can do that."

"Are you sure?"

She centered herself around the solid lump in her stomach. "Look, I need money. You need help. I think 'symbiosis' is the right term here."

He took a sheet of paper out of his desk, her name already printed on it. He'd known from the beginning that these terms would be agreeable. He'd known that whatever fire between them could be easily iced in the name of science. Instead of feeling reassured, her chest hurt as she signed the contract, the tax forms, the background-check release form. She would start tomorrow.

# CHAPTER FOUR

B randon had acted as a fence around Greta's graduate school experience, always there and marking the edges. On her first day of TA training, Brandon handed out informational packets. At first, she thought of him as Dr. Almond's minion. Larry Almond's Igor: a little too brawny to be brainy. He reminded Greta of a wrestler, and a year later, after a particularly acrobatic session of tangling under his sheets, she revealed her first impression of him.

"I thought you were moody," he said.

"Resting bitch face. Also, short haircut. Something about me doesn't scream 'damsel in distress.'"

"And you didn't need much help those first few weeks."

But he had pressed his help upon her, and it rankled. She found out later that he was required to mentor all incoming research and teaching assistants as part of his contract. As a final-year candidate and the winner of the departmental teaching award for PhDs for two years running, he'd been assigned to the care and tending of baby graduate students. While the other students in her year lauded him and, in some cases, searched him out to lean too casually against his desk, Greta never did. She made up half of a two-person anti-fan club for the first year. Only Max stood with her against Brandon. On the first day, Brandon committed the cardinal sin of making fun of Max's whip scorpion, who he had brought to orientation with him. "This is an arachnid-free tour," Brandon had said, smiling too large. The tour group had included a few incoming math PhDs who had missed their own campus tour and must have complained to "teacher."

*It's unfair,* Greta had thought, as Max was forced to leave the arachnid on the floor in the administration building. The whip scorpion hadn't been cute exactly, but it was one of the larger of the species that Greta had ever seen. It was a fascinating little monster, with front appendages like scorpion claws, and a ridged spine. In the wild, they would have a "whip" at its back, a feeling appendage, but the pets were whipless varieties. Greta knew without closer examination that underneath that whip were its secretion organs. The distinctive scent their spray emitted gave them their nickname. "Nice vinegaroon," she had told Max, and they had been friends ever since. She and Max, that was, though perhaps Gary was fond of her too.

Greta and Max's appreciation of small stinging animals and mutual distrust of Brandon were the first things that bonded them as office mates, even before they figured out that they had grown up thirty miles apart. Max was Ames stock—he'd graduated as a Little Cyclone. She had been a Madrid Tiger. At the time, she studied bees and he studied fruit flies and spiders. They both loved *Star Trek*, but her comfort re-watches were all Picard's crew aboard the *Enterprise*, whereas his ranged across every season. Trekkie that he was, he even, she found out one Halloween, had a Star Fleet lieutenant uniform that he wore completely unironically, combadge and all.

While Max learned to ignore Brandon, Greta had bristled under his offers to help. Brandon offered sample lab syllabi and an ear to listen to any concerns she had. He tried too hard. He acted too friendly while she was too busy to be friendly in return. Grad school was about learning to swim, and while she would swallow a mouthful of water every now and then, she wouldn't drown.

Now, years later, on her first day at Reiman Gardens she did feel like she was drowning. She took the bus to campus and by the time she got there, a docent was unlocking the doors, and Brandon was already in a meeting. An undergraduate student met her at the door of the lab. The student, Maura, handed her a white, USDA-required coat on their way in and had her sign into a log. "Because, you know, if there's an outbreak of some crazy tropical disease, we need to know who patient zero is." She laughed and swept her long black braids over her shoulder.

Greta recognized her. "Did I have you in intro bio last year?"

Maura nodded. "Yep. I got this as my work study job because of that butterfly lab you had us do. I got kind of, I don't know, intrigued." She took the log from Greta and put it in a drawer. Greta was glad to hear that, despite her terrible student evaluations, someone had taken something from her course.

Along the back and side walls of the lab hung plastic-coated cabinets with cheap hardware. It reminded her of an IKEA store. She opened the fridge along one wall and saw bowls of strawberries and peeled oranges. "For the butterflies in the exhibit," Maura explained, as she noticed Greta peeking around. "Release boxes are up there, above the cabinets. Have you really never been in here before?"

"No, just seen it through the window." Greta pointed to the last wall, the clear one at the front of the room that housed the emergence windows. The three glassy chambers measured as tall as a person and housed pupa, each as distinct as a fingerprint. Some of them had off-green, thin skin—an oblong tomatillo. Some were longer and browner.

Brandon entered, and Greta avoided thinking about the way he filled out a lab coat. He scrawled his messy signature onto the log and shoved it back into the drawer before hoisting a cardboard box onto the wide central countertop.

"Oh no. Specimen unpack?" Maura's tone hinted at an eye roll.

Brandon tapped a clipboard with a pencil. "And inventory."

Greta's phone rang in her purse. She could hear it outside of the door in the locked corridor between the main lobby and the lab. Brandon didn't look up from his box cutter as he drew it across the packing tape. "You can answer if you have to."

First day of work. First day working for an ex-boyfriend, who, despite everything personal, she knew to be immensely qualified for his job. Qualified in the itchy, too-perfect kind of way. He had to do things as dissimilar as taking butterflies to kindergarten classrooms and presenting research at national conferences, and could do each side of the teeter-totter as easily as the other. He loved research too. She remembered him filling out postdoc applications at her kitchen table and knowing somehow that he would get into the one farthest away. She joked with him, grabbing the pen out of his hands, kissing him on the neck. "You're too much of a distraction," he had said, and had gone to work in the living room without the hint of a laugh in his voice.

She didn't seem distracting to him now, but the

phone did. She held up a hand. "Sorry. I thought it was on silent." She opened the door, dismissed the call, and closed it again. Meg's number. In her head, she toyed with the words "future sister-in-law," and they tasted sour. Greta had expected an eviction notice days ago, and she guessed Meg looked forward to making that call.

Greta turned her attention back to the unpack. Some of the pupa emerged in transit, and Brandon made ticks on his inventory sheet. The too-early butterflies lay, wings twisted, on top of the layer of cotton next to the intact pupa. "We don't raise from caterpillar here," Brandon noted as he removed a long brown pupa and hung it in the first case. "Don't have the space or the license, but our domestic and foreign suppliers keep us pretty well stocked. Maura, did you take estimates in the butterfly house this morning?"

"Yeah, just a second." Maura scrambled on the counter for her notebook. "Found twenty deceased on the sidewalks. Are we doing a release this afternoon?"

Brandon nodded. He gestured to the glass cases without looking at them, his attention on the second layer of pupa underneath the first. "These chambers control for humidity, air flow, and temperature. We've been tweaking the variables but have gotten as high as ninety-five percent emergence." He turned to Greta, his palms covered in pupa the same texture as fall leaves. "Hands clean? Can you hang these?"

Greta nodded. "How many butterflies can you stock at a time?"

"Pop quiz, Maura," Brandon said, turning to his lab assistant.

"Eight hundred." Maura grabbed a pint of fresh strawberries from the fridge and began to slice off their stems and quarter them. "Give me a harder one."

Greta's phone buzzed.

Brandon didn't even glance at her. He was in his elements—all of them. Teaching and butterflies and performer, all in one. "All right, all right. We're only two thousand five hundred square feet, but we can support more butterflies than larger facilities. Why's that, Maura?"

"All our plants produce nectar," Maura said. "We don't rely on augmented food systems like food dishes. These strawberries, for instance, are just a failsafe."

"Aced it." Brandon gave her a fist bump.

Greta fit the rest of the pupa into the foam crevices lining the top of the window box. A toddler watched her through the glass, his palms on either side of his face, eyes wide. He tapped twice with his index finger, then turned his head to speak to his mother. Then, when his mother turned away, the little boy stuck out his tongue and waved it side to side. Greta returned the gesture before closing the door, and wondered if zoo animals ever liked some of their observers better than others.

Her phone buzzed again. Maura released the newly emerged butterflies, and a group of Red Hat ladies positioned their noses on the outer glass, a full foot and a half up from where the toddler had touched. Windex could sponsor this place. After a school group left, she squeegeed the front glass. She checked on the pupa again before lunch, and after she closed the window and washed her hands, her phone rang a fourth time. A pause, then a fifth. A pause, then a sixth. Finally, a soft knock came on the front glass that divided the visitor lobby from the lab. An elderly docent held up a handwritten sign: "Phone call for Great."

Brandon looked over at her from the lab computer. "I think that's you, Great." Despite his amused tone, his gaze spoke a boss's language.

"I am sorry. Seriously."

He turned his head back to his computer without clucking or agreeing, and she left the lab. The docent handed over the phone, and on the other end was Meg. "They moved Danny. He had a stroke. He—"

"What?"

"Check your voicemail." And Meg was gone again.

Greta's call history was all from Meg. She was glad to be alone in the hallway when she listened to the voicemails. First one, then the next few in varying degrees of panic and with the odd word jumping through the speaker like a knife in her ear.

*Vasospasm.*

*Life Flight.*

The word "surgery" sounded scary enough without adding the word *emergency* in front of it. Without adding the words "possibly life-saving." Did possibly life-saving mean most likely life-ending?

Greta didn't make excuses to Brandon or remember to remove her lab coat as she rushed outside. She got as far as the parking lot before she realized two things. First, that it was snowing and, second, that since she took the bus, she didn't have transportation to Des Moines. "Oh shit," she said to the flakes falling around her. "Fuck it," she said to an empty cement planter. "Goddamn," she said to the main door of the Reiman as she entered it again.

Brandon stood in the lobby. He wore his old "helping-newbie-lab-instructors" look. He took a large hand and brushed the flakes from her shoulder. "What happened?"

Greta didn't realize she was crying until her voice cracked. "Danny."

In five minutes, she had buckled herself into the front seat of Brandon's truck. She still wore her lab coat, but at least she now had her regular coat on top. On the drive, he adjusted the heat setting on her side to what she used to set it at, three degrees higher than his, and turned on her seat warmer to the middle setting. The creeping warmth along her back rubbed at her shoulders like his hands used to. When she got out of the truck, nearly jumping into the parking lot of Meg's apartment, she forgot to say thank you or goodbye.

She had a quarter tank of gas, just enough to go down and come back. Maybe there would be a pot of gold at the end of a rainbow somewhere along the interstate. The image helped distract her from turning over in her mind the worst scenarios on the drive. When she got to this new, even statelier hospital, she took off her coat and draped it over her arm. What if he had died while she squeegeed handprints off the emergence window? While she was sticking out her tongue at some kid? What if she arrived five minutes too late because she'd run headlong into the snow instead of thinking through the situation? She'd rather immunize herself against emotions than make mistakes because of them.

The elevator chimed open on an unfamiliar floor in the unfamiliar hospital. Unlike the recovery wing's lazy pace and hushed surroundings, the critical care unit ran fast but quiet, like a mouse on speed. Nurses moved at quicker paces, and she barely caught one's arm as he power walked down the hall. "Hey," she said, meeting his pace, "Daniel Oto's room."

"You new here?" he asked, looking her up and down.

"Just transferred." Hours ago Danny had been in a helicopter, whirling his way south, with blood vessels exploding in his head.

"Well, uh . . ." He paused and shuffled over to the nurses' station, which had obviously been his destination. A computer pointed outward, and stacks of folders hung in a wire rack. He tapped the rack. "He's in three-two-two-oh."

"Which is?"

He raised an eyebrow like she was testing him. She glanced down at his nametag. "Fallon" had a too-large mouth and thin eyebrows behind his glasses. "Down the hallway."

Danny's door was closed, but no one was around. This corridor was quiet and clear. Greta put her ear to Danny's door like she used to when they were kids, when she was up before him and wondering if they could sneak down-stairs together to watch TV. It was always more fun with him, with two overflowing bowls of Lucky Charms mixed with chocolate milk. After *Captain Planet*, the rinsed-clean bowls got stuck back on the shelf to hide the evidence (not incredibly hygienic, she realized). Now, like on some of those mornings, she didn't hear anything.

Just like on some of those mornings, she went in anyway. Not to wake him up, like she did in those days, but to watch him. She imagined telling her seven-year-old self that one day the only thing she would want would be to see her twin sleeping, and seven-year-old Greta would have gagged and made "you're crazy" spinning fingers round and round her ears.

She opened the door, then pressed her back against it like she was barring it from attacking zombies. Hospitals cost too much money to let a zombie in. They had rooms in hospitals for dead people, unlike dead butterflies. Maura said she swept dead butterflies from the exhibit paths each morning, or else they decomposed in the tropical garden that made up the biome.

She looked around the room, wishing she could find comfort in the place like she had in the recovery room. No worn leather recliner, no table for displaying "get well soon" cards. Did people not get well soon here?

The room wasn't designed for visitors, but machines. Like the inside of the Matrix, with wires and beeping boxes surrounding a single comatose human. Where was Meg? She had half expected to find her here, but instead she had discovered the inside of a clock—gears and ticking noises.

The door behind her opened, shoving Greta into the room with its force. She turned to face the doctor staring at her, mouth agape. "Who are you?"

"Greta Oto. I'm Danny's sister."

The doctor was tall enough to match Greta's height, and obviously pregnant. She could have set her clipboard on her rounded stomach. "You're not supposed to be in here. And you're not . . ." She gestured at Greta. "I should have security come. I should call the police."

Greta froze, her brain feeling as blue and exposed as Danny's skull. "What?"

"You can't impersonate a doctor."

"What?" Greta repeated, a record stuck in a groove. Finally she looked down where the doctor still pointed, at Greta's white lab coat. "I came right from work. I swear I'm not—"

The door opened, and the nurse named Fallon walked in. "I thought you were—"

"—I never said." And suddenly voices competed with one another. Danny didn't stir in the noise.

The doctor held up her arms. Greta and the nurse fell silent. "Out of here. He doesn't need infection introduced along with everything else. Come on."

Greta took a last peek at her brother and stepped into the hallway. The doctor straightened her starched coat, bright white, with a hangtag from the hospital. Greta looked nothing like a doctor with her wrinkled, ill-fitting mess of linen.

"I sent his wife home," the doctor said. "I'm Dr. Ambrose. I've taken over his case post-surgery. I've got more experience in brain bleeds."

"Fiancée. She's his fiancée."

The doctor paged through her notes as though there were a picture of Meg there. "And your mother. I sent them home, and I'm going to do the same to you. He won't be up for visitors for another day or two, at the very earliest. When I say that you could jeopardize his health, I'm not exaggerating."

Greta's head felt filled with mashed potatoes, stuck on a single phrase. "My mother?"

# CHAPTER FIVE

When she flung open the apartment door, Greta looked one way, then the other, as if checking a busy intersection for traffic. Actually, Greta felt as if she were the traffic looking for someone to hit. Meg was nowhere in sight. Instead, Martha sat on the spot where Greta had slept just hours ago. The pillows and comforter were shoved to the side to make way for Martha's patchwork purse. Martha didn't glance up from the deck of cards she was shuffling, until Greta stood a few inches from her.

"What are you doing here?"

Martha's curtain of brown hair parted as she glanced up at Greta. It was hard to say whether she looked the same or different than she had fifteen years ago. Mentally, Greta had tried to black out her hazel eyes and the mole on her cheek that she had always covered with concealer. Martha had the nerve to smile at her. "Good to see you too. Want to play something?" she asked.

The question felt as out of place as party balloons. "You're kidding."

Martha shrugged. "Your loss." Her voice had a tinge of Greta's own in it, the gravelly sarcasm that Greta swore was all inherited. Weekday mornings swam back into her memory, that voice before the first cup of coffee. That grouchy snarl that had always shoved Greta onto the bus until it wasn't there to shove any more.

Greta balled her fists. The bottoms of her feet sweat into her socks. She could feel the cotton working to absorb the flood. She didn't know what she was about to say before Meg walked in.

Meg's eyes were red and small. She carried a cup of coffee in each hand and offered one to Greta. "I didn't know how else to contact you. I knew you were at work, but—"

Greta repeated her initial question to Meg. "What is she doing here?"

Meg didn't make eye contact and placed the coffee cups on the table. "When I couldn't reach you, I made a judgment call. It's too hard to balance two sides of the family. So balance yourselves."

Martha smirked at her deck of cards. In the past few minutes, she had taken a card in each hand to lean against one another, long sides flat against the table. Another triangle, a few inches away, then a card set across the top to bridge the gap. Another triangle. Another bridge. Two stories, then three. It was a rainy-day thing they used to do. It was using Greta's own memories against her. She wanted to sweep the entire thing aside with the side of her palm, but part of her wanted to see how tall it could go. Strong buildings were made in triangles. Triangles leaning on one another. The tension—that's what built skyscrapers. The tense angles of steel that made New York a broken-toothed smile of a skyline versus Ames's seven-story brick buildings.

If only all tension could build rather than tear down.

Martha broke the silence "It shouldn't be left up to Meg. You should have told me that Daniel had an aneurysm. That's a thing a mother should know." Her voice was thin and taut, a tightrope.

Greta was as good at tightropes as she was at avoiding arguments. She plowed ahead, decibel-doubling Martha's voice. "You should have kept in contact if you think we owe you something. Jesus, I didn't know you were back in Iowa."

"I got a job at Student Health on campus. You knew that."

"How could I know that?"

"You should have tried to find out."

"*You* should have tried," Greta echoed back, harder. "*You* should have tried to keep our family going. *You* should have come to Dad's funeral. *You* should have called me on my college gradu-ation day, or Danny's."

"I sent a card."

"A postcard. From Vegas. Two months late." Greta tented a palm over her face. Between her fingers she saw Martha's hands stumble on the fourth level. That was always the one that sunk

73

Greta's towers. "Do what you want. Sure, visit Danny. Play nurse."

"I am a nurse." Martha let irony ripple under the remark, an eyebrow raised like a flag.

"Play mom, then." Greta said it like the word had grown teeth and bit her.

Martha reacted accordingly, the eyebrow lowering by degrees until it flatlined. Her eyes had new creases around them. Greta remembered enough of her face to see that.

"I'd like you to leave." Greta willed her voice steady.

Martha turned to Meg. Even though it wasn't Greta's house to kick Martha out of, Meg didn't open her mouth.

Martha picked up her bag. "You want me here, I'm here. You want me gone, I'm still here." The door closed behind her, the breeze from the door not enough to knock down the card tower. Martha's boots stomped down the hallway until the building elevator dinged and took those boots somewhere else.

Meg picked up the breakfast bowls that littered the countertop and brought them into the kitchen. Greta heard the noise of a dishwasher being stacked. The domestic noises she wasn't used to sharing with someone else. The card tower wobbled suddenly, provoked by nothing except Greta's glare. She had often wished, especially in her teen years, to possess Carrie-like powers.

She had a feeling they hadn't just materialized, however, especially once she noticed the air vent stationed above the coffee table.

Greta ran some water over her burning face in the bathroom. She left the tap on, staring at her reflection in the mirror for echoes of Martha that had come on without any warning. Without a comparison, without looking at pictures of her for years, Greta had never realized how her nose settled into a bony point like her mother's. Those attached earlobes. The arch of her eyebrows, so like Martha's.

A tap on a door, followed by Meg's voice. "Greta? You in there?"

"Obviously." Greta shut off the tap and, after a thought, flushed the toilet to cover the time lapse. The stress was getting to her, making her feel accountable for Meg's opinion of her. When she swung back the door, Meg was inches away from her with a knee-height brown dog behind her knees. The dog, Franz Liszt, was a shelter rescue and a Christmas present from last year. Greta remembered him only from pictures and had assumed she would hate him as much as everything that Meg loved. Instead, she found herself reaching a hand toward the dog as he ambled over toward her.

Meg watched Franz offer his nose for Greta to scratch. "You okay?"

"That's a relative term," Greta said. "I'm

75

breathing on my own and not strapped to monitors in a hospital, so everything is better than it could be. You could have mentioned in your four zillion messages that we weren't allowed to see him yet."

Meg cleared her throat, uncomfortable. Uncomfortable, like she hadn't thought about a machine breathing for Danny. Greta hadn't been able to think of anything else. And the sickest thing was that a joke kept popping into her head. She and Danny had been laughing just a year ago about his job being robot-proof. "No robot could teach music to middle schoolers," he claimed.

"That's because robots still have pride," Greta said in return.

He'd put his pointer finger in the pressure point beneath her knee and squeezed. Her weak spot, and Danny knew it. She might never have that again, one of those spasmodic laughing fits that made her hate him and love him. And here he was, a machine breathing for him, keeping that heart pumping.

Franz wandered back to the bedrooms, his fuzzy behind waving goodbye.

"Are you hungry?" Meg asked. She opened the fridge and peered inside at the pitiful contents.

"No."

"Me neither." She chewed her lip for a moment and turned back to the dishwasher. "Maybe you should try. You know. With your mom."

"I don't need advice."

"I don't need your attitude."

That stopped Greta, and she looked at Meg. "I am trying. I'm trying to find a new place, and I'm trying not to get fired, and I'm trying not to get kicked out of my program."

"Are things that bad?"

"I might get my funding revoked since I can't complete my research. I might get fired since I ran out from my job like a wild ape on the first day. And it's not like you want me to live here."

"You don't need to find a new place right away. I mean, I have the space." Meg rinsed the breakfast bowls in the sink and held one in each hand, examining them. "I hate this table setting."

Greta had nothing to say about dishes. She hated the automatic conversation people seemed to need to fill the gaps. All she wanted was for silence to scab over her headache.

"I mean, this pattern is terrible. Danny's old stuff from college. See this?" She turned the bowl for Greta's closer inspection. The blue-striped bowls still had tiny particles of cereal clinging to the rim. Their edges were marked with chips and fork scrapes in the enamel. Meg stacked the bowls. " 'Don't worry,' he told me. 'We'll register for new plates, and we can smash these one by one by one.' "

Sounded like Danny. Sounded like Greta too, actually. And their father, who took them skeet shooting with the wedding china after Martha left, even when they could have sold them. Some things were worth more than money.

"How did, um . . ." Meg's mouth tripped over the words. She clinked a handful of dirty spoons in her hand. "How did Danny look?"

Honesty came easier than lies. "Like death."

"Like death?"

"Like a scream mask. White face. Black eyes."

"Did they say anything about transferring him back?"

Her optimism made Greta want to scream. Meg's hope made her a bug stopped under a spyglass, temporarily stunned by the light. Stunned long enough for it to burn. Greta tried to never let herself get stunned; she would rather live entirely in the dark than let something throw her off, like Martha had. "Don't you get that he might die? Like, that he might never, ever badmouth the Yankees or play the harmonica or make his Rice Krispies again?" Greta emptied Martha's mug of coffee into the sink and handed the cup to Meg. Her headache beat behind her eyes, a drum urging her on. "He might never wake up."

"Don't talk like that." Meg held the cup, frozen in place. "Don't even say that."

"What do you care, Meg? You can pick any guy you want, but I can't pick another brother."

The mug slipped from Meg's hands and broke

in uneven shards around Greta's bare feet. Meg squatted suddenly, body curling downward and inward. Her pale face matched the broken ceramic pieces around them. Greta tried to move out of the kitchen, but Meg grabbed onto her pant leg. "Don't leave."

Greta didn't. Even if she'd wanted to—and she did want to—she had nowhere to go. She let herself sink to the floor next to Meg, and when Meg's head fell against her shoulder, she didn't move away.

Greta now had a whole new scientific discipline's worth of terminology to unlock. The first new term: "vasospasm"—the rupture of blood vessels in the brain. How it differed from an aneurysm or stroke, she couldn't yet articulate. All she knew was that for three days after the vasospasm, the drugs coursing through Danny's body had induced a coma—a coma stiller than his last one. With the possibility of brain trauma heightened further, the medical team wanted to stop the clock, to observe things for a few days. "Like a caterpillar going into a cocoon, hibernating," one nurse explained when Greta stopped by the hospital that night. She must have heard from Meg that Greta studied Lepidoptera.

"Actually," Greta told the nurse, her voice metronomic, precise, "larva—that's the caterpillar—eats itself inside the pupa. It digests itself—

imagine a caterpillar smoothie—until nothing but tiny discs, mock-up of parts, remain to rebuild itself in the goop. It doesn't hibernate. It breaks apart and eats itself for energy to finish its wings, genitals, legs, antennae. Did my brother become primordial soup before I came back?"

The nurse stared at her, mouth an em dash of displeasure. "You don't need to explain."

"You don't need to condescend. I understand the term medically induced coma."

Meg brought the nursing staff donuts the next day. Probably an unrelated act of kindness.

Greta did some extracurricular research on brain surgery—the mechanics, not the practice. She wasn't planning on becoming Dr. Franken-stein. The materials that Nadine gave her were useless for Greta's purposes. Nadine's proscribed curriculum about brain injury included too many touchy-feely pastel pamphlets for her liking. Instead of reading the caregiver guides, Greta chose a text that required the installation of a medical dictionary on her phone to peruse during free hours.

And less-free hours too. Greta completed her rounds with Maura and collected dead butterflies off the paths. Brandon stationed himself in the lab and instructed Maura and Greta to split the butterfly house duties. One of them had to guard the entrance of the wing. The entrance, a small glass room with locking doors on either side, was meant to be a place to explain the rules to patrons before they entered. Basically, don't touch, don't take, and don't go off the paths.

Since these warnings didn't always work, another staff member had to be inside the wing. Supposedly this staff member was there to answer patron questions, but Greta usually managed to exude enough antipathy to keep questions away. She sat at one of the benches, book open on her lap.

The only patrons, first thing in the morning, were usually parents of preschoolers desperate to get out of the house. Like clockwork, two families rushed into Reiman as the docent unlocked the door. Greta swore internally when she saw them. Perhaps she was a bad employee, but she was hardly alone anymore, between sleeping on Danny's couch and working in a crowded lab. Being alone helped her recharge, and her introvert batteries had been sapped lately.

One of the families—a mother and kid—wandered around the butterfly house while the other took off running to the conservatory. Greta heard the click of the entrance gate and Maura's voice wishing the pair a "good visit with the butterflies."

*Yeah, sure. They were real conversationalists. Ask them to tell you the one about the parasitic wasp.*

Even with her attention on the brain scans and medical terminology in her lap, she felt the presence of the family and tracked their progress around the stone path. The butterfly wing was small, but dense with plant and insect life. Insect life that the little boy was obviously unconcerned with. Instead, he went over to the only glowing screen in the wing—an identification program that only worked about half the time—and started fiddling around with it.

"Are you a medical student?" The mother's voice startled Greta, whose internal antennae had been set on the boy. Some little boys pulled wings off butterflies and left them wriggling on the path. Some little girls did too. Greta had before she knew better. She had thought, as a kid, that would make them caterpillars again.

"I am not a med student," Greta said.

The woman didn't push the issue. "Well, looks interesting," the mother said. Her words could have been taken as an indictment on Greta's inattention, but the tone was chide-less.

It was that tone that made Greta close the book. "It is, actually."

Strangers were easy. Strangers required little social energy. If she wanted to, she could talk to strangers all day. It was strangers that tried to get to know her that bothered Greta.

The mother sat on the bench next to Greta and raised her voice unnaturally loud, enunciating clearly so that Greta raised her eyebrows. "So, butterfly brains don't look like that, do they?"

"No. Their brains are much less complex, but . . ." Greta cleared her throat. Out of the side of her eye, she saw the boy watching, but she didn't turn toward him. "But their brains can do some cool things."

The boy turned reluctantly from the computer program, which had frozen anyway. It had a bug, she would have joked to Max. No one else liked puns.

Greta mapped a butterfly brain on her palm, showed him a relative size and told him about the crazy shit that fit inside such a small space, removing the expletive. Insect brains were more complex than people gave them credit for. Consider the sensory capacity of the average insect. Smell and touch meant life. Beyond the highly developed sense of smell, many butterflies could register colors humans didn't, like ultraviolet. The boy listened for a minute, and when his attention was drawn away again, at least it was by a butterfly.

As they left the wing, Greta instructed them to check themselves in the mirrored exit room for clinging butterflies. Hitchhikers. The mother gave Greta a genuine smile as they left, and Greta thought maybe she wouldn't be a terrible employee after all.

After work she brought the textbook to Danny's room. His transfer back to Ames was a relief. In fact, over the course of the last week she had spent more time with her brother than in the whole past year. Even living in the same town, their threads had become parallel after Meg entered his life. Now, knotted together again, Greta found that she wanted nothing more than to tell him about what she was learning about his condition. He would find something beautiful in it. Maybe, in the colored brain scans. Maybe in the complex terminology. He would somehow hear music in all of it that Greta desperately needed to hear.

Greta had a sandwich in one hand and a book in the other when the neurologist arrived. Dr. Traeger greeted her, then did his assessment while dictating his remarks to a resident. The neurologist was a man in his seventies with a monk's cap of baldness. Three brown liver spots dotted his forehead, reminding Greta of the finger holes on a bowling ball. "Heavy reading," Traeger remarked.

Greta grunted.

"What do you make of Steiger's case studies?" Traeger's voice smelled of condescension. Greta assumed he would offer her a wowwy pop next.

The cure for condescension in every scientific context she'd ever been in had been facts, repeated with cool certainty. Luckily, she had both facts and certainty, and added a dash of suspicion. "Well, I went back through his charts and noticed that you didn't follow the guidelines for a perfusion CT on day nine. The day of the vasospasm."

That iced it. "Recommendations, not guidelines," Traeger said, his tone careful. "And he had one scheduled that afternoon. If he had made it until the afternoon without incident."

The resident excused himself, and Traeger seemed ready to do the same. He paused at Greta's shoulder, obscuring her reading light. "What?" she asked.

He adjusted his glasses. "Recovery is never as simple as the books make it out to be."

"I haven't gotten to the recovery section yet."

"If you don't trust me as Danny's specialist, I'll let someone else take his case."

Greta didn't close the book, but she looked up at him. She had scanned the charts. She had read the recommendations for post-surgery treatment, and Traeger had complied with those. "It's probably just a shit situation."

"Your words, not mine." Traeger coughed and beat his chest with a fist. When it settled, he spoke again. "Let me be the doctor. Once he leaves, he'll need your help with things I can't necessarily foresee. He might not be the same as he was before."

Greta nodded, pretending she hadn't been imagining just that despite her research.

"I wish I could give you a solid answer on what life will be like. But one thing this field has taught me is that if you meet one patient with a brain injury, you meet one patient with a brain injury." Trager's shadow moved out of her light, and he opened the door to the hallway. "You might think about, well, talking to some people."

"I met *Nadine*," Greta said. Now her voice dripped condescension.

"There's a group," Traeger said. "Look in your packets for information. I think—well, I think it would add to your research. About the after."

The After. It sounded like the name of a parallel universe in *Star Trek*. Let's go to the other side of the anomaly, Mr. Data. Engage.

When the neurologist left, Greta stared at Danny's closed eyes and realized that she did, actually, feel alone. Alone in the room. Alone in Ames. Alone.

As if he could sense it, Danny's eyelids flicked open, then closed. An indictment. A shaming.

The boy in the butterfly wing reminded her of Danny, something in his hair sticking out at awkward angles. Something in the uncareful turned cuff on just one leg of his jeans. Something about the way he turned when something else caught his attention. But Danny never saw things like Greta saw them.

In fact, Danny was wired more like a butterfly. Pretty things caught his eyes. The Megs. That, and the fact Danny could see colors that Greta never could. The term for it came later, much later: synesthesia. But the experience came when they were both five. The whole family had been at a military band concert on the day of Dad's deployment. To Danny, the concept of "daddy leaving" only extended as far as he could count, which was to twenty. Count to twenty, then go find Dad. Greta knew it wasn't a game, knew Dad wouldn't be in finding range. He would be in another country; Martha had showed them a map, pictures from the encyclopedia of lumpy desert plains. "Does he get a camel?" was all Danny could think to ask, and he said if Dad did get a camel, maybe he could bring it home afterward.

"Camels spit," Martha had said.

"I spit too, but you keep me," Greta returned.

Greta had crossed her arms the whole concert, but Danny had never seen a conductor before and couldn't stop watching. It reminded Greta of the *Magician's Apprentice*, with Mickey swooping his hands over the brooms and them doing his bidding. Greta didn't care about the conductor. She watched the lines of her Dad's face crease and uncrease on the outdoor stage at the park. When the band kicked into the romping thump-thump of the first military march, Danny turned to Greta and tugged on her sleeve. "It's red," Danny said.

She shook her head and rolled her eyes in a way that mimicked Mom.

"Nothing's red, doofus," Greta had said.

"The music is red," Danny whispered, and Martha shushed them. Martha's eyes were wet, like shiny mirrors, but she hadn't been crying, or Greta pretended she hadn't.

Years later, when his ability to explain himself improved, Greta realized Danny saw colors. Saw them whenever he heard music. He explained it like a piece of colored plastic shone in front of a white light, but in his head. Whether that was tied to his musical abilities, she couldn't begin to guess.

What he would be like in the After, not even the doctors could predict. What she did know: even after the reading on brain injury, she felt constantly as she did on the day at that band concert, watching her Dad get onto a bus that would take him to a place she couldn't imagine. The lost feeling steeped like tea, darkening in her. She waited for a sign.

Then his eyes fluttered open and stayed. Coincidence is a funny thing. Coincidentally, his eyes opened at the same second that Martha walked in the door. Greta smelled her before she saw her. Her perfume was like a pheromone cloud.

Danny's eyes roved side to side. Blinked hard, slow, a first crack in an eggshell. After a blink, his lids glued closed again.

"Stay with me, Danny," Martha said from the doorway.

Greta got off the chair by the window and knelt, taking the place where Dr. Traeger had stood a few minutes earlier. "Hey, Danny. Dan. Wake up."

"Danny," Martha said, her voice unsteady.

Danny's eyes opened again. Greta had forgotten how green they really were. Freshly mown grass mixed with stripes of highlighter brightness. He turned those eyes again toward Martha's face as she reached out a hand to him.

The nurse must have seen a sign from the monitors in their nurse's station too, because moments later, white coats and scrubs crowded around the bed and forced them both from their positions. Greta and Martha were displaced into the hallway. There they stood, not speaking, positioned on opposite sides of the corridor. They might have been two queens on a very small chessboard, only a dozen squares between them to cross.

After a minute, Martha's posture changed, softened. She checked her watch. "Want to share an elevator?"

Greta didn't move. She had the position closer to Danny's room, and she put her hand against his doorplate. "Why? I'm not going anywhere."

Martha didn't break her gaze. "You should let the medical professionals do their work."

Greta scoffed. "Why would I think you'd start fighting for him now? How could I ever guess that the first thing you'd want to do was leave?"

"Greta, sometimes the best thing we can do is wait. And I can wait at home too."

"Jesus, I'm some kind of Sherlock Holmes now, solving the case of the missing mother. Turns out, she didn't do it because she never did anything." Greta slumped down the wall, crouching. "If you want to give up being here for him, go ahead. Seems like it's easy for you."

Martha rocked foot to foot for a moment. Greta didn't want to look at her face. Didn't want to see if there were tears there again. God, the tears hadn't saved her dad from getting on that bus, and they weren't going to restart Danny's brain either. When Martha left, Greta expected to feel the weight of her leave too, the weight off her chest. Her legs began to ache as she crouched, still feeling like she'd made the wrong move on that chessboard. She didn't know any other moves to make.

# CHAPTER SIX

Greta slept horribly on Meg's couch. Franz was a good dog, but he had the habit of licking her hand at midnight and bringing her the leash at six AM. The couch hated her, or at least it seemed that way from its lack of support. On top of that, she kept having a reoccurring dream focused on Halloween twenty years ago. Paired costumes: Hansel and Gretel. The whole thing had rankled Greta at the time, reminding her yet again that she got the "weird" name and Danny's was normal. Reminding her again that she was a pair, always, even though all they had in common was a shared uterus for nine months. In real life, they had gotten their biggest candy haul that year—their quaint faux-German apron and pantaloons winning over the houses sick of superheroes. In the dream, Danny and Greta got lost. Greta left behind Skittles to follow back. The witch's house wasn't candy, but as cottony as a spider's web, and Danny got caught. Greta tried to wrench him out, tugging his arms, legs, and failing, flailing.

So that dream wasn't great, and neither were the backaches she got rolling off the couch every morning, or the adaptation to someone else's schedule. Meg showered both in the morning, as well as the evening on nights when there was cheerleading practice. Greta showered every three days unless she actively spilled something on herself. Meg ate bowls of cereal with names like LeanFit Plus with smiling suns on it that totally would not murder you if they had the chance, nope. When Meg noticed Greta eating Reese's Puffs cereal, she had gotten about four words into a spiel about corn syrup when Greta interrupted to say that she must really hate the farmers, huh? Someone had to eat the corn.

Meg was built from an entirely different blueprint than Greta. Meg craved other people as much as Greta hoped to avoid them. Most nights, Meg took her social gatherings away from the apartment, but once or twice her closest friends, Ginger and Leanne, came over for mojitos and board games. They seemed skeptical that Greta didn't want to be included in their "fun."

Lately, it had been more personal arguments. Meg washed her bras in the bathroom sink. They dried, plinking aggravating drops of water into the bathtub adjoining the living room, where Greta spent most of her free hours. Because Franz scratched at closed doors—no matter what door it was—closing off the bathroom wasn't an option. Every few days, plink plink plink came the sound of the bras dripping. Instead of pointing this out, one Saturday afternoon Greta removed the problem—the bras—by putting them in the oven on the very lowest setting to dry. She had kept as careful an eye on them as she would have for any bra during this process. If Meg hadn't walked in and found Greta "baking my favorite bras," Greta thought she probably never would have noticed it happened.

"They are crispy!" Meg said, shaking a pink flower-patterned bra in Greta's face.

The strap not held in Meg's grip smacked lightly against Greta's cheek, and she took a step back. Greta only wore sports bras despite never having participated in any organized sport. She said, "I don't think anyone can tell."

"*I* can tell. Bra Pringles. That's what they feel like."

If Greta had liked Meg and wanted to be friends, she would have asked her if they were sour cream and onion or barbecue, but instead she said, "Okay."

"What do you mean, 'okay'? Do you mean 'sorry'?"

Greta did not mean sorry, and Meg knew it.

Three weeks of work without running into the snow coatless, but Greta wasn't patting herself on the back just yet. Three weeks of butterfly releases and maintenance, of sanitizing specimen cases and watching school children tap on the glass. Three weeks of switching her cell to silent the moment she entered.

Danny wouldn't die while she worked.

He wouldn't.

He would be one of the lucky ones, and everything would be fine. Was this how optimism worked, by willfully ignoring the truth? After two weeks watching patients in the recovery wing, Greta had enough of a sense of what it meant not to be lucky. Three other cases of brain injury were admitted. Two were traumatic—two motor vehicle accidents—and one was a stroke. The daughter of the stroke victim caught Meg's arm once while they were both visiting. Greta overheard their conversation in the hall, watched the way Meg laid a hand on the woman's arm. The next day, the stroke victim died, and they didn't see the woman again.

But that wouldn't be Danny.

She ignored the possibility like she had ignored an e-mail from her advisor for two days now. It sat, bold and unopened in her e-mail—a constant reminder of a red number one on the envelope icon on her phone's home screen.

Schrodinger's cat. The cat in the box was both alive and dead until someone opened it. She, the doctoral student, was both funded and not— in hot water and not—until she opened the e-mail.

"Coming tonight?" a voice behind her asked.

Greta looked up from her phone at the lunch table, from the e-mail she wouldn't check (whose subject bar said, "RE: Research Status" in Arial font, like all the other subject bars, but appearing so much more ominous). The speaker who had interrupted her was Mike. Mike from Marketing. Greta thought of him as Marketing Mike, with the Nikon camera, who obviously believed his photography and design degree was too good for the place it brought him. Marketing Mike with the hipster glasses and flannel shirt, as if he were dressing for Seattle autumn instead of Iowa winter.

"Coming tonight?"

"Coming to where?"

"Mixers is throwing a party. A bunch of us are going."

Marketing Mike reminded Greta of someone who would call any drink a cocktail. "Who's the bunch?"

"Well, me, Brandon, maybe some of the older research help—as in, legal age. It's a Democratic fundraising thing, you know, before the caucus."

"Oh boy. I'll get out my liberal spray, then."

Mike swallowed his yogurt hard as if she'd given him bad news. "Oh, I mean, I thought you were . . ."

"You do realize that 'conservative' isn't a dirty word, right? Like, I'm not going to go sticking a balanced budget up your ass or something."

Honestly, Greta wasn't conservative or liberal— or anything. Politics could be more divisive than religion in Iowa, and she was an atheist in both. Still, she knew that annoying this man would be her favorite interaction all day. It lived up to all hopes. Marketing Mike turned purple, about the same shade as his blackberry yogurt. It splooged out of the top of its plastic tube like he was an oversized, facial hair–wearing toddler. "I mean," he stammered, seeming unsure how to continue.

"Oh, I'll totally come," Greta said, surprising herself but enjoying the surprise on Mike's face more. "I need a night out."

When she finally opened the e-mail, it called her to the principal's office, or at least it felt that way. Trudging to the ATRB, she was a specimen prepared for dissection. She'd explained the situation with Danny via e-mail, but Plank responded that he still wanted to talk in person to discuss "options." If only she could still be collecting data in the cloud forest. Costa Rica and the resort could have been a sci-fi movie, or maybe her life now was. A parallel universe— make one choice, and it all went a different way.

When Greta was a teen, there had been a surge of reinterest in the theory of the butterfly effect. Magazines covered it, and experts were interviewed on *60 Minutes*. It was a dramatic time—September 11th and natural disasters. As the theory stated, if a butterfly flaps its wings in Argentina, there's a monsoon in Singapore. She understood the attraction then, and she understood it now—human beings like to think that everything they do matters. That Egg McMuffin was the right breakfast choice, Chuck. Look at the third-quarter report you gave to the board afterward! Not that she didn't think actions had consequences—her research had focused on climate change, after all—but if the butterfly effect were true, it was paralyzing. Sometimes shit just happened.

She met with Plank in his office before heading to the bar. Tom's office always gave an impression of something collapsing in on itself. Gravity worked differently there, and the rickety shelves full of academic journals and books leaned slightly forward. If one of the flies he studied were to land on the top of a teetering shelf, it might come crashing forward, but Tom's office worked magic. Even with its full-to-the-brim bookshelves, not a thing looked out of place. Except herself as she scrunched into a chair, fully aware she took up too much space.

"I'm concerned." Plank didn't beat around bushes. He, in fact, wouldn't have planted bushes anyway because they would have disrupted the ease of mowing his lawn.

"Don't be."

"I am. Larry's research continues without you—he can't stop the work. It's time sensitive. We can't stop the butterflies from mating."

"Have you tried putting their mothers in the room?"

Plank paused, then gave a hearty guffaw. "You're funny. More than that, you're a good student, but—"

"I can't leave my brother."

"I get it, Greta. I do." Tom took a deep breath and leaned against his desk. "I had a long chat with Larry, and he's finishing the research season solo. I've offered to supervise whatever project you do. I'm open to ideas—but you're slated to do your prelims soon."

"I'll be ready." She wished she sounded half as confident as she should have, saying that. She was an actor cold-reading a script. Preliminary exams meant writing for a week straight on any issue in the field they could devise, anything within the field of her general entomology coursework. If she didn't pass them, then nothing else mattered. She would fail.

As if sensing a lack of awareness of her screwed-ness, Tom continued. "Plus, alienating Larry isn't going to win you any friends."

"I swear I'll work on it." She didn't even know what she meant by "it."

"Sooner rather than later."

"I swear."

"Don't swear, show. And be ready for prelims in May." Like a gavel coming down, those words marked his judgment. She didn't get evicted, but she got a strong final warning. Science, if nothing else, studied a consistent set of observable conditions. Her current condition was ricketier than Plank's bookshelves and currently less valuable to the program than they were.

She swore under her breath the entire ride back to work. Succeeding in entomology was all she wanted to do with her life. To understand the vastness of the field by understanding its details, and now they were doubting her competence because of—what? A family emergency? She had to bite her lip not to spit out expletives in front of some fourth-graders while giving them a tour. At least she could go out and drink tonight. And drink she would.

# CHAPTER SEVEN

Having not had one that she wasn't related to, Greta didn't know the protocol for roommates and nights out. Usually, Meg was the social butterfly and Greta was the one preoccupied with the real thing. Should she leave a note at the house? Text Meg? Write a note on a Post-it and slap it on Danny's forehead? He was about as mobile as a whiteboard these days.

Although he was awake more and had even started making noises, Greta sometimes didn't know why she stopped at the hospital on her way home from work, even though she felt herself drawn there as surely as a compass needle drawn North. The nurses gave her a wide berth, knowing her schedule. She had been watching Star Trek's *The Next Generation* with him, season five. The show was her happy place, and aboard the starship *Enterprise* she could pretend she was ten years old again, watching it with her dad on a school night, homework ignored on her lap. Danny never used to watch it with them. While he might not have chosen to watch the show had he been conscious, she didn't feel bad running an out-loud commentary as the show played. Yesterday, it was the episode about the game that trapped the crew with its mind control. It made her think of Danny's comments about his middle schoolers and their cell phones. She wanted to inflict her taste on Danny when he was awake sometime, just to see if he agreed.

Tonight she wouldn't be anywhere near a hospital ward or the *Enterprise*. Tonight she would be in a den of lions with her ex-boyfriend, and as she applied eye liner to her lids for the first time in months, she refused to admit to herself how much she anticipated it. That didn't mean she wouldn't love some backup.

She texted Max. *Free tonight?*

An ellipsis. A pause. A response, finally: *No. Family stuff.*

She wasn't going to text back *Please,* especially after such a short response. She was half mad at him, but it was typical Max behavior. He always had family stuff. That was the problem with having two parents alive and in town. And parents that he liked and talked to, presumably, since he lived with them

Another ellipsis and another reply from Max. *Catch up later?*

*Yeah,* she said, but they didn't make plans.

The bar smelled like smoke despite the smoking ban in place for years. The entrance was blocked by a large folding table. Of all of the people in Ames, she recognized the woman staffing the table as Meg's friend Leanne. Leanne was a tall, thin black woman with a shaved head. "Greta!" she said warmly. "So good to see you."

Greta had no opinion about the goodness of the situation.

"It's a ten-dollar donation," Leanne said, patting a tall blue mason jar in front of her. "And feel free to take any lit you'd like."

Greta glanced at the brochures on the table. "No thanks." She handed over her ten dollars, Leanne shoved it into the jar with the other Hamiltons.

She was about to push past the entrance, when Leanne stopped her. "Hey," she said. "I know you're staying with Meg. You're Danny's twin, aren't you?"

She should be used to the question by now. Even in high school, she was "Danny's twin." She didn't think it was popularity this time that made the woman ask. "Yeah," Greta mumbled.

"How is he doing?"

It was hard to talk to strangers about Danny without defining a million data points. His recovery was now a game of Chutes and Ladders. Even after his coma ended, there would be a new scale: the Rancho Los Amigos Scale of Cognitive Functioning. Greta was a firm believer that there were too many acronyms in the world, but she knew she needed a way to shorten it. If she just called it Rancho, it sounded like either a salad dressing or a dude ranch.

If she called it Los Amigos, she pictured that annoying animated preschooler speaking Spanish at her. Whatever name she called it, the new scale would track Danny after he woke up and could respond to stimuli in a meaningful way. Her mind shuffled through explanations before realizing she didn't owe one. "Danny's fine," Greta said. "I mean, I don't know. Meg could probably fill you in just as well."

Leanne gazed at Greta for another long minute. Luckily, the door to the bar opened, and Greta had to cede her spot to make room for another round of supporters waiting to pony up their donations.

The bar resonated with bodies and voices, but the voices disconnected from the bodies in the small space so that everyone was a bad dub of themselves. Most of the lighting came from neon beer signs for defunct brands, and a corner of leather couches sat opposite the long bar. It took a minute to spot her group, but finally Greta noticed Brandon sitting on the arm of one of the couches, and Marketing Mike leaned against the wall so close to a sign that his hair glowed pink from the light. Greta went to the bar first and grabbed a beer to steady herself before approaching the group.

"Little lady," Mike said, though Greta was neither. Mike pushed himself off the wall and out of his Hollywood cowboy lean. The beam of pink light traveled down his shirt and returned his hair to black. "Glad to see that even a skeptic could come put ten dollars toward free community college and better health care."

Greta bit her tongue. If she wanted giveaways, she would go to a baseball game. That's what she wanted to say, but instead she said, "Yeah, well. A night out's a night out."

Brandon smiled at her. "How's your brother?"

"Same as yesterday. The flip-book version of his hospital stay wouldn't sell any copies, that's for sure." The leather couch was half full of people. The end farthest from Brandon had a pair of twenty-somethings, simultaneously texting and talking too loud. Brandon's arm, ropey and long, hung across the back of the couch and corralled the only free spot. She saw the place to sit but couldn't make her feet move toward it. To be that close to Brandon in a dark room, even with layers of winter coat and air between them, would feel like old times. Not that old, she knew—a year ago. Since before he left for New York. Long enough that her skin cells were completely sloughed from the last time his skin had rubbed against hers. She had a new layer of herself.

As she stood, rocking foot to foot to find her own bubble in the area, a body pushed past her into the circle of couches. The body, the person, fit herself into the space under Brandon's arm. "The line for the bathroom was so long I finished my beer while waiting and could have had a second."

"Need me to flag a server?" Brandon asked.

Greta watched the two of them like she might in a chemistry lab, observing for actions and reactions. When Brandon used to look at her, did other people see them this way? His half-closed lids, the swoop of his hair as he leaned closer to her to make sure she could hear him over the roar and laughter. Greta knew she could hear, this woman, because Greta could hear every word he said. Or maybe Greta still tuned into the frequency of his voice, catching its waves because she unconsciously searched for them.

"Oh, sure. If we can get someone in this mess," the woman said. She smiled at Brandon and glanced around so that her face caught the red light. In the dark, Greta couldn't get a good read on her details: Did she have blue eyes or hazel? Brown or dirty-blonde hair? It looked vaguely RainbowBrite-y in this light. Still, Greta couldn't help but notice the fineness of her face, as if carved. Plucked eyebrows, not a hair out of place. Thin, sloped nose like a ski jump. Greta thought of her own nose, slightly bulbous at its base from a softball pitch gone awry in high school gym class. They were different mediums, she and this woman. Granite versus Play-Doh. The woman must have caught Greta watching her. "You Greta?"

*Me Tarzan, you Jane.* Greta chose to respond in a full sentence, two if she could muster them. "I am Greta. Who are you?" She realized after she spoke how much she sounded like the help feature voice on a cell phone.

"Who do you want me to be?" The woman gave a wink of her much better eye-lined eyes, whatever color they were. The wink, plus Brandon's thin-lipped smile, wrote the story. This woman had no clue about Greta, not really. "I'm Eden. So great to finally be meeting some of Brandon's friends. He can be so secretive." Eden raised a perfect eyebrow at Brandon. "I swear he's a spy and not a butterfly house curator."

Brandon laughed. "Curator would be for a museum job. I'm more like babysitter, friend, mentor of butterflies."

"He's a bad influence. Buys them booze," Marketing Mike cut in. The line struck Greta as funny, actually. It would have been funnier if Greta had remembered Mike was there. When her attention snapped over to him, Mike took an actual step backward, as if she'd pushed him. Greta didn't relish being the third wheel, but being the fourth felt worse in some ways. *This couldn't be a setup.*

Oh, but that's exactly what it was. When Greta asked where everyone else from Reiman was, she got a shrug and the reply that they'd texted and said they couldn't make it. "They" could mean anyone, the undefined group of "them" that Greta wouldn't know the names of if Mike had spouted them off. She was new, but she wasn't dumb. When Mike offered to buy her a drink, she shook her empty bottle as if there were still beer there and said she was still working on this one. And when Marketing Mike tried to hold her hand during the "speaker" (the shouter, the spouter of clichés about progress), Greta leaned in so that he would hear her when she said, louder than she needed to, "I have less than zero interest in you."

He didn't market himself well, especially when he mouthed the word "bitch" and went to get a drink. Or *cocktail,* she supposed.

Brandon and Eden disappeared after the speaker finished. Greta didn't see them go, didn't know if they left together—her tugging him—or separately, with chaste kisses on the curb of Main Street. At the end of the speech, music started—dance music—and some men shoved the couches against the wall. Marketing Mike found some hippy (body-shaped) hippie (patchouli-smelling) chick to rub against, and soon everyone was grinding in pairs and trios to a song with a heavy bass beat. Greta stood for a few minutes against the wall, then closed her tab and left.

Pheromones and lekking. God, it all reminded her of Costa Rica. Danny had been right all along. Or maybe, in this flashing semi-darkness it was more like fireflies. Everything in science had a name. The enzyme that made fireflies luminescent? Luciferase. It reacted to another substance: leciferin. Both sounded like they were gifts of the devil himself, but really they shared the root for the word "light." Hell and brightness, two ends of the spectrum of a romance.

During her campouts in the backyard, she used to flash signals to the fireflies. Sometimes, flashing in the same sequence—timed just right—it tricked a few to swarm to her. She spoke their language, repeated it, even though she wasn't exactly sure what she was saying. Here, she didn't want to say anything to anybody. Part of her wanted to curl into a body, though. Pick a guy at random. Invite him back to—where exactly? She didn't have anywhere.

One thing she knew was that insects didn't masturbate. They were more virtuous than she was. She couldn't even do that. On the drive home she listened to classical music and opened the window a crack to let the cold air run across her face. The air didn't brush her face like Brandon's fingertips, warm and calloused. It wasn't his mouth, the way his lips cracked in the winter. His lips, crinkled paper against hers, until they softened. Cold, sobering air kept her from imagining Eden slip off her dress the way the nurse imagined butterflies shed their cocoons. As if a cocoon had a zipper down the back.

Danny's feeding tube came out, and Greta sat with him for his first meal. "Hope you like pudding," she said, sitting on the edge of his bed. "Not that this is pudding. It's maybe soup?"

Meg spooned a little into Danny's mouth, and he held it there before swallowing. "Drink?" Meg asked.

"No," Danny said. He'd started to speak again, single words. It would be a while before he could give his opinion about Picard's leadership in season six, but he didn't seem to hate watching the show with her. He never said no when Greta asked if he wanted to start an episode.

His voice sounded like he had laryngitis, but with every word, Meg looked at him like he was reciting an epic poem. She beamed at this rejection.

After Meg left—she went to Wednesday and Sunday church, for some reason—Greta curled up in the leather recliner next to the bed. It was the only thing she would miss about the hospital when Danny transferred to the outpatient facility in a few days. Greta let Meg handle the tours for that by herself—Greta couldn't handle nursing facilities. The smell of them always reminded her of the solution in her insect killing jars.

Greta's collection of jars was in storage. She

had four of varying sizes—weaponized mason jars primed with chemicals to knock an insect out without damaging it as a specimen. Yes, it went against the lease agreement of the facility to have deadly chemicals like cyanide in storage. Also, three full containers of acetate might be considered a flammability issue, but it was one of the most effective chemicals to do the job. Killing as a job. Bug assassinator.

When she was pining for a net in one hand and a jar in the other, Greta knew she'd been out of the field for too long. In quiet moments like this one, Greta fought off the urge to get on a plane and sneak back into Costa Rica. Her first paycheck safely deposited, she had enough money now for the flight. The fact that her funding for the project had been revoked, well, that was another issue all together.

Danny woke searching for someone. Not Greta, even though Greta was the one there for him. Probably Meg. "Do you want more food?" she asked.

"No."

"Drink?"

"No."

When Greta and Meg were there at the same time, Greta usually stood by and let Meg take over. Alone with Danny, all Greta craved was order, sense, and normalcy. She had the urge to shove a harmonica in his fist and tell him to get at it. Play, like he'd done every infuriating moment when they were kids. Constant music.

When they were five, Dad took her and Danny on a walk through downtown Ames. Danny pulled his hand from hers and got loose. They searched everywhere and found him in the music store, perched on a piano stool plunking out the notes to "Old MacDonald." Rather than get mad, their father asked about a layaway program. The owner had a better idea. A friend of his (he shouldn't be telling them this, he prefaced the whole conversation, since he was a businessman) had a free piano. A dozen of them, actually, in his barn. Whenever someone posted "free piano" in the paper, he picked it up in the hopes that someone would adopt it someday. The man used to keep cows but grew too old to tend to them. Now he kept pianos.

And they could keep one too—provided they could move it.

A buddy of their father's had a big enough truck, and together the two men had big enough muscles. Once Dad planted the piano in the corner of their living room, he said meaningfully, "This thing better get played, Danny."

And it did, as soon as it was tuned. The upper register of the old upright rang a little clinky and the lower, a little growly, but Danny's pieces mostly took him to the middle. Musical instruments sought him out after adopting the piano. Santa put a harmonica in his stocking. Mrs. Walters gave him the recorder in the fourth grade. The trombone and the oboe were gifts from a retiring middle school teacher when she heard they were downsizing their house to live in a mobile home. Was that generosity why Danny taught now? Danny slung a guitar around his neck in high school, like every boy in his class. After Dad's death he'd picked up a director's baton. If she slipped a baton between his fingers now, she feared it would fall to the tiled floor with a soft *tink tink* as it rocked back and forth and rolled under the bed.

He didn't smile like himself. In fact, his face reminded her a bit of someone with too much Botox. Stiff, slow swallowing. She remembered suddenly. "I brought you something."

He didn't reveal if the object jogged memories of them both riding the bus to high school, sharing earbuds during the only time of day they didn't pretend not to know each other. U2 and Coldplay coursed through the thin white wires on frosty winter mornings in a private concert. She would always close her eyes and lean against the glass, and he would have control of the "Skip" button to veto.

Greta lifted one of the buds to his ear and tucked it inside. His ears were shaped like hers— so narrow that normal earbuds were a tight fit, so she brought her own and fitted them in.

Greta put the other half in her own ears to make sure the volume was right. She spun the tracker wheel on the iPod, the screen jumping to life. She hadn't thought about the old brick for years, until last night, when she found it in a drawer in Meg's place. Plugged it in and it turned on. Wonder of wonders.

She selected "Beautiful Day," one of their unspoken morning anthems in high school. While their Dad might have said they were sullen, Greta knew they'd been finding their shells for the first time. Hermit crabs that knew they needed protection.

She didn't know what she wanted Danny to do when he heard the music. Did she think he would cry? Sing along? Blink twice? Whatever she expected, it wasn't what happened. When the music started up, the slow build of the rippling opening under Bono's voice, Danny started to moan without moving his mouth. The moan got more insistent as the song went on, and Danny's head started to move, then his shoulders, as if he were wrapped in a straightjacket but trying to move away from a fire. Greta took the earbuds out of both of their ears and stopped the music.

"Does that hurt?"

He started by saying no. Repeating no. Then single words built like Legos into a nonsense phrase, or at least it seemed that way. This time, he kept saying something. The word was all vowels and made no sense to her, but his expression did. His face cringed when he said it—he meant something, and it was something bad.

Greta heard noises in the hallway, and a nurse came in with fresh bedding and a cup of juice. "What's wrong with him?"

The nurse eyed the iPod. "He didn't like it with you either?"

"No, he started writhing. Like he was in pain."

"Our physical therapist usually plays music during sessions—pairing movement with music can help treatment," the nurse said. "In your brother's case, it made his muscles freeze up."

"Damn it," Greta said, to herself or Danny or the iPod—she wasn't sure.

The nurse looked nonplussed, explained that recovery could be unpleasant: everything felt magnified, but his pain was being managed. "Not to worry" was the phrase she ended on, like she was a British nanny.

Greta kissed Danny on the forehead. "I'm sorry for the music."

How many other things she should apologize for, she didn't know. Sorry for being a terrible twin. Sorry for not talking much in the past few years. Sorry for not knowing what to say when Dad died and Greta had literally no idea what they needed to do next. Call the cops on your Dad's dead body to report a murder? Call the mortuary like it was some hotel that took reservations?

Her first caught bugs had been those fireflies, caught on camping nights. Caught in baby food jars their mother saved to store buttons. Greta scattered the buttons on the den floor. Each button, pale and round and similar, came from a paper packet with one of her father's shirts. Each button represented a second chance if a button went missing. Greta didn't care about buttons. She had her jar. After caging a firefly with her hands, she slid them one by one under the lid of the jar until she had a dozen. They landed on the strand of grass she had there, seemed to stare at each other in the small space—a bunch of men at a party where they were told girls were supposed to be. When Greta brought the jar inside at bedtime, Martha stood in the kitchen with buttons in her hands. Both hands, full of buttons. She tipped her palms sideways and let the buttons skitter across the floor, bouncing unevenly on the cheap linoleum. "Pick them up," Martha had said.

Greta shook her head. Danny trailed inside after Greta as the screen door slammed.

"Pick them up," Martha repeated.

Danny offered to pick them up, but Martha sent him to bed, said she would be up soon to tuck him in. She eyed down Greta until Greta felt as large as the flies in the jar and just as trapped. They flashed wearily. Morse code.

In the end, after a few silent minutes, Greta had picked up the buttons. She dug them out from the cracks in the dishwasher opening and from under the legs of the chairs. She left them in a neat pile on the table while Martha watched with her arms folded across her chest. "Don't touch things that aren't yours," she said. She didn't tuck Greta in that night.

When Greta checked the jar on her bedside table the next morning and saw a dozen dead fireflies, she thought maybe Martha had cast a spell on them. Maybe, like the witch in "Sleeping Beauty" or "Snow White," she'd given them a potion because Greta was bad. It wasn't until she learned the next year in school that all animals—including insects—needed oxygen that Greta realized she herself had killed them. But it was too late then to apologize to Martha for hating her for a year over buttons.

When Greta got back to the apartment, Meg was sitting on the floor in the main room, with Franz asleep next to the television. She rested her back lightly against the sofa like she was afraid to disturb Greta's pillow on top of it. The sight of Meg in Meg's own apartment shocked Greta. After the baked bra incident, Greta had seen Meg more often at the hospital than her own apartment. Greta stretched the long days even longer by going to the entomology building on campus after work, and Meg left so early for the middle school, that Meg's presence hardly had a chance to sink in. But here she was.

"Sorry," Meg said, gesturing to the TV with a knitting needle. "It's almost over. It's live."

Greta glanced at the screen. Actors panted, arm in arm in a complicated dance, while a familiar soundtrack played in the background.

"Sit," Meg said. "Just got back from Danny?"

As if Danny were a place. "Yeah."

Meg nodded and kept knitting. "We were supposed to watch this together. It's his favorite musical. He got us tickets to see the show when it toured." Meg swallowed and examined the large wad of yarn perched on her lap, like it was a small, technicolor animal.

"What are you making?" Greta asked. She didn't really care, but she didn't want to keep talking about Danny. Meg's Danny and Greta's Danny couldn't exist in the same place.

"You'll laugh," Meg said, her voice cautious.

"Have you ever heard me laugh?"

"Fair enough. It's a cat vest. My friend Ginger has one of those hairless—"

Greta waved a hand in front of her face like she was shooing away a fly. "Never mind."

They were silent for a few minutes. A new song started up. The guy with slicked-back black hair dipped the girl on the screen. "I saw you bought dog food," Meg said.

Greta had. "Well, he was getting low. And I was at the store anyway."

"Thank you."

Franz growled in his sleep as if echoing the thanks.

A commercial for car insurance started. "It's our anniversary today," Meg said. Greta's eyebrows rose, and Meg took that as an invitation to continue. "Three years. You know, it's funny. You spend so long remembering a first date, and then after the wedding, it won't be the date that counts anymore."

"I don't want to talk about it," Greta said. Her stomach reminded her she'd forgotten to eat dinner. That was obviously the problem here, the twist. Hunger. It was so much easier to like Meg when she forgot that Danny loved her.

" 'It' being the wedding?"

" 'It' being you and Danny." Greta sat on the couch to emphasize the period at the end of her statement.

But Meg's head turned over her shoulder to stare at Greta. In a room lit by only the TV screen, Greta noticed the fineness of Meg's bones. Her pale skin. The freckles along the ridge of her nose. Meg scrunched the freckles into a line. "I don't like you either. I just thought I should tell you."

"That's good to know."

Meg's needles clicked together without her

looking at them. She narrowed her eyes. From this angle, Greta could see right up her pert little nose. "I know you're going through some stuff. I am too." Greta didn't say anything, but Meg took the silence in stride, like a part of the dialogue. "But do you ever let someone like you? Do you ever let someone get close enough to even try?"

"Danny."

"Danny would love a dog that bit him," Meg said turning back to her knitting. Her voice sounded decidedly less peppy than Greta was used to.

"Must be why he's okay with you."

Meg's laugh rang, surprised and genuine. She barely glanced up at Greta before adding, "You really are something."

Greta thought that being something was better than being nothing. She had felt like nothing before, and at least the solidness of someone's disgust bouncing off her made her feel noticed. "I'm going to bed," Greta said. She was going to couch, she meant. But it was a free couch, and it was hers. Meg turned the volume down way low, and despite the continued flashing light from the television, Greta was asleep within minutes.

# CHAPTER EIGHT

Greta pulled the whoopee cushion out of her purse. It was the self-inflating kind, the kind that revolutionized the fake-fart industry (or at least Greta assumed so). She put it on the just-greening grass below her and plopped down on top. The sound from a higher altitude was always better, she knew, and the sound needed to reach a long distance to get the message across. She felt the corners of the pink cushion try to reinflate where her butt wasn't covering it. She might have given it another go, but she saw another car pulling into the swerving P-shaped lane that made up the cemetery road.

"Sorry for no encores, Dad," she muttered. She kissed her hand and touched it to the flat stone. Her father's plot was on the edge of the cemetery, near a low chain-link fence. The location came with limitations on stone choices. For some reason, adjoining (living) neighbors didn't want to see tombstones sticking up like gray teeth in their backyards, so the first hill of stones needed to be flat. The flatness came with a slight discount on the lot, and necessity meant making cuts in funeral preparations where possible. Her father had only been fifty. An old army dog, he hadn't updated his will since his last tour of duty. He figured that if he wasn't killed in the Middle East, he was unlikely to die in the Middle West before he was a hundred. Heart disease disagreed.

Maybe her father's weak arteries should have cued her to be nervous for herself and Danny. At the time, she blamed her dad's heart attack to a lifetime of smoking. Two packs a day of Marlboros or, in a pinch, Camels encouraged that clot to dislodge itself. As she knelt in the dirt, she loosened the pack of American Spirits from her coat pocket and placed it on top of the stone next to the pennies and nickels left there by comrades over the winter. Not like the cigarettes could hurt him now, plus, if anything, her father liked graveyard humor.

Sudden movement made Greta survey the ground near her knees. A recent warm snap had left the snow melted and muddy, but she could see something. There, on top of the edge of her father's stone, was a beetle. She slowly leaned toward it, looking for identifying markers. She mentally scrolled through criteria, narrowing possibilities. It was small, black, and oblong, with thin antennae on its head that stretched a full body's length . If only she had a kill jar with her, she could take it home to get a sure identification. She took a twig from the grass and tried to turn the insect. Before she could identify it, the beetle identified itself with a loud snapping sound. "Tricky little bastard," Greta said, sitting back in surprise. As far as defense mechanisms went, click beetles had more bark than bite.

She verified the identification by flopping the beetle onto its back with a discarded twig. Sure enough, it arched and, with another loud click, flipped onto its belly before flying away.

She heard another click, this one louder and behind her. It was the metallic sound of a car door closing up the hill. Another mourner. That would make Danny happy.

One of the more surreal conversations she'd ever had with her brother was soon after the death of their father, as they toured cemeteries like they were comparing wedding venues. Cost, of course, was a consideration, but there were also half a dozen little things Greta had never thought about. For instance, there was the questions of what one informative website deemed "ambient noise"—how much road traffic could be heard from inside the gates. Danny and Greta's main point of disagreement came from the level of "foot traffic"—Greta couldn't laugh at the marketing speak at the time, but it came back now to her and brought a smile. Greta pictured a quiet plot, a place away from everyone with a pulse. Danny disagreed. "I want a living cemetery," he had said.

"For the record, I am anti-zombie," Greta said,

and made a cross with her fingers in front of her. Danny hadn't smiled; he'd waited next to their father's hospital bed for him to catch his breath from a dive that wasn't going to end. Her comment didn't bring a smile either.

"I want a place where I see people driving around and visiting, you know? So even if we aren't here . . ." Danny had taken a shaky breath, and Greta wished, not for the first time, that she were a thousand miles away, that it was ten years ago and their father was hiding their shoes in the freezer like he used to when they lived at home. She remembered an Easter egg hunt at a park, and her thawing saddle shoes. Maybe death was her dad's biggest prank. He'd pull a Tom Sawyer at the funeral. "I wanted to hear what you jerk-wads really thought of me," he would say, pulling Greta in for a rough hug and giving Danny a noogie. Danny was so tall he would have to lean in.

It wasn't a prank, and they'd buried him in this cemetery because it was visited. It was more expensive, but they bought a spot on the chain-link fence road. The cemetery manager had asked if they wanted to buy adjoining plots, and it had been then that Greta cried for the first time because not only had her father died, but she had also been asked by a stranger if the closest relationship she would form for the rest of her life was with a now-dead man, or if she wanted to buy an additional plot for a relationship she might never have or which might also end in acrimonious divorce like her parents'. This stranger was asking her if she would probably, like everyone expected, not start a family, or if she did, if they would visit her in a cemetery next to the grandfather they never knew in a chain-link adjacent plot that was probably quiet, no more foot traffic any more. She'd felt guilty for crying for herself, but the cemetery manager didn't know the difference between self-pity and grief. Just one spot, she had said. Just my father's spot. She could only figure out one death that day, the one that had already happened.

And she hadn't thought Danny's had been a possibility at all, and here they were three weeks from an avoided funeral. Where she was kneeling would have been turned over black dirt, with a fresh stone.

Greta blinked the image away as she heard footsteps behind her. In reality, they were gloppy boot steps in the still-muddy grass. Greta noticed the figure, shadow short and stubby. "You shouldn't be here," Greta said.

"Did you bring Danny?" Martha asked.

Instead of answering that Danny wasn't out of the hospital yet, Greta swallowed. She held back a comment about how he was beginning to string words together, the memory of him holding an oversized pencil in his fist, for physical therapy.

Instead, she gestured around to the solitude in the cemetery. After a second of silence, Greta said, "He's not yours."

"Who? Your dad? Danny?"

"Both. You gave them away. Come back when I'm done."

"There's plenty of memory to go around," Martha said. She had lipstick on and that was indecent. A seduction of a dead man. As Martha squatted next to her, Greta tried not to notice that their thigh bones were the same length, some genetic joke of duplicated bone structures.

Greta stood, erasing the similarities in their stance as she had tried to erase their similarities in everything else. Her mother was a nurse; Greta blocked medical dramas from her Netflix queue. Her mother liked Robin Eggs Whoppers around Eastertime. Greta pretended to share Danny's preference for Peeps. She couldn't delete her earlobes, bow legs, or narrow wrists, but she could pretend they came from modeling dough instead, or her father (though his earlobes hung so loose from his head that he used to wiggle them at restaurants to distract them when their food had taken too long).

Martha stayed squatting and didn't look up at her. Greta made it halfway to her car, rummaging in her pocket for her keys, and came out with them gripped between her fingers like she was in a dark parking lot. She let them fall into her pocket again and turned to where her mother still stared down at the gray stone she'd had nothing to do with choosing.

"You can't pretend you've always been here," Greta shouted back from beside her car.

"It was fifteen years ago."

Greta took a few steps toward Martha again, blood pulsing in her throat. "It doesn't matter. That's the thing. It doesn't matter. You chose someone else over us."

"That's not what—"

Greta took a deep breath before interrupting Martha's interruption. "And that would have been okay. Right? Like, I could have gotten over it. But then you left him. You left your better option, your greener grass."

"This isn't about a man, Greta. And if you'd just let me—"

"No." Somehow the argument had dragged Greta off the street and back into the mud. Just five feet away from the gravestone again, she saw the gray roots of her mother's head as she looked down at the gravestone.

"If I thought you wanted to talk like adults, I would talk," Martha said, still not glancing up at her. It was the same time-out voice Greta remembered from childhood—that achingly calm voice in the face of a tantrum.

Greta grabbed her keys again, cutting her palm against their sharp edges. Her tennis shoes sank in the mud as she stomped back to the car. Parked below was Martha's car, an unassuming white Camry. No one would guess that it belonged to the bride of Satan, but you know, she would probably leave him, too, if there were better options. When Greta sat on the front seat, she set off the whoopee cushion in her pocket. A low, loud belch of air under her. And suddenly she was gulping air between loud gasps of laughter. *That's what I get for American Spirits, huh, Dad?* Her car kicked into gear.

She dialed Max's number, cradling the phone between her ear and shoulder as she pulled out of the cemetery. The phone rang. Rang again. Where the hell could he be on a Sunday afternoon? His family went to church, but even Greta knew that was a morning kind of thing. When his voicemail flipped on, she didn't even leave a message, though there were a few seconds between the beep and her turning off the phone. Empty air on his voicemail.

Meg's words rang in Greta's head: *"Do you even let someone try to get close to you?"*

She felt like she was trying to draw on an empty bank account with Max. How much could she exploit his good will?

But there were other people who tolerated her, right? Or used to.

She shouldn't have done it, but she drove past Brandon's place on the way home. Brandon lived on the other edge of the chain-link fence. Turned out, the houses were rentals filled with PhD students on a budget. It also turned out that the first time she and Brandon had sex in that house, Greta got up afterward and noticed something strange. The neon Marlboro cowboy, which served as ironic decoration in a nonsmoker's man cave, fell off the wall during a freak breeze from a window that Brandon didn't remember leaving open. In the car on the way home, she warned her dad that he needed to stay out of her personal life, whispered into the air like he inhabited the pine tree air freshener hanging from her rearview mirror.

It wasn't her father she was trying to exorcise as she pulled into Brandon's driveway. It was four o'clock in the afternoon on a weekend. This was a normal friend kind of time to drop by, right? With or without prior authorization, it was less bad for an ex-girlfriend to stop by unannounced when it was daytime on a day when people somewhere sat in pews and folded their hands. She knocked on the door.

Eden answered, her almost-metallic blonde hair in a balletic bun poised on top of her head. Even on a Sunday, she had a full face of makeup in the way that Greta identified with women not from the Midwest. Thick mascara, purposeful eyeliner, and a soft-pink lip. Below this getup, she wore slouchy sweatpants and a pink sweatshirt. The pristine condition of both reminded Greta that Eden didn't need to work out, or didn't sweat if she did. "Hey, Greta," Eden said, because of course she would remember someone's name she'd met only once. She waved Greta in with a wide smile. "We were just watching some hoops. Right, babe?"

Brandon waved a hand from the couch. He had a section of newspaper draped across his lap— exactly how Greta would have chosen to watch basketball too.

Eden perched on the edge the white loveseat, the one that Greta had once fallen off while making out with Brandon. Her gray eyes tracked the movements of jerseyed figures on the flat screen above Brandon's unusable fireplace. In Greta's back pocket, her phone started to vibrate. Probably Max returning her call.

Brandon patted a seat next to him, and Greta slipped off her shoes. The mud from the cemetery coated a fine ring around her ankles and socks, so she stripped down to bare feet. She tried to hide them under her as she sat on the couch. She wondered if Brandon had watched Eden put her makeup on in the mirror that morning, his arm slung around her waist as he looked on while she painted herself. Once Greta and Brandon had walked through the Younkers makeup section, accepting every perfume sample offered to them—up one arm and down another. Pausing at a makeup display, Greta had grabbed an oversized makeup brush and pretended to apply blush to her butt. "That's how those monkeys get red asses," she had said. He'd laughed. They both stunk so badly that her car smelled like a greenhouse had exploded inside it for weeks. Brandon maybe wouldn't know that Greta actually knew how to use makeup, though. She felt self-consciously naked—her feet and her face and everything, she guessed.

"So, what's up?" Brandon asked.

She shouldn't be disappointed that he didn't remember her father's death day. They weren't a couple when her father died. She usually observed the anniversary alone, but still she kicked herself for not being more open prior to this moment so that she wouldn't have to explain everything. A full Greta recap. She knew she couldn't really talk about everything, or anything, with Eden here and thousands of roaring fans cheering for and against two teams she didn't have any connection to. "Got into a fight with my mother," she told him.

"That sucks," he said, his voice careful. He was obviously mining his memory for any mention of a mother in the past. He wouldn't find one. "You okay?"

Eden stood up, fists pumping. "Tar Heels!"

Brandon didn't roll his eyes. It was his nature to be a good boyfriend. He'd never made fun of the stupid shit she liked, either. He'd always watched at least a few minutes of *Star Trek* before he picked up a book. "Right, well, I'll get over it." Greta stood up. "I'm not sure why I came."

Brandon stood too. "No, I get it. I mean, we should hang out sometime. Maybe you can bring someone."

*Someone you're seeing. Someone you're kissing and someone who's seeing more naked skin than your toes.* "Yeah, sure. That'd be . . . something." Greta rolled her socks into a ball and crammed them into her pocket. She slid over the heels of her shoes so that her bare feet met the wet insoles of the sneakers with a gush.

Eden waved and broke eye contact with the screen. A commercial break. "Sorry to be a bad host," she chirped. "Twenty Final Four appearances can't even compete with this guy's rugged good looks. But I was a Tar Heel before I was with him."

*And you'll be a Tar Heel after,* Greta thought as she pulled out of the driveway. Those loathsome thoughts that danced from one lobe to the next with glee. In her head, she didn't have to pretend she didn't mean it.

Max left a blank voicemail, too, in return for hers. When she got back to Danny's apartment, she logged onto Facebook and sent Max a message:

*Today SUCKED.*

He sent back a beer emoji with a question mark after it.

*I don't want to talk to anyone ever again.*

*We don't have to talk,* he wrote back.

*Okay,* Greta texted, and they made plans to meet.

# CHAPTER NINE

Even on Sunday nights, Greta was afraid to run into students at bars in town. Once, two years ago, she happened to be at the same bar as a student celebrating her twenty-first birthday. The student practically fell off her stool while her friends handed her more shots. Greta had felt like one of those creepy, leering men on family dramas in the eighties talking about high school girls. "I keep getting older, but they just stay the same age."

One of the only places to duck students were the dive bars on the other side of the railroad tracks. Greta and Max settled on Mikey's. Ames didn't have motorcycle gangs exactly, but there were motorcycles parked out front. While in her hometown, twenty miles away, there would be rips in the leather jackets around her, in a college town these were intact, with their patches carefully sewn on, like it was a meeting of a Boy Scout troop on wheels.

At five on a Sunday, the crowd in Mikey's was thin and lazy—thin as in few people; the men had plenty of girth. The whole place smelled like popcorn, even though the popcorn machine was empty. Like at Brandon's, some basketball game played in the background. Max was already there when Greta arrived. He was reading a thick book that looked like a presidential biography, under the light of a hanging lamp. He turned when she approached and stowed it before she could ask what it was. She missed the days before the aneurysm, when she'd had time to read horror and sci-fi and fantasy—to escape into something that was wholly in her head but apart from herself. Now, all the reading she did was either about brain injury or bugs, with little room for space exploration or ax murder. If anyone could conjure up free time where there was none, it would be Max. Max had been the single most organized person Greta had ever met, and while she had never told him so, he would have made a good doctor had he not dropped out of medical school after the first year. He said he'd been "winnowed out," but she always suspected the truth was something murkier. Even in the bar, he looked like a young professional, ready to slip a thermometer out of the pocket of his pressed button-down. He didn't fit into the bar dressed like that, and he would never have fit into her hometown. Maybe that was why she liked him.

Greta took the stool next to Max, but he had switched from focusing on his book to his phone, and didn't look at her. When her own phone buzzed, she realized what he was doing. *No talking,* his message said. He caught her gaze and gave a half smile. When the bartender approached, she held up two fingers. She didn't know what they'd get by just specifying a number and not a product, but it produced a result. Two mugs of watery beer appeared in front of them. They clinked them together and drank in silence. Almost silence. The soundtrack was her, slurping, and him, sipping, and the bar's country music and sleepy middle-aged men yelling at referees someplace far away.

Beers acquired, he sent another text. *We'll start with the good stuff. Promise.*

She barely had time to question what he meant when she noticed a tablet perched on the bar in between them. Max opened Netflix and scrolled to the downloaded shows. He had an entire season of Star Trek *Voyager*.

She was about to text her protest, when the first episode began, and by the second she was three beers in and enjoying the flavor of the show more than her drink. Max knew that she never strayed beyond *The Next Generation*, but for once, she didn't feel like fighting. She didn't love Captain Janeway's crew, but Max had started at an exciting episode during a Borg attack. The Borg episodes from *TNG* had been some of her favorites. The Borg, half humanoid and half machine, lived in colonies like bees. They were even called drones, with a queen as their head. The entomological connections in sci-fi were one of the things that drove her love of the genre. Somehow the imagination of writers drew connections from insect to alien so easily that these trails were everywhere. At the end of the second episode, it was clear that a Borg was joining Janeway's crew, and slightly tipsy Greta had to admit it was an interesting turn of events. Not that she would admit that to Max.

Not saying anything at all felt so good that Greta was silent the rest of the night. When she got back into the apartment, Franz Liszt nosed his way out of Meg's bedroom and curled up on the couch next to Greta. He was a cute dog. A Wheaton terrier mix—she'd done a little digging around. She thought she would have named him Wil if it had been up to her. Ensign Puppy. Why weren't there any dogs on the starship *Enterprise*? Data had that cat. She'd never been around a dog much, but she liked the silence between them. It was like he could sense the things she didn't say, and soon they both fell asleep, his wet muzzle resting on her leg.

Monday morning, Greta spoke again. This time, to the nursing staff, and it didn't go well. She had woken up with a plan to protect Danny from Martha.

"I didn't ask if it was easy. I asked if it was possible." Greta's hands on her hips defiantly. She didn't know if it was a genetic predisposition to cock one's hips when making a stand or if it reflected learned behavior. Someone's dissertation could come from that stance.

"The patient's wishes need to be taken into consideration," the nurse responded.

"And once the patient regains the power of complex speech, then maybe we can ask him."

The nurse bit her lip 'and referenced her charts. "Look, I've been helping your brother for two weeks. He lights up when your mother comes around."

"He's developed phosphorescence? You might want to note that in his paperwork. Probably a side effect of some drug or another."

"If you ask me—"

"I didn't. I'm listed as the next of kin, right? So take her off. We can take care of him."

*We.* Meg and Greta, an unlikely superhero pairing. How to explain to the nurses that sometimes it isn't better to have loved and lost. Sometimes it's better to pretend like you never loved at all, since that person acted like they didn't love you. Danny didn't need someone who was just going to leave him again. Greta had put down roots, planted herself back here, and she would be damned if Martha came and fucked everything up again just as she was rebuilding what little family they had left.

After Martha had left fifteen years ago, her father hadn't stepped up; he had shut down.

Greta hadn't taken over her mother's workload either. If anything, Greta's chores got easier without Martha. Greta sorted and folded the laundry like she always had, but there was a full load less without Martha there. Greta unstacked the plates from the dishwasher as she always had, but time between loads of dishes went a little longer. Danny, on the other hand, tried to fill himself into the holes that their mother had left behind. He carried them for the first month on his shoulders, or tried to, at least until the social worker came. He was the one who made their birthday cake that year. He had walked around with this guilty dog look like he had done something to make her run, and it was remembering that face now that made Greta plant her feet in the hallway, restate her request.

"I don't want her here."

Trying to create a plan with Martha involved felt like trying to plant a garden in the winter. Better to go at it alone, or with only Meg. Greta might not know what she was doing or how she could help Danny, but she would figure it out fast if she needed to.

She needed to, she realized.

Still more noise in the hallway.

The nurse raised an eyebrow at Greta. "She doesn't sound happy."

Greta nodded. "Is there a back stairway?"

"Emergency exit only."

And this doesn't count? "Oh, so not coward exit only."

The nurse didn't say anything, but her lips curled in such a deliberate way that Greta would have suspected that the nurse called Martha herself if she hadn't been with her this whole time.

Martha stood by the nurse's station, where one hallway crisscrossed with another. Acoustically, it was the best place to make one's stand for attention. Martha's body turned toward Danny's room as she raised her voice to the nurse at the desk. She turned her attention as soon as Greta stepped in the hallway. Martha half-ran up to her, so mad that she spat. "They say I've been put on the no-contact list. The no-visitor list?"

Greta felt the cross-hairs on her, and with no option for the flight response, her heart began to beat. Fight it is. *Ready the photon torpedoes, Worf.* Her voice raised in pitch and volume, like the knob broke off inside her. "Are you the aneurysm fairy, here to exchange his recovery for some sort of favor?"

Martha let the sarcasm slide. "What did Meg say?"

"Meg doesn't know."

"That's right that she doesn't know. Neither of you know how long this road to recovery is going to be. You can't do it alone. I'm here. I'm allowed."

"You're *allowed?* You got your license renewed to come be a mother again? I think that's up to both of your children, isn't it?"

"You cannot shut me out. Danny does better when I'm here. Would you rather he be alone all day?"

They were in step toward the elevator together now, her mother following her. Greta could still feel the eyes of the nursing staff trailing them. "I would rather that he doesn't slide backward in a week when his support system crumbles because it wanted out."

Three floors down, then the entry level. "I'm not making excuses for leaving your father."

"Not just 'my father.' Me. Danny." Greta turned, lowered her voice to a normal volume, hoping her mother would take the hint. "In the animal kingdom, you did your job—birth to infancy, to early childhood. You kept us from getting eaten by predators. Thanks. And bye."

The door dinged open and her mother stayed inside the elevator, mouth agape. Greta heard her name called before the door dinged closed in front of her, a curtain closing on the act. Greta jogged through the lobby before it could open again.

As she drove away, Greta kept waiting for the moment to feel triumphant somehow, like beating a boss in a video game. Explosions of gold coins and experience points enough to level up. She should feel different facing Martha down, but she didn't. She was too mad to go home and instead drove twenty miles south to the town she'd grown up in. She skirted along the old neighborhood past her old house. A bike in the front yard, dead grass, a flag at half-staff. Her father had put in that flagpole the year before they moved, hit it into the ground with a mallet. Every day it wasn't raining or snowing, he'd go out at dawn and raise the flag, sometimes with Greta at his side and sometimes alone. Danny learned "Taps" and played it on the trumpet they rented from the school. They left that flagpole behind, with all its memories and weight, when they moved away. Sometimes it was untenable to keep that big a part of yourself. Even big things—especially big things—you had to jettison to stay afloat.

Martha's perfume hadn't diffused in the hallway when Greta got back to the apartment. Before Meg said anything, Greta knew Martha had been there.

Meg knit on the floor. Franz occupied the same spot on the couch where Greta had left him that morning. As if expecting an argument, he covered his head with a paw.

"So, Martha stopped by." Meg didn't say "your mother." She meant to say the sentence casually, but it still sounded weighed down with rocks.

"I'm not talking to her again." Greta tried to

141

walk into the kitchen to end the conversation, but Meg trailed behind her.

"I didn't ask you to talk to her. I just wanted to tell you she was here."

Greta poured a glass of water and took a sip. "What, so she wanted you to override me?"

"You know I couldn't. Legally."

Meg stood too close, and Greta wanted to tell her to back off. She wanted to duck. She wanted to avoid this conversation, fast forward it, because she knew she couldn't stop herself. "I thought maybe you'd feel sorry for her."

"I do feel sorry for her," Meg said.

That admission was all it took for Greta to let it out, let pop that kernel she'd been holding close inside for three years. *Fuck it.* "Oh yeah? Probably because she was a cheater too."

Greta saw Meg's demeanor change, saw the tiny crack in the dam open. Her voice was quiet. "Leave, Greta. I've given you time. Get out."

Greta took a final sip and slammed the glass down on the counter. No shouting, no tears or begging, and no bargaining. She skipped the stages of grief—as if there were grief in breaking off a temporary truce. Greta's things were packed in five minutes, and she was gone. Nothing as big as a flagpole to leave behind— only the small face of a terrier pressed to the second-floor window of an apartment that Greta refused to look at as she drove away.

# PART TWO

## Spring

"Can I even walk on the land without gutting it? Maybe not: Acts have their consequences. If it does happen that without being aware of it in time, we immutably change and destroy what we have sought and found, we will, of course, not be unique."

—Paul Lehmberg, *In the Strong Woods: A Season Alone in the North Country*

# CHAPTER TEN

On the first night after getting kicked out of Danny's apartment, Greta slept in her storage unit. She'd rented it for the semester, after all. It wasn't heated, and after one sleepless night she abandoned that plan. On the second night, Greta got a room at the cheapest motel she could find in town. It stood on an industrial road leading to a highway, one of those long, two-tiered motel structures with metal railings along the top balcony. The scratchy bedsheet covered a lumpy mattress, and the side table didn't even house a Bible. If Jesus didn't want to hang out there, Greta should have been more nervous. The hotelier had cut so many corners the room should have been round. But nothing in the world—not cheap amenities, not even bed bugs—would send her begging to Meg again. That door had closed.

Language shaped perception. Even Greta, who nearly failed her humanities requirements in college, could prove that. For instance, the story *The Very Hungry Caterpillar* was most kids' introduction to the process of metamorphosis. Wasn't it cute to show a caterpillar eat tiny hole-punched holes through everything? It was all a question of perspective. If the story was told by the strawberries and oranges and sausages and slices of cherry pie, the caterpillar was a menace. It didn't even finish what it started. Just because butterflies had pretty wings at the end of it all didn't make the destruction they left in their wake any less real.

So, the story of the relationship of Danny and Meg from the Eric Carle perspective might show a meet-cute scenario in a middle school parking lot. Meg had just finished her job interview. Still clad in some adorable, probably pink skirt and pantyhose (Greta imagined Meg was the type to wear pantyhose in August), she offered to help Danny. Danny needed to load a bus full of instruments to bring to a band competition because his parent volunteers had ditched. The first hole through the first piece of fruit.

Danny liked her, but maybe it feels good to be eaten—not in the sexual way. God, she didn't even want to think about sex and Danny and Meg and biological urges and all that. She meant "eaten" in the falling for someone kind of way. If Danny had been her only piece of fruit, her only apple, it wouldn't be an issue. It was those multiple pages of greed that made it all a problem.

He didn't lie about who Meg was, not even the first time when she had seen them together at the movies. She had only been down there to do some Christmas shopping; it had been a fluke. Her twin two rows ahead of her, his lips smashed against the lips of a girl with long blonde hair wrapped in a red kerchief. Greta waited for them by the 3D glasses recycling case outside of the theater and caught his arm. "Who's this?"

"This is my secret girlfriend, Meg," he told Greta. He wore that infuriating wry smile, a kid with his hand caught stealing a candy bar. "I'm the other man."

Meg turned pink, but Danny's mouth tilted sideways. "It's okay," Danny said. "I chose this. You didn't kidnap me."

Greta could have slapped him, but she wasn't given the chance. They disappeared out the front doors of the movie theater, released into the wider world.

That night Greta called Danny. "What's the boyfriend's name?" Greta asked, even though she didn't know why. Maybe she wanted to remind him of the implications. Maybe she wanted to remind him of the feeling of being left on the porch while Martha drove away with someone else.

"It's her fiancé."

Greta swore at him but heard discussion in the background. Soft voices.

"Ex-fiancé," Danny clarified, this time into the phone again. "They've been taking a break."

"How much of a break? Does he know?"

Silence on the other end.

Dad had been dead for a year. Good thing, too, or this would have killed him. It was enough to have a cheater for an ex-wife, but a son? Greta's thoughts outpaced her mouth, for once. If he hadn't died, though, Danny could have stayed at Oberlin. He wouldn't have dropped out of his performance program, and he'd be touring the world. He wouldn't have had to come back to Iowa to finish college. He wouldn't have gotten a job teaching music. The debt would have still been there, but in hibernation. Waiting to emerge. He wouldn't have met her, done this. "Break it off, Danny. What's that story about the wise man building his house on rocks or sand or some such shit?"

Danny had the nerve to laugh. "Are you trying to quote parables to me? Seriously?"

"I don't remember it, but this is a bad foundation. Do you want her to cheat on you? She can't change her nature."

"And you can't change yours, Greta. She is the first thing that's made me feel solid in years. She makes me feel like—" Danny said.

"Don't give me a music metaphor, Danny, or so help me."

He laughed. "You'll like her when you get to know her. You'll love her."

"You love too easily."

"And you hate too easily."

"I call that discerning taste," she mumbled, but she could tell he wasn't listening.

Another conversation out of earshot. Then,

"She's telling him tomorrow. And then it'll be official, okay?"

But it hadn't been okay. It still wasn't okay. So they'd stopped talking, she and Danny. And now Danny needed her and so like an itch she got used to, like an infestation of a pest that you had to live with, she tolerated Meg. She tolerated Meg until she couldn't anymore. She even lived with Meg, and side by side they made their pilgrimages to Danny's bedside. Danny was their common religion—that was too dramatic; Danny was their common language, maybe. They could speak Danny together. Now, they couldn't speak at all.

Not surprisingly, Greta's motel didn't offer premier internet service included in the price—it didn't even offer a bagel for breakfast. The lobby didn't even have furniture outside of a moth-eaten couch and a long check-in desk with laminate coating. When she got to work, she logged onto the Reiman Wi-Fi to check her e-mail.

Another e-mail asking about her research.

*Shit.*

She should have guessed that the lab wouldn't want to fund someone for next year who had no research, no goals, and no fucking idea of what she wanted now that Costa Rica was gone.

She knew she still needed to stay in the program, even if it meant digging her fingernails into the ledge to keep herself from falling. Entomology had been the first thing to really make sense to her. There were more insects than humans on the planet, and understanding that larger group made her feel better about not understanding the smaller one. Maybe she could scrape together the money tomorrow to fly back to Costa Rica and finish her research season on her own dime. The cost of the butterfly transmitters started to total in her mind. It was more likely that Danny would contract a new species of lice in the hospital, and he could be her test subject. He needed to grow his hair back faster in that case.

When she turned around, Brandon was behind her. She tried to stow her phone in her lab coat pocket without him noticing, but he did. "Hey, sorry. Writing to Plank. Funding shit." She couldn't speak in a full sentence. The nerves choked her English abilities.

"You look terrible." He didn't mention her showing up at his door two days ago, and his not mentioning it made the whole thing a million times more awkward.

"Haven't been sleeping well."

"Couch problems?"

"Lack-of-couch problems. Got in a fight with Meg."

Brandon gave her the barest smile. When they used to fight, Brandon stood and took her yelling, her insults, her complaints, and her concerns. He let her walk away from a fight when she needed to. He took her anger in like a black hole sucking the light and matter out of the universe. It wasn't even arguing in a vacuum, it was arguing *with* a vacuum. He sucked up every-thing and shot nothing back except a blank stare. She could have been speaking in German for all he noticed.

It had been like that for their last fight, the one about his post-grad opportunities. She knew it was improbable for him to stay in the Midwest, but part of her still wanted him to. A one-year position for a visiting lecturer in New York came up, and Brandon was floored when he was accepted. Other acceptances rolled in, but Greta knew he would pick the one farthest away— which he did. He told her they could still date long distance. "What's the point?" Greta barked. "How are you here for me when you're over there?"

"It's only a year."

"Which is longer than we've been together."

He had shrugged, which made her madder. "If you can't wait a year, then I guess that this isn't the right relationship." He had said it so calmly, not a single caps lock moment. She left anyway, slept in the car in the middle of the winter. It was even worse than sleeping in her storage unit, seeing as her face nearly froze to the car window. The next time they had seen each other he spoke so evenly, with such control, that it lulled her. She might have called him a snake charmer if it didn't imply she was a cobra. After that fight, they'd shaped a relationship past its expiration date. They had stayed together, in a kind of frozen animation, for the three months until he left. If he hadn't been so cool and collected, they wouldn't have had those three months. Those three summer months of hikes in Ledges Park, swatting mosquitos by Gray's Lake, and eating gelato.

Getting a rise out of him took too much energy. She missed that, about their fights. She always wore herself out crashing into his silence. He always let her get a word in edgewise, and in fact, offered his edges for her to throw words at.

"I'm homeless, and I'm doing prelims in May and learning to fence the other grad students for a spot in the fall TA lineup."

"Anyone need research assistants? Funding there, maybe?"

"Unlikely."

"You could always work here." He grinned at her and gestured around. "This is the Taj Mahal of butterflies, no? We've even got a coffee shop across the hall."

"And complete my dissertation when exactly in this nine-to-five job of yours?" Two adolescent girls watched their discussion from the other side of the plexiglass. She worked in a goldfish bowl—if goldfish bowls could be full of butterflies.

"Get creative, Oto," he said, and with that, he left the lab.

She turned back to the pupa. Inside each of them, the soon-to-be-butterfly was reassembling itself to accommodate wings. Most of them, at least. She touched the pupae in turn—cool, cool, cool, warm. She picked up the warm one. It was for a swallowtail, or it had been. She held it up to the light, and it looked dark and splotchy. The cremaster—the tip that attached with silk to a branch in the wild—had split. It was the warmth that was the first clue. They died in transit sometimes, or some just failed to fully metamorphose. Change or die, the common rule for both business and nature. Greta disposed of the pupa in the hazardous materials bin in the lab and washed her hands.

Above the sink was an article with Brandon's face on it. The text detailed some experiment he had run about wine and butterflies—local news in Ames was so thrilling. But his open smile beamed at her as she ran water over her palms. She realized, suddenly, that he'd had no purpose to come into the lab earlier except to speak with her. Despite herself, despite the embarrassment at his apartment, despite him being her boss, she felt her cheeks warm.

# CHAPTER ELEVEN

Episode's over." Danny said it too loud, but at least in that loudness he sounded like himself. That, paired with the fact that Danny seemed to actually like Captain Picard, nearly brought tears to Greta's eyes.

She shot a glance sideways to check if the guy in the bed next to Danny's was still asleep. The rehab center's dual occupancy rooms were the only ones approved under Danny's insurance. Danny had been in the center for two weeks, and Greta still hadn't seen the guy in the bed awake. She had, however, noticed a pair of knit mittens for him on the side table. Meg had befriended him somehow, and Greta felt that the comatose guy had taken sides. "You don't have to be so loud. Jesus. I can hear you," she complained.

"I didn't rise from the dead," he replied

"You might recover, but your humor doesn't stand a chance."

Danny sometimes tripped over his thoughts the way Martha's fabric used to fold over in the sewing machine when she wasn't watching. She always made their Halloween costumes, and the zippers and seams ran crooked, turning in on themselves.

Greta had so much she wanted to ask Danny,

and so few things she wanted him to find out in return. It was easier to turn the focus on him. After so many weeks in the hospital, he was used to that anyway. Greta finally asked the question that had been weighing on her. "What did it feel like? How did you know what happened?"

He sighed. "A headache."

"Oh God. Don't make me paranoid about headaches."

"But it started that way. One of my students raised his hand and asked what was wrong with my face. Some of the kids laughed." Danny paused, yawned. "But then I thought about Dad. About seeing him in the hospital bed, dead. And then suddenly I couldn't think anymore."

"That was the worst day of my life."

"Can worst days be tied?" Danny laughed. "A smart-ass eighth-grader saved my life."

"I thought smart-ass eighth-graders only saved the world in books."

"He didn't save the world. He only saved me."

Greta didn't say anything for a moment, afraid for him to hear the fear in her voice. *Same difference,* she would have said. She had only been alive ten minutes without him in this world. Ten separate minutes in different spheres—he inside, she out. Martha had said they used to kick in unison inside her, like choreography. "Has the whole music thing gotten better?"

He looked at her straight on. His hair had

started to grow back in uneven patches. "I lost it."

"What?"

"Music. And the colors," he said. "And there's this constant sound. I thought maybe it was something in the hospital, but you don't hear it, do you?"

Greta shook her head.

He closed his eyes and leaned back against the pillow. "It's like the sound beneath a lake. Like swimming, the pressure and the swish of water against water. Like that. All the time."

"Maybe the colors will come back," Greta said. "Maybe the sound will disappear."

Maybe "maybes" would start meaning something too, but that was unlikely.

How many piano recitals had Greta sat through in her life, watching her twin's fingers sail up and down the keyboard like they were possessed? Private performances with "Taps" played to a silent neighborhood while her father folded the flag into reverent triangles. She had been to more band concerts than any sister should ever be forced to sit through. She had even helped record his audition tape for Oberlin. They'd borrowed a camcorder from a teacher and sat in the music room of the high school. Greta knew she would go to Iowa State—it was nearby, it was cheaper—but she blindly scrabbled in the dark for what to study. Here was her sure-footed brother bounding up the side of his mountain. Even as they recorded the video, and although she didn't have the musical knowledge her brother possessed, she had known he would get in. No surprise to her when the thick envelope arrived. The only surprise had been his surprise. She realized then that he truly had no idea how good he was.

If he had been allowed to stay, to finish that program, where would he be now? Sick or well? Famous or unknown?

It had been ten years since that envelope arrived. His right hand clenched and unclenched against his thigh, closing jerkily like a Venus fly trap. She caught herself watching the movement and noticed the lingering silence between them. When Danny didn't say anything for another moment, Greta checked her watch. Almost the end of her lunch hour, always just enough time for an episode on the *Enterprise* and not much else. "Are you tired? Want me to get out of here?"

"Are you watching out for Meg while I'm here?" he asked. He closed his eyes and couldn't see the expression that crossed her face.

In fact, she had hardly said anything to Meg since their fight three weeks ago. "Something like that."

"She's not like Mom."

Greta ignored this. "Get some rest. You're

getting out of here in a week, and we're gonna train for a Starfleet Academy fitness exam to celebrate."

He didn't laugh this time, already half asleep.

That afternoon at work, Maura and another aide rushed into the lab with the release nets in hand. They wore identical lab coats and frantic expressions. Maura said, "Dr. Utz, we have a problem. There are these ants—"

Brandon didn't ask a question, didn't even let her finish her sentence. Instead, he pushed through the locked lab doors into the butterfly dome. Greta was two steps behind. "Show me," he said to the aides at his heels.

Maura cleared her throat, catching her breath from the sprint. "There's this line of them. I think they might have come from the new tree."

Brandon swore under his breath and then waved a hand toward the docent at the door to the exhibit. "Put out the velvet rope for a while. We're doing some maintenance in here."

The line of ants drew a red thread across the rocky path. It led directly from the base of a bulbous tree, across the walking trail through the exhibit, and into the center garden of flowers and ferns. "The damn gardeners and their damn new plantings," he said. "I bet they hitchhiked in on the new rubber tree."

The pairing made Greta think about that stupid

kids' song about rubber trees and ants. "High Hopes" was one of Martha's favorite songs—she used to whistle it sometimes while she cleaned. These ants were harvesters, and the damage that a harvester colony could wreak in a place like Reiman was unimaginable. Besides having lots of plants to build habitat in, the butterflies also had access to food plates scattered throughout the garden. These spots gathered the insects for better patron viewing. Even without those delicacies, the plants themselves were sweet and full of pollen. Ants would take down the most delicate plants that the butterflies needed to survive for their food and building materials. "Should we use ant traps?"

"For this big of a problem?" Brandon raised an eyebrow.

"Fumigator?"

"And risk damaging the butterflies? It's not like we can catch all of them. Or leave things closed for that long. It is winter—this is the only reason people are coming to the gardens." She could see him formulating theories and solutions, a chalkboard behind his eyes. "We can't use industrial-strength poisons. And narrow poison usage would still seep into the rest of the habitat," he muttered. "We can't rip everything out."

"Well, start smashing, then, I guess," Greta said, and she stamped her foot on a line of brown bodies. She felt a delicious schadenfreude as her foot cracked their carapaces in one go. She looked at Brandon, whose eyebrow was cocked. "I'm sure it's moments like this that make you miss me," she said.

"Move over," he said. "We'll have to figure out a plan for the long term, but for now my feet have a bigger surface area."

"Plenty of ants to go around, boss," she said as she made room for him. She didn't admit how nice it was to have a distraction. She didn't admit how good it felt to crush something.

One week to go. One week, and Greta couldn't imagine what it would be like to have Danny out of the hospital. When she admitted that to Nadine in their weekly meetings, Nadine pressed a handout into her hand for the third time. It advertised a support group for caregivers that met in a hospital conference room. "It would help Danny if you knew a few people who were in it for the long term too."

Greta glanced up from the paper. "Does Meg go?"

"Not that I know of," Nadine said. "She seems just as reluctant as you."

And that comparison was all it took to get a rise out of Greta.

If Greta were to make a list of things she didn't like, touchy-feely conversation would rank on the top of the list, closely followed by bad coffee and uncomfortable chairs. The fiendish combination of all three in a single location could only have been designed by a social worker, also on the ever-growing list of dislikes. Still, she forced herself to go. Greta had to admit she was not handling things well, however. She had even considered starting text therapy, but the intake form on the therapy website was so personal that she closed the tab before the form asked about bra size and worst memory from the sixth grade.

When Greta arrived in the conference room on Tuesday evening, two men and a woman were busy dragging the chairs into a blobby circle. One of the men, an older gentleman with a short-cropped gray beard, waved her over. "Care to grab one?"

A circle had an infinite number of points along its outer edge, but this circle, once complete, contained only eight stiff chairs. A bearded man poured coffee from an industrial carafe. He offered a cup of the offensive stuff to Greta, who shook her head. Styrofoam cups were on her list of dislikes too.

After a few minutes, the rest of the participants in the support group arrived. What did they call themselves, the supporters? The groupers? Some of them looked like fish: older people with jowls and thick jaws. Since she'd always been tall and prickly, Greta rarely felt young. It's hard to picture a miniature saguaro cactus. The groupers settled into chairs while Greta hung back. When it seemed like the meeting was about to get started, a woman in a teddy bear sweater gestured to the only empty chair. "I assume you're Greta?" she asked. Greta was wearing a name tag that declared this, so she did not take offense. This woman, this middle-aged woman who introduced herself as Pam, could have been any casserole-bearing neighbor from Greta's old neighborhood. She had permed brown hair, and Greta was just deciding whether she would bring a tater tot casserole or a chicken enchilada bake, when she told Greta they were about to begin.

Reluctantly, Greta sat down. "Everyone set?" Pam asked, turning expectantly around to each person. "Well, then let's bow our heads for a minute of centering and silence."

Heads bobbed around the room, but Greta's stayed upright. She wished she'd accepted the tarry coffee to give her fingers something to tangle around besides each other. Greta didn't know if the groupers were praying or falling asleep; she didn't do the former and it was usually hard to do the latter. After a second, and as if on some peripheral cue, the heads came up together.

The bearded man next to Greta cleared his throat. "I'll start," he said. "Lisa's been better this week. Her hips aren't bothering her, and she's mostly been sleeping through the night."

"That's great," Pam said.

"Angelo's birthday is next week," the woman next to Pam said. "He invited the kids because he's convinced it's his last. I mean, we thought that it might be his last 'last' year, you know, and so one of our sons can't leave his work. Vacation time, you know? As if this is a vacation."

"That must be frustrating," Pam said. And so it went around the room—status report. The entire bare-your-soul-and-kumbaya business made Greta squirm. The room swelled with an echo of uh-huhs, of "I understand." Right. They understood. Greta watched them nodding to one another in empathy and felt more and more like she'd made a mistake. Finally, Greta's turn came. She could tell by the way they turned toward her, smiles plastered on their faces, as unnatural as the ones on the teddy bears.

"No thanks," Greta said. "I'll sit this round out."

"Well, who do you care for? Can we start there?" Pam asked. She obviously thought Greta was shy.

Greta was not shy, and she prickled against the hint of condescension in her voice. She stood up. "My twin. My brother. Can I end there?"

Pam gave a soft tut. "Oh, sit down."

Something about her tone made Greta do just

that. Greta forced her glance up from the parade of grinning bears on the woman's sweater to her face as she continued, "We were all new once. Just tell us something. What kind of care does he need?"

"Uh, brain injury," Greta said. "He had an aneurysm."

The group nodded as one. "I can imagine that is hard," the bearded man said, his voice neutral and slow as a jazz announcer's. "And do you have much help?"

The question nearly set Greta off again. She pictured Martha, hands on hips in the center of the hallway of the recovery center. "His fiancée."

"Good to have an ally," Pam said.

Greta didn't have anything to say to that.

"When's the wedding?" the man on Pam's other side asked.

"October. I mean, it's supposed to be."

"Having a goal to work toward helps recovery," Pam said.

Greta swallowed and her stomach congealed. Coming was a mistake. A room full of strangers with more advice she didn't need. Greta was about to stand when Pam continued.

"My husband had a stroke, and his recovery has been slow. I love all of you here," Pam said, smiling at the people in the circle, "but I know we face different challenges. Ed lost his wife to breast cancer, and Heather's son has severe epilepsy. I can't say that I know what you're going through, but I do know that my experience of recovery hasn't been easy. Caregiving for brain injury can mean grieving in real time, even as you're trying to take care of the person, and they are different."

Greta's hands hurt, and she looked down only to realize that she had balled them into tight fists.

"But we're here. Five years on, we're still here. A few months in, I made a reservation for a cruise and told him he needed to be healthy enough for it by the time we shipped off. He worked on walking with me every day because, he said, he didn't want to stay in the cabin the whole time."

"He didn't want to snuggle with you the entire time, Pam?" one of the other women said.

"Well, you can only canoodle so many hours," Pam said, laughing. "We know it's hard. It's hard to be one and a half people when your better half is a bit less than himself. But things change, for the good and bad. Glad you're here." Pam bridged the distance between the cheap plastic chairs and put a hand on Greta's arm.

The woman's warm fingers made Greta's arm hair prickle. Out of shock more than permission, Greta let the hand rest for a second before she shook it off. The whole ride back to the motel, Greta felt the imprint like the woman had marked her with inky fingerprints. It was the first time someone had touched her since Meg had in the kitchen. Greta realized what it was about the group that bothered her. It went against everything in her nature to convene like that. It was dangerous. Those ants, for instance. Without their telltale line and shared living quarters, they might have lived in the butterfly house for years, scavenging and surviving. Most insects, as a rule, lived alone. It was the rare social insects that drew attention to themselves—those ant hills, with people buried in them, in the Old West. That was what the meeting felt like, being buried in ants, and Greta doubted she would go back.

# CHAPTER TWELVE

The ants returned after a week. They reconvened their forces, and for once Greta wanted to thank the little demons. The ants had bought her some time.

"It could be worth considering." Greta produced her preliminary observations for Plank. She had secured ten minutes to make her case before he rushed off to a faculty meeting. "Besides chemical analysis and studying the behavior of the colony, there could be an eradication method we need to invent to fix the problem. Since toxins are out of the question, we need to be creative. We're not the only butterfly house in the country, and many of them are for-profit ventures. If we come up with something, those product applications could actually reach the market."

Plank rubbed his beard. "Are you planning this as your research focus now?"

She chewed her lip. "Yeah." The point of a PhD program was to finish a PhD program. She wanted the research, the connections, the experience, but she needed the letters after her name too. Ants, though? The ants had a smell to them, especially after being smushed. "Smushed" was her internal term—eradicated might be the more procedural one. The first day that she and Brandon went into manual eradication mode, she went home smelling earthy and sharp, like sour milk mixed with pine needles. The acetic acid in their defensive glands was the same primary ingredient as the sprays of whip scorpions and cockroaches. She dreamed that night of ants lining up to her bed because she smelled so much like their pheromone trails.

"Your coursework would support it, and I would still feel comfortable overseeing it as your dissertation. Especially if you could get Brandon to sign off on the project."

Greta cornered Brandon that day by the specimen cases. He was unloading a shipment of pupa, removing the tissue paper and holding the specimens up to the light to check for imperfections. "Sure, I'll help. I think this has strong potential. Actionable. I know it wasn't your first choice, but look." He dug into the box in front of him and pulled out a cotton-wrapped lump. "I ordered something for you. For your other research."

He handed her the cotton, and she unwrapped it. It was a small pupa, half the size of her pinky, but she knew it would contain the transparent membranous wings she saw swooping in Costa Rica. "You got a glasswing."

"Four, actually," he said.

Four. She breathed out and placed the pupa in the covered glass chamber. "Thank you, Brandon."

He took the box from her hand and flattened it against his body so that it folded, ready for the recycling bin. He didn't say anything for a moment. "Return the favor by helping me unpack the rest of these. And by 'favor,' I mean that I'm paying you to do this, so get to work." He wasn't smiling, but his voice sounded like it.

The first time Brandon had asked her out, she'd had grass stains on her ass. Spring semester of her first year of graduate school. Central campus was arranged like a clock's face, with a ring road around its outside. Just near the midnight point on the clock was the Memorial Union and the campus's bell tower, the Campanile. On sunny days, undergraduates lay in the grass and strung ropes between trees to tightrope walk on them. Normally, Greta wouldn't have been caught dead around so many people, but she had an odd break between classes that gave her time to stretch her legs and read outside. Brandon had snuck up on her and commented on the series she was reading at the time. Something with pirates and fantasy and other worlds. He had not read it. He asked what it was about, and she wouldn't tell him. Her exact words were, "I am not Google."

"But I can't ask Google on a date."

She glanced up from her novel then. His large body blocked her reading light, the sun shining around his edges like an eclipse. It hurt her eyes to look at him, and so she stared back down again as she rejected him.

By the time he asked again the next fall, he had read the book—and its sequel. It wasn't her reason for saying yes. That was something different altogether. She had been on dates before—albeit not many, not recently, and not consecutively with the same person. Strangers were easy when they were strangers. She had the skills to window-shop the variety that the internet provided, swipe her finger in one direction or another, and send brief messages. The resulting dates were nothing like her date with Brandon. He knew her and had asked her out anyway—twice.

"Why did you ask again?" she had asked him over that first dinner.

"You're smart. Funny. And I don't really get you, so that's interesting to me."

"Well. You're in for a treat." She had cocked an eyebrow and tried to sound droll, but his interest surprised her. His curiosity, for her thoughts and her interests and her turn-ons. And the longer they had dated, the more secondary goodwill came her way. People in the department started treating her differently, as if light passed through him to her, that aura from a hidden sun. They couldn't see what was good about her, but they figured Brandon had.

And that was the situation now. Even if her

committee hadn't been gung-ho on the ant proposal, they trusted Brandon.

She scarcely realized she had crossed the line into flirting with him again. A bad habit, that was all, like a smoker's urge during a concert. Hard to believe that a year ago he had slept next to her. Never curled into her, because she couldn't stand the feeling of someone else's breathing patterns not matching up with hers—it made her hyperventilate. Instead, she slept on her stomach, and he, curled into a letter C next to her.

Danny had once shared a theory with Greta that people fit one of the basic character types in *The Wizard of Oz*. Martha had forced them to watch the musical annually, under the guise of tradition, so the repeated viewing obviously gave him time to consider the applications. People could be all sorts: cowardly, brainless, rigid, meandering, a dog, or a general witch. Greta knew herself to be one of the latter, good or bad, depending on the day. She liked to be in charge, to make things happen. Danny admitted to being a Dorothy, or at least he used to be— overly idealistic and a world saver. Greta thought Meg was a Scarecrow. Max was Tin Man— unflappable, clear-headed, calm when everyone else flailed. From his appearance, Brandon looked like he might be a Lion, but he was a Wizard. A little too smart for his own good, a little self-interested, and a lot mysterious. Even after dating him for a year, she couldn't quite guess what he was thinking.

For instance, what did he think of his girlfriend? Greta observed Brandon, past the last papery pupa she was hanging, trying to make it look like she wasn't. She remembered he and Eden had made a nice-looking couple, objectively speaking. He'd started growing a beard, and Eden seemed like the type who might buy him beard oil for an anniversary gift.

Greta tore off the long strip of packing tape from the bottom of the cardboard box and rolled it into a clear ball in her palm. "Do we need to do a release this morning?"

"I have about thirty ready. We're low on morphos, so time to restock."

He grabbed the release boxes from the upper shelves. They were solid cubes on every side but one, which had a netted opening that worked a bit like a lobster trap. The butterflies could be put in easily, but they couldn't escape. When Greta first started, catching butterflies was the part of the job that required the most practice. She had studied the anatomy of a butterfly, its life cycle, and its mating patterns. She had held butterflies singly to attach sensors, and she had dissected dead butterflies and observed their smallest organs. It was a very different thing to catch butterfly after butterfly between two fingers to hold it still. She couldn't shake the feeling that she damaged the butterflies the first twenty times she caught one, especially after warning visitors not to touch them every day. After a while, though, she became as confident at catching them as the aides were. Maura was especially good and held the highest record for quick catches of most butterflies at one time. The aides stuck the folded wings of a butterfly between each finger like insectoid gloves. Brandon once caught Maura and the others at this game, and instead of scolding, showed how in his huge hands he could catch two butterflies between each finger, snapping them out of the specimen case like Mr. Miyagi with his chopsticks in *The Karate Kid*.

They didn't show off today. The aides weren't scheduled to come in for a few hours, and she and Brandon worked steadily side by side. She caught a few blue morphos. Their scales were the color of night sky just after dusk. Funny thing about the morpho was that for all the attention they got in the exhibit—kids pointing them out, photographers reaching for the cameras around their necks—it was nearly impossible to get a good picture of them. When they landed on a surface, they closed their wings tightly to camouflage with the bark around them. Their dull brown underwings sported eyespots to warn off predators. Useful in the wild, but nothing to compare with their photogenic scales. The blue, like stilettos or skinny jeans, attracted mates. The morpho shared some habitat with the glasswing—they belonged to the same family, too. Greta had to wonder how they appeared to each other. Iridescence versus invisibility. Just showed you how different members of a family could be.

Brandon held his release box close to his chest. Inside, Greta could see flutters of color rising and falling as the butterflies knocked into one another in the crowded space. An external butterfly-run heart. He smiled at her, and her own heart tightened in her chest suddenly. "Have time to help release before you head off?"

She checked her watch. "Yes." Her own box looked less full, but between the two of them, they removed most of the emerged butterflies from the case. She liked to leave at least one behind. Kids peeking in the window liked something to point at, something just emerged and fluttering. Plus, the swallowtail in the emergent case was so freshly out of the chrysalis that its wings were still too damp to fly well.

Before leaving the lab, they removed their white coats and hung them on hooks. He handed his release box to her wordlessly as he shrugged off his coat, and then she handed both boxes to him so that she could do the same.

The walk from lab to exhibit took only a minute. Brandon and Greta crossed the wide hallway and passed the pegboard with butterfly specimens pinned to it. Brandon scanned his badge, and the door unlocked. When Greta opened the release boxes, the butterflies scattered upward and outward like bubbles floating up in soda. She squinted at the morning light coming through the glass dome. The air was humid and hot—had to be to keep the ecosystem in working order—and the dome had the barest rim of condensation around its base. The path had low flowering plants on either side, with small trees spotted with tropical fruits and laced leaves. The center of the exhibit housed the water feature, rocks spilling forth a little waterfall from five feet up. One of her favorite visiting couples was seated on the bench in front of it. The couple were probably in their mid-seventies, and she held a sketchpad while he flipped through a novel. The butterflies flitted over and around them like fairy guards. In moments like this, Greta felt sure that she belonged here, but unfortunately, at this moment, she couldn't stay. She checked her watch again. "I gotta go," she told him.

"Good luck," he said.

Moving her brother home wasn't a thing she should need luck for, but just in case, she said, "Thanks."

Greta got to the rehab center just a few minutes before Danny's release time. She paused outside his room at the sight of Meg and Danny together. Meg rubbed Danny's hands while he looked out the window, neither of them speaking. She hadn't seen Meg in weeks, and the only change was that her long blonde hair had been cut into a bob. "You cut your hair," Greta said.

Hearing a compliment that wasn't spoken or meant, Meg said, "Yeah. Thanks."

Or maybe she was thanking Greta for noticing the change, this change amid changes. Greta's eyes kept shifting to their hands, interlocked on Danny's knees. He sat in a wheelchair that he'd been using at the recovery center. But he was going home with a walker, had been practicing with one for two weeks. He still could barely raise his arms past his shoulders, and his right hand didn't close fully. According to his treatment plan, he needed more physical therapy to rebuild the damaged neural connections.

"I can load up the car," Greta said. An excuse to leave again. She didn't know why having Meg there made her feel so anxious. Greta knew her brother and his needs better than Meg could. Hell, she had known him in the womb.

If only bringing Danny home was like releasing butterflies in the wing. Instead of a netted box, there were suitcases, a stack of books, and a plastic canister full of medication bottles. Framed pictures of Meg and Franz Liszt—the dog, not the composer. Greta carried these items to Meg's Outback and put them in the trunk. Typical for spring in Iowa, the weather didn't know if it wanted to snow or rain, and the sleet coated Greta's hatless head before she could get safely back inside the lobby to get another load.

Danny's guitar case came next, dusty and untouched for the duration of his stay. Why had Meg even brought it? Hadn't Danny told her about the noise in his head?

They had learned to swim in a lake in northern Iowa with a mud bottom, cloudy water, and fish that nibbled toes. Greta and Danny would jump off the side of their grandfather's boat when he docked, and they played shark. One shark victim and one shark. Chomp. Their grandfather would drink beer and do crosswords under his big sun hat. Under the lake water, she could never hear her brother calling. She understood what he meant about water rubbing against water. It sounded like gloved hands clapping, like whispers. It was so toneless and unmusical that it stuck with her. And Danny heard it all the time now.

When she got back to Danny's room, hair wet and fingertips white, Meg was sitting on Danny's bed, with Danny still at the window. There were tears in Meg's eyes, and Danny rubbed his skull with his closed fist. Greta didn't notice the nursing staff lining the wall near the door until she entered the room fully. Two white-uniformed male nurses stood, lips pursed in matching frowns.

"What happened?" Greta asked.

Meg shook her head. "Nothing."

The taller nurse cleared his throat. "Danny had an incident."

"He just shouted a little," Meg said, speaking toward the bedsheet as if it took her testimony.

"Anger is normal after brain injury," the shorter nurse cautioned, "and it can come from unrelated causes. It's just something to be patient with."

Meg nodded. "I know."

Lucky her. She knew everything.

"You folks ready to go home?" The taller nurse's tone had flipped into false brightness.

Meg eyed Greta warily. "Now or never." She handed a folder to Greta and kept one for herself. Glancing inside, Greta found duplicates of the release instructions, the list of physical therapy sessions, and the schedule of follow-up neurology appointments. "I put stars on the ones I can't take him to. Could you check your schedule?"

Greta nodded. Shared custody. "Sure."

And with that, the nurses led them to the car.

"Got to pack the last baggage. I won't fit in the trunk," Danny said, too loudly, as Greta wheeled him down the long corridor to the lobby.

The taller nurse held an umbrella over Danny as they loaded him into the passenger seat of the car. Greta noticed that Danny had lost some weight in the past few weeks. He used to have a tire of fat around his waist, but it was a flat tire now, and the skin remained loose under her hold. Still, it took the two of them to load him, especially with Danny helping so little. Once he was in the seat, the nurses said goodbye and went back inside.

Greta stared at her brother, settled on the seat. She knew he could move more, that it was choice, not ability, that made him limp. He would have to walk when they arrived at the other end.

Meg closed the car door and turned to face Greta. The sleet had stopped, but the wind whistled past and caught up Meg's words.

"What?" Greta said.

"I'm scared," Meg repeated, louder this time, each word punctuated with a period. The short haircut made Meg's face older, but not by much.

"You've got my number," Greta said.

"Yeah, you're in my phone under Bug Lady."

"I've been called worse."

"Danny's doing."

Danny shifted in the front seat, head leaning against the window.

Greta chewed her lip and said, "Thanks for letting me stay with you a few weeks ago."

Meg seemed surprised, and that surprise made her look younger again. "You're welcome," she said. And even though she said it like it was a question, the tone didn't annoy Greta.

Greta watched them drive away before getting in her own car.

Brandon was still in the butterfly wing when she got back to work. While the day outside was still gray and windy, the inside of the butterfly wing radiated warmth. So did the smile Brandon gave her. "Everything okay?"

"Okay" was an odd term for it. "He's home," was all she could say.

Brandon pointed at the notebook in his hands. "Just finished soil tests. Want to check the ants while we're still here?"

The dome housed more than butterflies, of course. The exhibit accidentally housed all manner of creatures: snails, worms, and the occasional errant frog brought in on a new planting. Frogs delighted visiting toddlers and drove the curators crazy. They had identified four species of ants in the facility. Most creatures were harmless, but harvester ants were slowly multiplying. When she thought about armies of ants, she now thought of them literally. These little pests could be as destructive as cannons.

It didn't take long to find one of the harvester mounds in the corner of the exhibit. Since their original encounter with the ants, she and Brandon's discussion of them became increasingly specialized. It went from, "Ah, an ant!" to "Let's look at the morphology and try to determine genus—can you tell the antennal segment count under this microscope?" Ten-year-old Greta with her ant farm (complete with plastic tractor) would have been pleased, she knew.

In order to gather data, they needed healthy base-level measurements on damage, as well as proof of the widespread outbreak. When Brandon had first mentioned to her that they wouldn't take action—not even to step on ants—for a month, she scoffed. The scoffing stopped after she realized that waiting meant building research for her dissertation. Something wanted to eat up the habitat, and she had to let it in order to make sure it never happened again. Without proof of the problem, they wouldn't be able to find funding for a solution. They mapped each of the ant mounds and checked them daily. They had tacked some of the sensors to a few of the ants to help map the trails—that idea had been Greta's. At least her butterfly research hadn't been entirely wasted. Scientific method to the rescue, per usual.

Max had once forwarded her a web comic with the title "Scientific Meth-Head." Good data could be addictive, especially when it supported a favorite theory, but maybe not that addictive.

A morpho alighted nearby on a bell-shaped yellow blossom by the ant mound. It flitted its wings for a second, winking blue at her before closing them again. Its proboscis uncurled and dipped into the flower like a soda straw. Greta turned from her notes to watch it drink. Even after years of studying them, she still admired the ingenious head anatomy of a butterfly. Eyes to see, antennae to sense, proboscis to drink, and all-purpose palpi in the center to comfort, to touch, to wipe away excess nectar from the eyes like windshield wipers. Nature provided solutions.

Kneeling in the damp corner of the butterfly house, she thought of her brother, of the nameless something eating his spirit and the look on his face when she'd tried to play music. If only they could see it like the mounds of harvester ants and the steady stream of workers in and out. Five workers carried a carcass of a dead moth between them, its desiccated yellow wings resembling wet, ripped paper. It hadn't died because of the ants, maybe, but the ants would eat it now. It would make them stronger, make them grow. This dead moth would feed into the butterfly effect, would it not? Feed its enemy and expand its strength and territory. Greta's forced inaction meant more destruction. She wished nature provided more obvious solutions for all of its creatures. Nothing had taken Danny from her yet, but darkness was trying to drag him under. She didn't know what action she should be taking or what inaction to continue, to help him heal.

She shivered as she stood up and rubbed the dirt off the knees of her pants. "I hate this job," she told Brandon, meaning it and not meaning at the same time. Forced observation of the life cycle.

He finished his marks on the folded piece of paper. "I know. Me, too, some days."

# CHAPTER THIRTEEN

On Tuesdays Greta offered to transport Danny to and from his appointments. Meg had staff meetings Tuesday mornings and detention duty after school. When Greta offered to help, Meg seemed so grateful that Greta blushed. At eight, Greta mounted the stairs and helped her brother into his coat. The baggy garment drooped on his slim shoulders. As she adjusted it, she noticed bare patches on his half-grown-in scalp. His head looked like a dead lawn, but Greta kept that opinion to herself. Two and a half months ago, he had been in the hospital. In some ways, the recovery seemed miraculous—after all, he was alive, walking, talking. In other ways, it felt impossible. He was sullen and silent during the entire drive.

He must be different for other people. The staff in the clinic waved at Danny when he arrived. His charm for strangers recovered faster than the rest of him, and the nurses smiled in his direction like he was a cookie cake and balloons.

Danny and Greta resembled each other, but few people actually guessed they were twins. He had bright green eyes, where hers were more hazel. Danny was an inch taller than Greta's five-ten, and while they technically had the same hair color, Greta's was always referred to as "mousey" while Danny got the less gendered "light brown" description for that color.

No one had ever looked at Greta like the people at the clinic did, not even on her best days. Her father, maddeningly, would have blamed her for not smiling enough. Danny's default expression was a grin, while Greta's was what she thought of as neutral. Greta worried people could see the things that she thought about them. She liked to call her suspicion "intuition"; her school counselor after Martha's disappearance had called it "fear of abandonment." Either way, she had never made friends easily, even before Martha left. Caterpillars emerge from eggs with all the potential for butterflies. Dissecting a caterpillar, Greta once removed the wing node. It was a near-microscopic organ of pure potential for flight and color. Deep inside of Greta, she knew, had always been those wings to get away from predators.

Harder to overcome those innate characteristics. Greta tried on a tight smile as she transferred Danny's hands to the physical therapist. The PT was built like a tennis player, long tight muscles and height. She could picture his long brown hair tied up with a nylon headband, but stopped herself before she began imagining him grunting and swinging on the court. "I'll be back at one," she said after clearing her throat. It had been too long since she had grunted and swung with anyone. She blushed.

"Two today," Danny said quickly. "It's going to be two. In the lobby."

"I'll be there," Greta said.

She had her own appointment for a birth control shot a few floors up. When she got into the elevator, she checked the e-mail that Meg had sent her about today's schedule. Sure enough, the time said one. Greta sat in the lobby at the woman's clinic and checked the e-mail once more. One o'clock in bold serif font. Maybe the stress had gotten to Meg more than Greta thought.

Her first semester in graduate school, she had shadowed an apiarist. He was a thick-set man of sixty with more salt than pepper in his hair. This was back in her pre-Brandon days, back when the problems of bees seemed like the ones that fascinated her the most. The apiarist gave her a veil and jacket, putting one on himself, and they went out in the hottest part of the day, when the bees were most likely to rest. He brought her to the field containing the ten-frame hives. When full of honey, the hives weighed nearly sixty pounds, but he steered her toward one that could be easily shifted. "This one swarmed two weeks ago and lost its queen," he told her. "And about sixty percent of its workers."

The hive was distinctly quieter than the others

around it. Only a low hum came from inside. "So what do you do?"

"I wait. Bees usually sort themselves out," he said.

"But it's so quiet."

"My suspicion," the apiarist said, "is that a virgin queen is in there eating her sisters and mates. She'll take over and re-establish the hive."

The day Martha had left them was the day of Greta's first period. Ever since she'd been little, Greta couldn't handle the sight of blood, and seeing it come out of herself made her hate her body in a way she hadn't known was possible. It was like her body had driven Martha away. In her mind, for years, the two events were inexorably linked as if there could be only one grown female in a house, one queen bee in a hive. But Greta hadn't been a queen bee, she'd been terrified and grossed out even with the health class lectures.

The day Martha left was warm, too hot even, though it was autumn. It was nearly Halloween and their carved pumpkin nearly rotted in the heat wave. Besides the smoldering temperature and a new strange cramp, Greta hadn't suspected anything was off in her teenage universe. Life ran in the courses it usually had—her father worked his metal and polished his bow for deer season. Danny took his piano lessons and fiddled around in the band room after school on actual fiddles or whatever else he could get his hands on. Greta dodged packs of other girls at the bus stop and buried herself in sci-fi novels and her bug collection. Martha did what she had always done: work as a school nurse and then disappear for hours at night and on weekends. Continuing education, she said, though Greta never thought to ask what she was educating herself in.

Greta's dad never asked questions, not about any of them. He never pushed them on their answers. Greta didn't know if he had always been like that, or if the change came after his tours of duty, but the way she remembered her father was as a man who didn't like confined spaces, either in life or in his relationships. He didn't corner her or Danny for an account of how they spent their time. Knowing would somehow make it his responsibility. He never checked on them to see if they went where they said they did, and he hadn't done that with Martha either. If Greta or Danny had been different kids, their father's laissez-faire attitude would have been trouble. But although Danny occasionally drank in high school or stayed out too late, he never lied about it to their dad.

Martha lied, even when not pressed on it. She must have, because the day she left she told them she hadn't had a job for a month. The mornings getting ready for school, eating cereal all together, and Martha's blue or green or pink scrubs—lies. The day Martha left, the day Greta started to bleed, a strange man waited beside a strange car in front of their house. Martha gave him a peck on the cheek before heaving the suitcases inside his trunk. It was October, but Martha had worn cut-off jean shorts on the day she left and a sleeveless, floral top. The details burned into Greta's mind like she might have to report them someday. No one had ever asked for them, though, and her stomach had cramped and contracted as Martha said, "I just have to go. I'm sorry. I'm so, so sorry."

Every twelve weeks when Greta got her birth control shot, she thought about Martha leaving. A little pinch, a prick, no blood except at the sight of injection, and the memory of being left at fourteen with a rust-colored spot on her underwear.

They had gotten postcards every few months for the first year. Danny kept his, and Greta threw hers away. Eventually, the postcards stopped coming too, but she had an eye for hand-writing. Maybe it came along with identifying the finer characteristics of genus and species. When she returned to work at Reiman that day, she studied the note left for her in her mailbox and knew instantly where it had come from. Greta still recognized the short "m" and looping, bulbous "e's." Martha had written, "Call me,

Greta" and a scrawl of digits that Greta knew she wouldn't ever call. The act felt like a shot into an empty sky on the off chance of hitting something. Greta wouldn't let herself be hit, not that easily. Martha wouldn't get a reward for coming to her workplace. As if to spite her, Greta entered the number in her phone as "Don't answer."

Brandon had already led the butterfly wing cleanup before she arrived. It was morbid most mornings, counting the deceased on the path and entering totals in the spreadsheet. Since he couldn't hand count the butterflies, averaging was the next best thing. With their short life spans, the time and expense to tag the butterflies didn't make sense. Anyway, the butterflies' main duty was to exist and fly around in a pretty way, so it didn't matter too much if they were off their counts by a dozen. The research was mainly done in the lab, prodding pupae.

She was about to put on her lab coat and sign in when Brandon grabbed her arm. "Hey, one second. I wanted to show you some trap ideas."

He pulled her down the main corridor toward his office. She hadn't been inside since the interview a month and a half ago. His desk had a new decoration, a framed photograph of Eden. Her mouth gaped wide open in a laugh so hard that her eyes closed. Even without having ever heard his girlfriend laugh, Greta knew Eden would sound like a tinkling music box. The laugh that would come from a girl whose nickname used to be Princess when she was little. Meg had a laugh like that.

"Okay, so take a look at this." He passed a sheet of graph paper across the table.

Greta eyed the schematics warily. The box mimicked a starter apiarist kit. Bees and ants didn't construct the same kinds of structures, however. She shook her head. "I purposefully didn't major in engineering in college so I wouldn't have to do this kind of stuff."

"Examine it like an ant might."

"Ants don't rely on sight as their primary sense. I can't exactly sense the pheromones on your image."

He took the picture back. "Well, we'll try one. Maybe a few designs. I think you should work one up too, so we have a few to compare to because . . ." He rapped his fingers on the desk in a drum roll. "I may have gotten a paper on the subject accepted at a conference."

"What the hell, Brandon?" She stood up without realizing that she did.

His smile faltered. "What's the matter? I thought you'd be thrilled. Orlando. September. Butterfly breeders and curators, all in one location. It's not as stuffy as a normal academic conference, I promise."

She didn't know exactly why she was mad.

Maybe because this wasn't the project she had wanted to make her name on. Maybe it was that she would be adjacent to projects she would have loved to work on, but she was squishing ants instead, or maybe it was the fact that Brandon didn't ask for her say-so on the application. Maybe the fact that nothing had gone as she planned for the past three months, or year, if she included their breakup. "I don't know," she said. "I mean, that's great but . . ."

"Great nothing. This is where connections are made. This is where you find the right lab to join. You will graduate in, what, a few years? This is the kind of stuff that will find you a home."

"Don't talk to me like I'm a child. I know that."

"I thought you'd be excited."

"I am. I am." She took a breath and felt for the first time the rush of endorphins after someone told you they liked you. It was a rush she hadn't felt in a while. "I just can't believe they accepted it."

"Well, we've got a lot of work to do."

She swallowed. Six months to get data and write it up. Doable, but not ideal. The idea stuck in her head for a second, a skipping record. Then she caught the gaze of the picture on Brandon's desk. Eden's eyes laughed with the rest of her, laughing for Brandon. Laughing at a joke he told her. Or laughing at the way he touched her.

He pushed a piece of blank graph paper across the table, breaking her concentration. "Start drafting, Gret."

At two o'clock, Danny waited by the front of the clinic. He was quiet for the first minute of the drive, a repeat of the morning. Greta had steeled herself for silence when suddenly he spoke. "You all came in shifts. While I was in the hospital."

"Who is 'all'?" Greta asked. The real question was, did he mean Martha? The letter at work had gotten under her skin, as if Martha had invaded her castle. Greta assumed he didn't remember enough about the early recovery days, didn't remember enough to know that she had been there for a week or two. God, Martha didn't even fight hard enough.

"You, Meg, and Dad."

Greta glanced sideways at him, then back at the road. "Dad is dead, you know."

"I know," he said. "He sat with me in my dreams. We talked."

"Talked? That really doesn't sound like Dad."

Danny tapped his fingers on the armrest. "He had a lot of papers with him, and he laid them all out. A program from my first-grade school concert, my acceptance from Oberlin, the FAFSA filled out for the scholarships I didn't end up getting enough money for, the birthday card he sent the day before his heart attack, the stack of bills we got in the mail a month after his death. And do you know what he said?"

"In your dream?"

"In my dream," Danny confirmed.

"No, what?"

Danny leaned against the window and the finger tapping ceased. "He said he was sorry. 'Sorry, I died. Sorry we had debt. Sorry I made you drop out of college.' "

"Better late than never," Greta said, even though she was thinking, *But really, this is never. This is all in his head.* The aneurysm was all in his head too, though, and look how real that had been.

"And you know what I told him?" Even out of the side of her eyes, she could see his face screwed up like it always did before a punch line. Danny had no poker face. "I didn't want to be a star anyway, because stars burn out only after a million years. That's exhausting. Teachers burn out after twenty and get good pensions."

"Jesus, Danny," Greta said, a laugh escaping against her will. After a second, both stopped as if caught by something.

They pulled into the parking lot of Danny's apartment building and sat there for a few minutes. "Someone else is teaching my kids. I think it'd be jazz band right now."

"You'll be back before you know it," Greta said.

"Will I?"

Greta didn't have anything to say to that. His face didn't look the same. Even if she hadn't stared at his face more often and longer than any other person's she had ever known, she would have seen it. One eye drooped, and he was thinner. She knew he might never be the same again—the neurologist had warned as much. But what was the same? Was anyone really the same from day to day, and wasn't that the whole freaking issue with people? At least with Danny, un-knowableness was a known quantity.

He clicked off his seatbelt, and she did the same. "Hey," she said, catching him before he could open the car door. "I'm sorry for being an asshole last year. For us not talking. For everything actually."

"Fuck, it only took an emergency to get an apology from you?" But he was smiling, or almost smiling. "Greta, you know I love you, right?"

The words embarrassed her, even from him, her other half. "I love you too."

Her arm ached where she'd gotten the birth control shot that morning, but she kept herself from rubbing it. She walked with him into the lobby, but he stopped her there, telling her he could ride up on his own. A feeling of helplessness bloomed in Greta's stomach as she heard the elevator lurch upward. She didn't know how to be his family more than this, this watching him go behind a closed door and disappear. She wanted to understand him.

That night, she went back to the caregiver group.

# CHAPTER FOURTEEN

Mikey's bartenders had grown used to Greta and Max's wordless beer meetings. Weekly they poured a beer before she even sat down, and they didn't mention the tablet propped on the bar. She couldn't pretend they were onboard *The Enterprise*. The bartender wasn't Guinan— or at least, Greta hadn't seen Whoopi Goldberg hanging around Ames yet, but Mikey's was homey enough. There wasn't even a Ten Forward in *Voyager*, just the crew mess. Something about that felt like a cop-out. If she were in space with access to a replicator, there would be more drinking.

She and Max had made it through a whole season, but still Greta didn't know what the actors sounded like. Max put on closed captioning, and they watched the dialogue with the endless twang of country music behind them. She had muted herself too. It was three weeks in before either of them broke the silence rule. Greta had a cold that night, and her constant nose blowing unsettled a stack of napkins on the bar top. After an especially big sneeze, Max said, "Bless you."

Greta side-eyed him, deciding for a moment

not to say anything in return. He raised his eyebrows before looking down into his beer like a wishing well.

She didn't want to disappoint him—not the only office mate who hadn't complained when her papers and figurines took up too much space. Not the only person she had in her life who didn't mind the friend who preferred lab reports to personal e-mails and dissection to self-disclosure. She could tell him that the relief of these nights wasn't the weak beer or the clack of pool balls in the background, but the fact that no one expected anything of her. If that were so, he might think that it was only because she considered him no one. That wasn't true at all. She cleared her throat and pushed "Pause" on Max's tablet. "Thanks," she said, five minutes too late.

Max must have had his own internal monologue going on, because he looked away from the screen, startled.

Greta called out to the bartender for two more beers, and he seemed just as surprised to hear her voice. When the beers arrived, Max rubbed the condensation with his finger on his mug, a pensive expression on his face. After taking a sip, he asked, "What does six months mean to you?"

"What, twenty thousand light years closer to home?"

"Not to *Voyager*, to you."

"I don't know. A growing season." Greta said. What she actually thought was that six months equaled her lost time in Costa Rica, the length of the grant that had disappeared as quickly as a lightning flash.

Max's fingers traced the glass. Patterns she didn't recognize, which could have as easily been chemical structures as stick figures. "Aren't you going to ask me what six months means to me?" he asked, finally lifting his glass to drink. His tone was calm, but with something behind it that Greta didn't quite catch. She wanted to hear it again, to sample.

"No," Greta said honestly. "The idea didn't occur to me."

He laughed and put his glass down. "Figures."

"What?" she asked, not joining his laugh. Something about it didn't invite joining. His laugh pointed at and indicted her.

"Greta, you need to ask the reciprocal question sometimes." He took her pursed lips as an invitation to continue. "When someone asks how you are, what do you do?"

"Answer them."

"And do you ask how *they* are?"

She blinked twice. "Why?"

"Because you should care."

"I care. Do I have to parrot back whatever someone wants me to say to show I care?" Her beer was empty already. She'd been glugging it down in the uncomfortable silences in the conversation. Silence a few minutes ago had felt like a warm bath, but it was boiling now.

"Jesus, you're as bad as the Borg."

She felt his judgment acutely, like her personality was twisted in a funhouse mirror. "I'm a scientist first."

"Which precludes you from caring?"

"No, it just means I'm used to asking and answering my own questions. I'm used to answering when prompted."

Max was only too happy to take counterpoint in the discussion of her vices. "But you're also a teacher, so you should get used to asking questions too."

"I'm not a very good teacher," she defended. They had both seen her evaluations. Hitleresque in all caps was a memorable comment.

He laughed at that, a laugh that she would have joined in on this time, but his phone rang. When he saw the name on the display, he cleared his throat and slapped a ten-dollar bill on the bar. "Next week?" he asked.

She nodded. "Talk to you then."

"Or not talk," he said, pulling his arms into the sleeves of his leather jacket.

"Either way," she said, and he gave her a grim smile on his way out, just as hard to read as his tone had been.

· · ·

Despite those reassurances, Max cancelled their next night out and the one after. After the second week, she sent a reply text. *You get bubonic plague or something?*

*Just busy.*

She almost offered to stop by, but the idea was ridiculous. Shit, they could have watched Netflix every week at his place if he had wanted. She always got the impression he was ashamed to live with his parents. Or more likely, he was ashamed of her, her messiness. She pictured their barnwood-floored house, the neatly stacked bookshelves that would be in their living room. Her edges would scrape up the corners of his tidy life. Suddenly, she wanted him to think good things of her, to erase the chalkboard of their friendship she had scrawled all over. He had seen her in manic study mode, cramming for exams; and with her mouth open, drooling in deep sleep on her desk afterward. Of course he wouldn't want to take her somewhere that people recognized them. Take her to his house.

Even if he wasn't ashamed of her, if Greta came over there would be layers of interaction. At departmental picnics, it was easy to dodge one-on-one conversations with your friends' parents. In private, it would not be. "Chitchat." The word—so flippant—inspired dread in her. It was a talk that required back and forth. The chit—her end, she assumed. And the chat, the response. What the hell would she ask about? *"So,"* she imagined herself saying to an older-looking version of Max, *"your son dropped out of medical school and now he plays with spiders and beetles all day. What's that like? You super proud?"*

Without the silent or otherwise outings with him, a plug loosened in her, and she began to talk at the caregiver meetings. It was more like confession than chitchat. She didn't want a dialogue or to offer reciprocal questions. It helped not to study the faces of the men and women around the circle. They were too earnest, too hungry, too empathetic. She spoke toward her knees or with her eyes closed. She could have been talking in her sleep. She could have been mumbling on a subway in a foreign country, surrounded by people who didn't know her language.

At the third week of cancellations, she didn't respond to Max's text. What would she tell him anyway? Weeks passed with so little change in some ways and so much in others. She wanted to show him her ant trap design. Greta modeled her eradication device off bamboo cane. The idea came after watching a nature documentary. What her motel lacked in amenities, it made up for in last-minute flashes of inspiration.

One bottle of wine, ten channels, and a lukewarm shower—that described the average night these days. She had a clear deadline to share a prototype and decided with Brandon on which to move forward with. Though half a sketchbook had lost its life to meandering scribbles, she hadn't come up with a convincing idea. When the documentary about ants came on, Greta almost shut it off. It was like watching someone reading a children's book version of her dissertation, but suddenly there was this shot of the inside of a palm plant, teeming with ants, and Greta dropped her remote. It broke, but paying a fee counted among the least of her concerns. She could picture what to make, she knew what would show well at a huge international conference, and she knew that if she pulled it off, she was going to be a doctor, dammit. If the price of that knowledge included a universal remote, well, she could stand that.

She brought the trap into work and stood it on Brandon's desk. It wobbled unsteadily for a moment, then settled. She'd used the chop saw station at Lowe's on her own, and somehow her high school shop lessons hadn't stuck well enough to make a clean cut in the ductwork. Whatever. It was just a prototype. She saw Brandon's sign on the floor in the room, nearly identical to an apiary box. She also knew immediately that Brandon should know that would never work. Brandon didn't even need convincing. Hers was placed in the exhibit in the highest area of ant concentration.

After they anchored her prototype in place, Brandon placed a hand on her shoulder. "Nice work, Gret."

She was almost glad then not to be seeing Max. She couldn't tell Max about the warmth of Brandon's hand on her shoulder, the sudden clench in her body like it was trying to staunch a wound. She couldn't tell him because she didn't know what it meant. And she didn't know what it meant to worry what Max thought of her crush.

The hospital conference room smelled like cigarette butts. It wasn't the room's fault that the percolator broke during the first pot of coffee in the most dramatic way possible: exploding. The nozzle mechanism had failed during brewing and leaked hot coffee everywhere, including onto the power cord still plugged into the wall. Luckily, no fire alarms—they would have cued a hospital-wide alarm. Greta imagined the chaos of trying to evacuate a hospital—birthing women, kids recovering from appendectomies, men limping fresh from their vasectomies. "Blame it on bad coffee, gentlemen," Greta could say, watching them careen out of the whooshing front doors, holding their junk.

The meeting's drink offerings became limited to

powdered lemonade. Greta grabbed a lukewarm glass and swirled the cup to dissolve more of the sugar. Pam settled next to her, and soon it was time for centering and silence.

Over the past two months, Greta had learned to let the touchy-feely language of the sessions dink off her shield without noticing it. During centering, Greta still didn't bow her head like the others. The gesture always made her aware of her nose. Fluids wanted to flow from her nasal cavity in the recycled air of the conference room. Instead, she eyed the crowns of her groupmates. Bodies, from the insect to the human and anything in between, could be discussed in two ways: morphology and anatomy. Morphology detailed external characteristics. As she gazed, she saw that some of the men had thinning hair; some women had roots long unattended and growing in a highlighter of white. The anatomy described the internal. Brains, those dripping cavities. She hadn't been able to completely not listen to these people over the past few months, so she knew that in those skulls thoughts about sick wives and husbands, parents and children loomed large. Thoughts didn't fit into either category—harder to map, like the clouds that obscure views on an island.

A door squeaked and heads came up, a bit too early for Pam's liking. The facilitator was particular about timing, especially for silences.

She shot a glance to the door, and Greta saw her face soften. "Welcome," she said.

Greta reflexively turned as well. She knew it was an inborn habit, some long-lasting remnant of the fight-or-flight response, but her heart hammered as Meg walked into the room.

Meg caught Greta's glance—or glare. She knew Meg did, but still Meg accepted the seat Pam offered right between her and Greta. "Thanks," Meg said with a forced exclamation mark at the end. She wore a pair of thick-rimmed glasses high on her thin nose. Meg didn't wear glasses. If Greta thought of this woman as the possibly un-evil twin of Meg, maybe she could stay. Greta's mental gymnastics were about as stellar as her actual gymnastics skills had been, unfortunately.

Pam started the group off, just like on Greta's first night there. Greta suspected it was all a ploy to get the new person to talk. She saw it transparently now. Make the newbie feel like the room was so full of other people's stories that their own felt safe to tell—like pee in the swimming pool. No one will notice if someone just lets it out. Well, hell if it hadn't eventually worked on Greta too. Each of the circle members was sharing additional details that Meg wouldn't know were for her benefit, defining the characters in their individual dramas. Greta caught herself glancing at Meg out of the corner of her eye, watching her fold and unfold her hands like bird wings.

The man next to Greta—Tim-with-the-lymphoma-daughter—finished up. In a bigger city, these groups would all be sorted more rigorously. All brain injury, all heart attacks, all cancer, but Greta liked the ragged mix of horror that could happen to the human body. It felt more honest, less likely to lead to one-upmanship. *My cancer is worse than your . . .*

Greta's concentration broke as she felt the weight of expectation shift to her. She swallowed. "Pass."

"That's your right," Pam said, even as her tone undermined that.

"Pass," she repeated.

"Well, welcome to the group, Megan. If you'd like to share anything with us tonight, we'd love to hear about you. If not, know that you're free to pass."

Greta thought about how hard Pam had pushed her on her first night to say something. Old Pam was losing her touch. She made a mental bet about whether alternate-universe Meg would talk—Megan, she would be called. Or Nag-em. That was pretty good. She hadn't quite figured out what side of the bet she would take before Meg spoke.

"Hi, I'm Meg."

The group repeated her name and a greeting

like they were working toward their next sobriety chip.

"I'm here for Danny," Meg said. She assumed it meant something. Meg probably saw a flicker of recognition in Pam's face. "Danny's therapy is going well, or so the experts tell me. They say his dexterity is good and he can skip again as of last week, but it wasn't like that was a skill he missed, you know?"

Pam chuckled, and Meg gave her the barest smile. "The problem is that I don't know how to make him better. The parts of him that don't skip. I mean, I talked to Nadine, and she suggested . . ." Meg gestured around the room, took a breath. "Sorry. I'm not making a lot of sense."

"Take your time," one of the men said.

It was Greta's time too. Her time. "Maybe I do want to say something," Greta said in the silence that followed.

Pam, whose patient grin usually refused to waver, frowned. "You had a chance. Let Meg talk."

"Because Meg will air Danny's dirty laundry? Because she can leave if she wants to, but he's my blood?"

The room iced over like a pond, a thin solid coat on top with roiling movement underneath. "Greta," Pam said, her voice calm but loud. The tone that said she saw someone double-dipping at the picnic and to knock it off. "Give her a chance."

Greta hadn't realized how far forward she sat in her chair, a woman on a ledge about to jump. She closed her eyes and raised her eyebrows in a single gesture, simultaneously as dismissive as it was permissive.

Meg spoke, slowly at first. "We made microwave popcorn the other night. He started to be able to watch movies on our big screen again—they made him motion sick before, and the music . . ."

Meg rubbed her eyes under her glasses with her thumb and forefinger. With the glasses replaced, she started again like she couldn't work without that gear engaged. "Well, anyway, he said he could make the popcorn. Swore up and down and sideways he could do it himself. I sit on the couch—literally the other room—and I hear the plastic open, and I think, *Good*. The microwave opened, and I heard that too. You tune in for the noises, you know? You think yourself through the process from the other room and you just wait."

"And you hold your breath," Pam said. Greta noticed no one yelled at her at for interrupting.

"Exactly," Meg said, and the relief in her voice was so thick it made Greta hate the story before it even was told. "And I heard the beep of the buttons and then the pop of the popcorn. *Pop*

*pop pop,* and I heard this big noise, and I knew it wasn't popcorn. I go running in, and there's Danny on his knees in front of the microwave with his hands over his ears."

Greta sat with her shoulders so high they nearly covered her ears. She didn't want to think of Danny and Meg alone in their apartment. She pictured them as a music box that turned on when opened, their figures moving about in her viewing.

Meg kept on talking, quieter but faster. Unspooling. "And I thought maybe something was wrong. Another aneurysm maybe. I hit the 'Cancel' button on the microwave, and the popping eased off, and after a minute he stares up at me and says, 'Why are you looking at me like that?' And he was mad I stopped it because the pain would have stopped in a few minutes, he said. I told him, 'It's just popcorn. I don't need popcorn,' and we ended up not watching the movie at all because he was so tired. I was too honestly. And I feel so guilty. I don't want to fight. I won't fight with him."

"Why not?" Greta asked. The question was out of her mouth before she could stop herself.

"What do you mean?" Meg asked. She turned sideways in the chair to fully face Greta.

If Meg didn't understand that to fight was to claim someone as equal, she wouldn't explain it to her. The opposite of love wasn't hate, but apathy. She'd gotten at least a "C" in philosophy class. "He's not a child. He deserves to know what you think."

"You don't get it," Meg said.

Greta thought she did, though. She thought Meg treated Danny like a project, not a person. He was getting better every day. Maybe he was different from before, but he was still Danny. "Never mind."

Meg glanced back down at her hands. "We're making it work. We will make it work."

Pam wrapped an arm around Meg's shoulders, squeezed them. Greta felt a ghost squeeze on her own shoulders. That touch from months ago, that warmth that drove her away—Greta felt the lack of it now, a phantom coldness.

*Fuck this,* she thought. Or said. She didn't know which. A minute later, she was in the hospital corridor, with the burnt smell of coffee sunk into her clothes.

# CHAPTER FIFTEEN

Even after living at the motel for so long, the room hadn't gotten any homier. In those moments between closing her eyes and unconsciousness, Greta wondered whether, if her father had still been alive, she would have returned home to live with him through this saga. After Martha left, the three of them moved into a trailer and got a cat. Greta tried to convince herself she never missed their old house, an old clapboard thing with dingy curtains and rolling carpets. The trailer was newer, and while there was a certain chemical stringency in the air originally, weeks of waffles, frozen pizzas, and deodorant quickly wore it out.

The neighboring trailers had window boxes of daisies and kids riding tricycles in the alleys. If location were everything, their trailer had it all. Close enough to the railroad tracks to have the omnipresent white noise. Walking distance from the metalworking shop where their father plied his trade, and the last stop on/first stop off the bus route to the high school. The cat Greta could have lived without, but it wandered into the trailer court on the day they moved in and survived until the week before her father died, like it knew its reason for being there had ended.

Moving from having their own rooms to sharing was easy in retrospect, though tough at the time. Their old house hadn't been large, but it had space enough to keep their interests separate. Danny's music sounded louder in a smaller space, so he had to join garage bands with his friends who had garages. Greta's bug collection could remain as long as she kept only dead specimens.

If Dad had been alive when Danny had his aneurysm, she wouldn't have come home at all. Or she might have come and left again. Found the money somehow and fled. Instead, she had scratchy sheets and ex-boyfriend woes and the constant weight of the unknown in her brother's skull. She couldn't parent a brother. Her father had barely parented, or he did so with such a light touch that their choices seemed recklessly independent to her now. Perhaps she could notice now the feather-light influence her father had on their college choices and afterschool activities. It wasn't that their father was distant; he was close. He never left the house after work and waited up for them when they went out.

Once, she had snuck out to the state park at night to walk in the woods, only to return home to her father waiting in the threadbare recliner in the front room, his stubble visibly longer than at dinnertime. He grew facial hair like a chia pet—vigorous and thick and weedy. He had to shave twice daily to prevent a full beard. That night, when she got home, he hadn't said anything to her, hadn't mentioned time or curfews, only acknowledged her presence and gone to bed.

Few insects demonstrated paternal care, but Greta remembered one from a research expedition to Montana during her second year. Seven grad students piled into a university van and went off for a long weekend of hands-and-knees exploration. Brandon had driven them, thrilled to show off his home state and thrumming with excitement at the crossing of each state line. She and Max had played license plate bingo in the far back seat. After their arrival, they'd camped in a wilderness area near a creek bed. On the first morning, Greta saw a *Lethocerus americanus*, a giant water bug. He was truly giant at four inches. His carapace was light brown, with mandibles like fork tines protruding from his head. Greta followed his limited route to and from the bank, where he guarded tiny, marble-like eggs laid on a patch of weeds. Every so often, he splashed the eggs to prevent desiccation. Greta snapped a picture of the male, refusing to add it to her kill jar. She didn't want to strand the eggs. In other orders, in other places, male water bugs carried their eggs on their backs. It prevented flight and further mating, but it protected the eggs.

When her grandfather died, her father sold the fishing boat. Even boatless, they still went to the lake each summer. By the time Grandpa had died, a few months after Martha left, she and Danny had grown out of Marco Polo-ing. Instead, they used to sit beside Dad on the dock, their toes lightly resting on the top of the water, as if feet would bait the fish. Each of them had a pole threaded into the water. Danny was always indifferent to getting a catch, his hands metronoming the pole side to side gently. Greta grew more interested in the darting dragonflies and water striders. Surface tension made water particles cling together like film on the top of pudding, providing enough substance to let the water striders pull a Jesus and walk on water. They looked almost like ice skaters, four skinny legs dimpling the lake surface. How easy they made it seem to run away.

Often during those summer days, she brought a jar to catch a strider, but they evaded her. Once, her eyes were so focused on them, she nearly lost a pole when a fish tugged the line. When she finally caught a strider, it lapped the surface of an aluminum nine-by-thirteen-inch pan on the counter of the trailer's galley kitchen. Danny watched over her shoulder as she tested a hypothesis. She took the dish soap from beside the sink and let a single drop fall into the pan. It was enough to break the surface tension, and suddenly the strider was Jack in *Titanic*, without a door in sight. She caught the thing on the tip of a pencil before it could drown, and let it out in a puddle outside.

That tension. The tension of the line with the fish, the water surface for the striders, the card tower on Meg's table.

A breath hitched in Greta's chest, and she opened her eyes. She would never get to sleep. She propped herself up on elbows and considered the clock. Past midnight, and that meant they were a year older. Before Meg, she used to call Danny at midnight on their birthday. After Meg, she was always there with him. Hadn't that been the silent accusation in the hospital conference room? *"I'm always there,"* Meg seemed to say. *"You're not really there, Greta. You're not there."*

Or maybe that was how she'd always felt each word from Meg, even before the aneurysm. Meg and Danny worked and played and slept together. Even now, she was there every moment that Greta was except Tuesday appointments, and Meg would be there tomorrow for the party.

*Goody.*

Greta dug around in the storage unit for a gift for Danny, and there she found the largest silverfish she had ever seen. She grabbed the plastic container that had held her sandwich and caught it. It rammed into the side, wheeling over on itself in a thirty-legged cartwheel. Its feathered body righted again. Ancient insects—simple. One of the few that appeared identical from its newly hatched form to adult stage. Greta squinted at the creature before she snapped a picture on her phone. She thought about all those months ago and the forgotten caterpillar at the airplane pickup. She sent both picture and the words, "Does Gary want it?" to Max.

Three floating bubbles appeared, and Max texted back. "Now?"

Greta carried the Ziploc container with her and placed the writhing bug in her passenger seat. "I can drop it off at your place."

He texted back a thumbs-up.

After finding the picture she was after, she locked up the storage unit. She realized on the drive over that she missed Max. It was more than just being used to him, this missing. She found herself thinking about him and the way he ran a hand through his hair when he was working on a hard problem. The way he sketched ridiculous cartoons on the corners of his notes. Even the scent of Old Spice from the next cubicle over, or the next bar seat in Mikey's. She wondered if he would invite her in—worried that he might. Parents. Handshakes. But she also worried he might not.

She parked in front of his house. The porch featured a swing and a dozen potted plants blooming in welcome.

The front door opened before she had a chance

to knock, and Max stared out at her from behind the screen door.

She held the container up and showed him. He opened the screen door a crack and accepted it, holding it up to the light like a jeweler might. The screen door closed behind him as he stepped out onto the porch. "Big one. I'm sure Gary will be thankful."

"You can tell when a whip scorpion's thankful?"

"It's all in the eyes."

A breath. A pause. "Okay," she said. "There's still time to come to the party if you want. Give me cover from Meg."

Max chewed his cheek. "You should be nicer to her."

"Can't."

"Won't?" he asked. "Sorry, I have to go. Happy birthday."

Danny was napping when Greta arrived. Meg was in the middle of hanging blue streamers around the apartment and tying inflated balloons to every lamp in the place. Greta noticed Meg didn't meet her eyes. It also figured that Meg didn't wish her a happy birthday. You don't do that with the people you hate. "Here," Meg said, and handed Greta a roll of paper.

"What do I do with this?" Greta asked.

"Make it festive?" Meg said, that questioning rise in her voice.

Greta had always been shafted on their birthday, the one who didn't get her locker decorated in high school. Once the entire pep band serenaded Danny while the bus pulled away—"Happy birthday, dear Danny." Dear Danny. The words flowed so easily, but few people had ever considered her "dear Greta." She didn't even want to pretend this party was for her, but she was also having trouble helping set up this one for Danny. Was the party more to soothe Meg's sense of normalcy, or did Danny really want one? Either way, Greta's decorative imagination being as limited as her patience, she tore a dozen arm-length strips of crepe paper before deciding where to hang them. Meg had hung paper from the ceiling fan, looped it from the corners of the room to the drapes, and whirled it around chairbacks. The room looked like a Smurf had a cold and left discarded Kleenexes everywhere. Greta attached her blue crepe paper to the furnace near the window. It shook, waving blue ghost arms when the fan kicked on and fell into limp piles when it stopped. Good enough, or at least good enough for Danny, who, she knew, couldn't care less.

On the other side of the room, a balloon popped, inflated too much. "Oh shit," Meg said.

"I didn't know you swore."

"Well it's not going to un-pop this damn balloon," Meg said, her voice thick. The scraps of rubber lay scattered in twenty different directions around her feet.

Danny groaned from the other room.

Meg heard it too. "Shit," she said again rushing off to the bedroom.

Greta trailed a few steps behind and lingered at the doorway. She hadn't seen Danny's bedroom since he'd come home. Hell, she hadn't been welcome in the apartment. Danny's walker stood in the corner, ready to be returned to the medical supply company. A more streamlined walking stick would take its place. A sentinel of pill bottles lined the dresser. With Meg's back turned from the doorway, Greta pressed herself against the hallway door to listen. Meg spoke to Danny in soft tones. "I'm sorry, babe."

His eyes were open, and he reached an arm over to the night table to grab his glasses. The hand fell on top of the glasses but didn't close enough—a weak claw game, losing the prize.

"Let me get those," Meg said. She placed them on his nose, which wrinkled under her fingertips.

"I need to do this myself."

"I don't mind."

He swatted his glasses off his face with his left hand. They fell onto the bed next to him, and Meg didn't say anything. His right hand closed around the glasses, and he raised them slowly to his face, but the temple piece on the left side wasn't open and swiped against his forehead. Meg waited. Greta waited, the jamb of the door pressing against her forehead. He lowered the glasses to his lap and took a deep breath. He pressed one wire temple, then the other, and slowly lifted them to his face.

Danny sighed, glasses in place. At that, Greta let out her breath without realizing she had been holding it and went into the living room to pretend she had been there all the time with the overpriced, dyed toilet paper.

A few seconds later, Meg beckoned Greta to follow her into the kitchen.

Danny's favorite dinner before had been pork, sauerkraut, and beer. Each component was a problem now. Danny couldn't cut with a knife well. He couldn't drink with the meds he was taking. Also, in Greta's opinion, sauerkraut was disgusting.

Meg bought beer-less beer, the kind pregnant women on television shows used as cover before they showed. All the flavor of beer minus the buzz. Meg's solution to the knife debacle was pork burgers with optional sauerkraut topping. Meg explained she didn't want to cut up his food in front of other people when they had company. Greta's eyebrows rose at the word "company."

Just a few of their friends, Meg said. The past few months had been hard on them all. Meg listed off birthday meal elements—burgers, veggies, cake—using her fingers to mark each course.

Greta shifted her weight. "I forgot to get the veggie tray."

Meg's smile skittered to a halt. "Greta, I asked you for one thing. There's still an hour before anyone else gets here. HyVee is, like, three blocks away."

Danny stood in the doorway. "I can come too."

Meg bit her lip, but the action failed to stifle her nag. "You sure you don't want to rest more?"

Five minutes later he was in the car. Greta hadn't seen him move that fast since his recovery began. "Happy birthday, big sister."

"Bigger by all of ten minutes. Anyway, happy birthday, little brother," Greta said as they merged onto Lincoln Ave. Greta might have cut off a pickup truck in the process, and the driver switched lanes and gave her the finger.

Danny laughed at that, the first laugh she'd heard from him that day. "I survived just long enough to die in a fiery car wreck," he said.

"Yeah, well," Greta said. "We don't have to tell Meg about that."

"Worried you'll lose privileges?"

If she was, she wouldn't tell him that. "I'm afraid to get demerits. Detention. Is that how they do it at your school?"

"And you won't get to have field day with the other kids. Parachutes and popsicles and the whole nine yards."

"You think pretty highly of yourself if you think you're as good as field day was."

"It's my birthday, so give me a break."

It only took five minutes to pick out and pay for a black plastic tray with a clear clamshell cover. The platter contained squat orange carrots and thirds of celery stalks with a small bowl of ranch dressing in the middle. For their ridiculous cost, the carrots should have been cut with an ancient, magic scimitar. After they paid and got back into the car, Danny put his head against the window and stared out at the parking lot.

"Want to go for a drive?" Greta asked.

"Sure," he said.

Danny didn't like music in the car anymore, so the road noise hummed under the tires as she made aimless turns past the mall, into the Somerset neighborhood, circling by the horse barns on campus. Max's voice prodded her: *Ask him how he is. Ask him. Ask him.* She cared, but she didn't want to know, afraid to hear his answer out loud.

# CHAPTER SIXTEEN

They returned to the apartment an hour later. The celery looked as flaccid as the only other limp thing Greta could think of, but she plopped it on the entrance table and forgot about it. In the time since they had left, Leanne and Ginger had arrived at the apartment and now sat with Meg on the overstuffed blue couch, sipping nearly empty highballs. The accusing clink of ice cubes against glass sounded as the three women fell silent at their arrival.

"Happy birthday, Danny-boy," Leanne said, rising. She wore a white turtleneck, which accented her dark skin. Her head had been freshly shaved, and she was the only person in the room with less hair than Danny. Ginger pulled Danny into a tight hug while Leanne turned and offered Greta her hand. "Nice to see you again, Greta."

Greta just nodded.

Ginger moved to the couch after greeting Danny and waved a hand lazily. "We've met. I'm Ginger. Remember?" Ginger had a round face and painted her mouth in a dramatic red. She wore a black chin-length bob, as neat as Greta's hair was eternally mussed. She reminded Greta a little of Madeline Kahn in *Clue*. Leanne took one of Danny's arms and led him to the couch. Danny had quite the entourage of women.

"Where are your guy friends?" Greta asked.

Danny looked over his shoulder toward her spot in the entrance hall. From her perspective, with the blue balloons and banners draped around the room, it could have been a baby shower with Danny as the expectant mother.

"Busy," Meg said. "I mean, I wrote to some friends, but . . ."

"Henry's on tour, if that's what you mean," Danny said. It was what Greta meant. The one guy friend that Danny clung to from before Meg. From Oberlin.

"Sure she's not asking to be set up?" Meg asked, elbowing Danny.

If Greta had been drinking, she would have choked. "No thanks. They can help themselves," Greta said, gesturing vaguely at Leanne and Ginger.

That seemed a hilarious thing to say, because all three women erupted into laughter.

Talk descended into a flurry of conversation that Greta didn't track. Names and places that didn't mean anything to her. She shuffled into the kitchen to sniff out the alcohol that the others were consuming and leaned against a counter to check her text messages. Quiet.

It was okay to be quiet. What did she expect, Brandon to text out of the blue? Meg's offer bubbled into her head. Be set up? By Meg? *God forbid*. She'd be just as likely to eat leftovers off someone else's plate.

She found the liquor above the refrigerator and took a steadying shot.

As they ate, Franz circled the dining room table, shark-like. Franz always breathed loudly—Greta had noticed that when she lived there, so his begging lacked a stealth factor. Danny hardly touched his burger and slid the sauerkraut off the top into a soggy pile on the side of the plate. Greta noticed Danny palm a chunk of burger and lower it below the table level, much to Franz's noisy satisfaction.

After Meg cleared the dinner plates away and returned with clean forks, Ginger glanced at Leanne. Greta noticed they were holding hands under the table and blushed to remember the raucous laughter earlier when she'd suggested they get set up.

Leanne cleared her throat. "We have some news."

Ginger freed her hand from Leanne's, and it rose above the tabletop.

"Oh wow," Meg said. She sounded shocked, then adjusted her tone—turned down the contrast and upped the brightness. "Oh wow. That's wonderful."

Leanne held up her hand too. The rings were identical—black platinum, dun at first, but when Ginger wiggled her finger, something starry caught the light. "They're kind of subtle," Leanne said, "but we didn't like a lot of the traditional rings."

Ginger cut in, "Not that we don't like your ring, Meg."

Meg touched the small stone of her ring with a finger, then removed it as quick as though she'd touched a hot burner. "No, of course not. Did you set a date?"

"We were thinking July. August maybe. Nothing fancy, but something simple, summery." Ginger looked to Leanne now, and their hands disappeared under the table again. "And you? How are wedding things going?" Ginger smiled her widest, reddest smile.

Meg glanced at Danny, but Danny's body language replicated the slump of sauerkraut that had just been cleared. "Things are fine."

"October fifth, right?" Leanne's tone was conspiratorial.

No glance needed this time. "We're delaying it a bit. Because of Danny's health . . ."

"And the bills," Danny added, his voice sharp. "Don't forget about those."

"Anyway"—Meg dragged out the word, half-singing it, filling the pause—"we still have to officially call it off, to get most of the deposits back. So, we'll let you know. When we reschedule."

First Greta had heard of it, but then again, she hadn't asked.

The birthday cake was chocolate chip, the little Dalmatian spots mostly hidden under a white buttercream frosting spread thin and unevenly. Thirty green candles ringed the top like a dartboard.

Meg lit a piece of uncooked spaghetti with a match and touched each of the candles in turn. By the time the last was lit, the outer candles sweat wax onto the white frosting. Meg turned out the light so that their faces were ghostly in the flicker.

They obviously didn't know about Danny's aversion, and Greta felt him tense next to her as Ginger and Leanne broke into the birthday song. Greta saw him cringe out of the corner of her eye. Leanne's voice squeaked on the high note, and Ginger harmonized the bottom.

When they finished, Ginger shoved the cake closer to Danny's spot. The flames of the candles wavered like drunks, but remained lit—like drunks again, Greta guessed.

Danny stared at the candles.

"What, do you want us to leave you to blow these out alone?" Meg asked, her tone joking. She was unable to help herself, or really, unable to help herself from helping him.

"I'd like a piece of cake without wax, please," Leanne said.

Danny stood from his chair and shoved his hand over the flames before anyone had a chance to react. Meg stood too, her chair knocking backward with a slam. His palm was only big enough to flatten half of the candles in the first swoop, but he shot his hand to the right and left like a windshield, knocking the candles flat on the cake.

Thirty little fires hit his palm and went out. With them, went the rest of the lights. Greta moved near the wall, a shadow in the shadows. Danny sat back in his chair with a deep breath. The room breathed too, the undercover breath of a stowaway avoiding capture. After a minute, Greta reached for Danny's hand.

Lights went on, revealing Meg's face frozen with a smile that resembled that of a kid terrified of a costumed character at Disneyland.

Together, Danny and Greta examined his hands, globs of green wax stuck like points on a map. Greta barely noticed Meg helping the guests collect their things, find the door. Alone now, Danny let his hand rest in Greta's, still sticky from its contact with the frosting. She suddenly remembered holding his hand at their father's funeral. Her hand in his, two people alone together in front of a hole full of dirt. Even with so many guests, everyone from their father's old unit—old coworkers, and church members—she had needed no one except the brother next to her. He had sung. She had given the eulogy. They shook hands with the attendees, and after everyone had left, they only had each other and a table full of leftovers in strangers' Tupperware.

"I forgot to give you your birthday present," Greta said, wax finally peeled off Danny's palms. She dug the picture out of her purse. She had found that silverfish yesterday in the box of photos; the photos themselves had been hole-ridden so that this one had gone swiss-cheesey at the corners. Its sacrifice to Max's pet seemed appropriate, like the picture had been the one at fault. *Lepisma saccharina*—so named because it consumes polysaccharides. Sugar, book glue, paper, photos. This photo was of Danny, Greta, their father, their mother—all smiling and holding up fish they had just caught. Greta stood at the edge of the picture; both she and Danny were nine years old. While Danny's face had lengthened, grown manly and stubbled, Greta could have been part-silverfish herself. In many ways, she looked the same now—flat jaw, closely set hazel eyes. She was tall even at that age, and thick with prepubescent fat. Greta's fish had been a prop, caught by their father. She hadn't caught a single one that day. It was almost like the silverfish had known the photo was a lie, because it ate around the corners, starting near Greta. But Greta had caught the silverfish. Greta had done at least that.

"I love it," he said.

Quietly, Greta said to him, "So, what did you wish for?"

After a surprised second, something like a laugh came out of Danny. "A different brain, maybe." He leaned against her shoulder.

She should ask him then how he was. She should ask him, and she could ask him, but she wouldn't. "Hoping for a tornado to sweep you up into the sky? See the wizard?"

"Greta," he said, "I would miss you if a house fell on you."

She elbowed him, but gently, so gently that he wouldn't lose his perch, leaning against her. The reassuring weight of his head on her shoulder would anchor even the lightest thing in a tornado.

Greta wasn't exactly lying to Brandon—at least, it wasn't a lie the *first* time. So maybe it had been months ago that she thought she heard Meg tell her to pick Danny up at one. Maybe she had continued to leave work at twelve forty-five to have a long lunch every Tuesday before picking up her brother. What was Brandon going to do— tramp down to Noodles & Company and wreck the place? It wasn't like she was working on issues of national security. Honestly, things were going so well with her ant-eradication prototype that she doubted Brandon would care that she took a little extra time—off the clock, mind you—for herself.

Her pad Thai was getting cold. She closed the book she had been reading—saving the known universe from an alien pathogen would have to wait until later—and slurped the rest of the noodles down.

She had always wondered what happened at Danny's appointments. When she was a kid, her mother had insisted that she and Danny both take gymnastics. The place had a balcony where parents could watch over the railing while kids who weren't Greta did twirly, flippy things that Greta didn't remember the names for anymore, while Greta tried not to sprain an ankle. The parent balcony also had a snack machine that was the ultimate bribe if she and Danny were "good." Nine-year-old Greta would do nearly anything for Oreos. Greta reassured herself that thirty-year-old Greta required at least a full sleeve of double-stuffed Oreos to consider doing things in leotards.

The building that housed physical therapy was called Medical Arts, which made her feel vaguely like it belonged at Hogwarts. Despite picking him up for weeks, she hadn't ventured inside. Danny usually waited by the curb when she pulled up. Greta assumed that he was ready to get home, tired, but as she pulled into the parking spot this time, she had a thought that maybe

Danny didn't want her to meet his friends. Or his therapists or whatever they were. Maybe he was embarrassed about her.

Greta knew she wasn't the easiest person to get along with, but the one person she had always managed not to piss off too badly was her twin. Unwillingly, she thought of birthday candles and microwave popcorn. Of that day Danny left the rehab center. Maybe Danny was different. Not like a different person, but more like he was muted under striations of rock.

With a whoosh, the clinic doors spread apart and closed behind her. The clinic walls were stuck with decals of Easter eggs and demonically cheerful rabbits. Greta tried to avoid their gaze as she went to the check-in desk and tapped the bell lightly to get the attention of the woman in the cabinets in back.

"I'm here for Danny Oto. I'm his ride."

The woman rifled through some paperwork. She was broad, with expansive shoulders only made larger by her *Looney Tunes* scrubs. "Danny? I think he's gone. It's already one thirty."

"What do you mean?"

"You might be his ride, but I can't actually tell you about his treatment. HIPPA."

Greta blinked twice, at first picturing hippos on a riverbank with paperwork. She consulted her watch-less wrist, then the cell phone in her pocket. The time was, as she said, one thirty. But it wasn't two, and that was the important part. "I'm his sister. I'm here to drive him home."

The woman sighed and headed toward the cabinets, Daffy Duck and Bugs Bunny on her scrubs wrinkling with each movement. She spoke over her shoulder. "My best guess is to check in the cafeteria. It's in the building across the road—main floor. Follow the signs."

Greta crossed the street and found the aforementioned signs. Sans serif, all caps: "CAFE-TERIA," with a bold arrow pointing the way. Oh, this broom closet isn't a dining center? As she grew closer, she was also led by the telltale smells of mass-prepared food. There were tater tots somewhere nearby, and Danny might be with them.

When she turned the final corner toward the line of cash registers, Danny was walking toward her. He stared down, his face blank, but he had a smudge of ketchup near his cheek that she could see from a distance.

"Hey, dork!" she shouted at him. The hallways of a hospital, it turned out, made perfect acoustics for the echoing of sibling insults. "You've got ketchup on your face."

Danny stared at her, wide-eyed. His eyes were lighter green today, his mood-ring eyes that changed colors, and he blinked them twice before taking a step toward her. "I thought we said two o'clock."

"Came to surprise you. I didn't know you treated yourself to some culinary delights after your sessions."

"Just on Tuesdays."

"Just on your sister's watch, you mean." Greta caught his left arm in her right. Even to her, her voice sounded falsely cheerful. He had lied to her. Under her fingers his muscles tightened. Whether because of her gesture or her words, she didn't know, so she continued, "I won't tell Meg, if that's your issue."

"I'm not a kid. Like, I'm not under house arrest."

They didn't speak much on the ride to Danny's apartment. When she parked outside the front door, he bristled in the seat next to her. "You don't need to park in the handicap spot."

"I'm dropping you off."

"You don't have a sticker."

"I'm leaving in two minutes. I can help you upstairs."

He unclicked the belt with his left hand. from Greta's position in the driver's seat, his elbow appeared to be bent wrong. "Don't want help. Don't need it." He hit the car door closed with his hip and was at the front door before she could stop him.

She rolled down her window as he fumbled with the door code. "Fine. But you've still got ketchup on your face."

# CHAPTER SEVENTEEN

Preliminary examinations: invented by the devil and the dean and judged by everyone who could secure her success.

Maybe the devil actually had inroads here. She should investigate that.

Brandon had given her a week off during exams, out of pity—or maybe friendship. The exams were like some dastardly reality show. In a single week, the department assigned a topic, from outside a candidate's specialty, on which to write a research paper. Besides this, she would have to present her dissertation and general knowledge before a committee. Her randomly assigned research topic wasn't butterfly mating, carpenter ants, or even honeybees. Her topic: genetic alterations in mosquito populations for reduction of malaria.

*Because of course it was.* First on the list of things she couldn't care less about: the medical applications of her field. Some of this disregard came from her feelings about her mother's job as a nurse. Beyond that, Greta had spent so much time in hospitals lately, and, well, while she could dissect any insect specimen, kneel in the dirt for hours, and barehand fistfuls of maggots, she hated blood. Mosquitos wouldn't be her first, second, or millionth choice.

After she received the assignment in her e-mail, she decided to move into the Iowa State library for the week. Literally. In her car, she had a sleeping bag small enough to fit into her backpack—meant for use in Costa Rica—several boxes of energy bars, and a canteen. The price of the motel had added up. Or rather, it subtracted down. Even with the steady paycheck, financial worries nudged at her. To reserve her old apartment, the one she'd been subletting out that semester, she needed an entirely new deposit by the middle of the month. Subletting had forfeited her old one. The contract came via e-mail and made her mouth water. Her home, that cozy eight hundred square feet.

A partial financial solution? The library stayed open 24-7 leading up to and during finals week on campus. She knew enough secretive corners that she figured she could get away with sleeping there. To ensure it, she reserved one of the "study rooms" from two to six AM every morning. She figured no one would reserve it after midnight anyway, so she might sneak in a full undisturbed five hours.

An imposing four-floor stairway led from the library's lobby high into the stacks, but that route took her right by the busiest sections of students with the most amount of foot traffic. Any chance to avoid human interaction was worth a few extra steps. She walked through the main floor and circled around the Grant Wood paintings to climb the back stairs. A large mural greeted her on the second floor, a bright painting full of cyclone shapes hidden in springs, a girl's hair, and a replicated DNA sequence. After passing through rows and rows of dusty books, she came to a lone table in the corner. Campus lore whispered about this part of the stacks as haunted. Greta knew enough ghosts now that this didn't trouble her. She plopped her large backpack on the metal table and dug out her laptop.

Mosquitos.

She opened a Word document and at the top typed, "Fuck mosquitos." She then saved her document as Fuckmosquitos.docx, the suggested name—thank you Microsoft. Finally, she opened a research database and got to work.

When she paused, four hours had passed, and she needed to use the bathroom. It was tricky to decide if her place was safe enough to leave for five minutes. She weighed the odds until her bladder won out, and she abandoned her computer. For once, her reluctant bet paid off. Human beings were essentially good—or at least not around, which was better—and her things were untouched when she returned.

At hour five, she ate a vanilla chip energy bar and choked it down with two swallows of water. Her chapped lips proved she was not taking good care of herself, but at least she was learning about the procreative weak links of certain species of mosquito. Some of the stream-of-consciousness notes she was taking included the impressive number of times that mosquitoes procreate in their short lifespan.

Procreation wasn't a goal of hers, but she didn't consider herself a failure of the species. She'd slept with Brandon, but, like any good scientist, she'd required multiple sets of protection against the elements. The sexual equivalent of rubber gloves and hand wash. It wasn't so much that she wanted to be "child-less," though that was part of it. It was more like she wanted to be science-more, research-more, travel-more, and not being a parent often went hand in hand with that. Insect success was measured on the number of sets of offspring produced. She didn't lay any eggs in stagnant water, to hatch and infect the population around her, and her main goals in life weren't to suck blood and die. She was exempt from the biological imperative. My, what would Darwin say about her?

If she had begun rationalizing her reproductive choices, she needed a break. Facebook hummed with notifications about acquaintances' birthdays she had missed and the next big meme. Brandon had never unfriended her after he left for New

York. She'd never unfriended him either. His photo hadn't changed. It was a picture of him holding up a kite he'd made with his grandfather. Greta knew that was a picture from the last time he'd ever seen his grandfather alive, but she wondered if Eden knew. Below Brandon's name and basic information (he was a Gemini), was the line "In a Relationship with Eden Palatino."

It was Eden's fault that she didn't have better privacy settings. What person over thirteen didn't know how to adjust their account so that any ex-girlfriend in the world couldn't go waltzing onto it? The things Eden loved were on display everywhere. Her favorite bands, "Tar Heel Nation" groups, and recipes that Greta couldn't picture Brandon liking—even though he "liked" the posts. He didn't eat bacon, for one thing. He didn't like pork—how the poor guy ended up in Iowa was beyond her.

Footsteps behind her. How could someone creep up on her at midnight in the library? Clippy, save me! It was the perfect tagline for a boring horror movie. Or it was a ghost? The figure cast a shadow across her work. She felt the presence before she turned around. Once she saw who it was, her body untensed as she laughed in relief.

It did more than untense. She felt her cheeks warm as Max smiled at her. "Hi."

"Hi," Max returned. "Prelims?"

She nodded. "You?"

"I got fig wasps and related plant-insect pairings. What did you get?"

"Mosquitoes and malaria."

He looked like he was weighing the topics in his mind. "Yeah, I'll keep wasps."

"As if we had a choice."

He leaned against her desk and lowered his voice. Considerate, even with the lack of anyone around them. "Gary enjoyed the snack you brought. Sorry for being weird the other day."

"Me too." There were too many spinning plates in the air above her head to create any real apology. Danny nearly getting kicked out of the program, and her dissertation topic change. She feared that pausing long enough to consider any of those problems would make them all come crashing down on her.

"Well, good luck. I mean, good defense."

"No, good luck is fine. I'm going to need it."

Max stood, staring for a moment like he wanted to say something else. Finally, he shook his dark hair out of his eyes. He seemed as tired as she felt, but she knew they both had hours to go before they slept. He turned to walk farther down the dusty corridor of books. "Hey. Max," she called.

He swiveled around to face her again. "Yeah?"

"I reserved a room in the third-floor study section all week to sleep. If you need a place to crash between academic journals."

He gave her one of his rare smiles. "I've got an actual bed to go home to," he said. "But thanks, Gret."

At one thirty, she closed her laptop and unrolled her sleeping bag on the confetti carpet in the study room. In the atrium outside, she heard the faint whirr of an industrial vacuum and dreamed of getting sucked up in a cyclone made of DNA and mosquitoes. She woke at six on Tuesday morning, her eyes as crusty and heavy as if she had applied rubber cement as a beauty mask.

The main level of the library housed a coffee shop. Although the air in the shop smelled over-roasted, anything would improve Greta's breath. Her mouth tasted like an animal had farted in it, and as she sipped her first cup of coffee, she bemoaned her forgotten toothbrush, somewhere in a box in her car. She didn't see Max again before she left at noon, but didn't go looking for him either. Her stomach grumbled too loudly to start a search party. Woman cannot live on energy bar alone. As she drove away from campus, she had a thought. Why not meet her brother in the cafeteria for one of his illicit lunches? She'd kept his secret, so now it was time to cash in. Her body had been running on oats and corn syrup for the past two days, and maybe an item from every part of the food pyramid, plus a little sibling ribbing, was what she needed.

And ribs—but what kind of hospital made ribs? Probably not this hospital.

Her legs burned as she walked the distance from her car to the door. Too much sitting the past few days. Her eyes burned too, from real-world things more than six inches from her face. PhD programs should come with pages of warnings. Hazardous to your health, love life, muscle strength, family relationships, and sense of humor. Her head was full of mosquitoes, and she hoped that the cafeteria coffee came in refillable all-you-can-drink cups.

Danny wasn't there yet, but it was only 12:55. Maybe he had changed his routine too, but that was unlikely. Danny liked routines. He always had. When they were kids, he insisted on having the same lunch every day for seven years: peanut butter and jelly, yogurt with fruit on the bottom, and a banana (with no brown spots). He had started making his own lunch at age eight because their mother bought grape jelly once, instead of strawberry. Although he outgrew his love of peanut butter sandwiches, he still liked things just so.

Greta filled her hospital tray with a pound of food: meatloaf, mashed potatoes, cottage cheese slathered with peach slices, and a mixed green salad topped with pickled beets. Her plate held a rainbow of comfort food in individual plastic bowls. She paid—cheaper than campus food—

and her mind formulated reasons to visit the hospital more. It would be good for the budget. Sure, it would be better for the budget to learn how to cook, but that was as unlikely as her turning into a giant lizard and knocking over the Campanile.

Seated at a table facing the entrance to the cafeteria, Greta picked at her plate and watched for her brother. She had the perfect view to see him enter. A woman walked ten paces behind him, a woman who had been ghosting Greta since January.

Greta stood up, leaving her food on the tray, already shaking her head. "All this time?"

Danny stopped, feet flat and fingers still for the moment. Martha stepped forward and put a hand up as if to break up a fight. "Let's do this somewhere else."

"There is no 'this.' I'm an adult," Danny said, his look forcing her hand down. He turned to Greta. "Why did you ban her in the hospital?"

Greta couldn't believe she was being put on the defensive. "She was taking over."

"From who, the doctors? You're the one that impersonated a doctor."

"I didn't. It was an accident." How had he heard about that? She was on shaky ground, and she knew it. "Does Meg know? About your little meetings?"

Danny ignored her question. When he spoke

again, his voice was calm. That tantrum-control voice. He must have inherited it. "Greta, you're the one barring the doors. She's been knocking on them for years," Danny said. "We started talking last October, before all this. I wanted her here."

The revelation made her eyes sting. "I don't get it. Why didn't you say anything?"

"Like you would listen." His mouth twitched up again. He knew the worst parts of Martha, and he still wanted to talk to her. "I have a right to make my own choices, and Mom and I—"

"You're calling her 'Mom' now?"

"Mom was telling me about Dad, about Dad before. And it's helping me get through this."

Greta scoffed audibly. And as she did so, she thought she could hear why the sound was called a scoff—this scuffing of an "o" sound, disgusted, against her palate. "Like she knew Dad."

"I knew the man, not just the father," Martha said.

"Look," Danny interposed, "we're going to have lunch, like we do on Tuesdays. If you want to join us, you're welcome. Otherwise, I can get a different ride home."

The comment stung. Tuesdays were their time together, just them. The time that, between appointments and Meg and work, she felt like she had family. If there was one thing Martha knew how to do, it was break apart a family. Greta's chest hurt.

"I need to get back to the library." Her tray of food spoke as she abandoned it on the table. Her lies smelled like meatloaf and mashed potatoes.

Martha put a hand on Danny's arm, and Greta flinched as if her mother had reached for her own arm. After Danny had been taking piano lessons for three years, Martha had insisted that Greta try it too. The rationale: "It'll be good for you." Martha always imagined duets, the four peaceful hands of her twins working together in ways they never did when they washed dishes. In the end, all that happened was Greta had made the piano teacher cry, and Danny had to apologize. Couldn't Danny feel the looming disaster?

"Ten minutes in the same place," Martha said. "Think of it as aversion therapy." Goddamn if Martha and Danny didn't have the same patronizing grin.

Greta's eyebrows contracted, but she didn't pick up her tray. "Ten minutes."

Martha held Danny's tray and walked a step ahead of him while he chose his items off the buffet. He couldn't grip things steadily, but Greta saw how she made Danny scoop his own pudding, spear his own pickle. She pushed him, and more than that, Danny glanced at her when he grabbed the tray from her hand and insisted on carrying it. For approval? For support? It didn't matter the reason behind it, because the look on his face rewound time by twenty years.

Greta disappeared from the table before they returned.

The door to the study room opened, sometime past three or four AM, and a flashlight shone in. "Ma'am?"

Greta sat up in her sleeping bag, her arm falling off her eyes. She'd never been "ma'amed" before, and she'd aged ten years in the two hours she had been sleeping.

The lights flicked on. A library page—gawkish and wide-eyed—stood with a campus police office. "Ma'am, I'm afraid we're going to have to ask you to leave the premises. You can't sleep here."

"I go here." Greta rubbed her eyes. "I'm a PhD student. I'm catching a nap before I get back to studying."

"You'll have to go home to do that. It's a safety concern to have people sleeping in the library."

The bag unzipped as Greta moved her legs. "If I weren't a 'ma'am,' would this still be a problem?"

"This would be a problem."

The library page scurried out of the room, but the cop waited until Greta collected her things, and escorted her to the entrance of the library. The campus slept at four in the morning. Without the campus buses shouldering her off the road, she could walk in the middle of the street, and that was just what she did. Ames had so little pollution that she could see the stars. She'd never taken an astronomy class in undergrad. Looking up hadn't been her habit, since her studies more often led her into the dirt than the heavens. As she walked, the stars kept her company, though she didn't remember any of their names. It was like every party she'd ever been to. She was alone and unobserved and the least shiny thing around.

It didn't take long to fall asleep again in her office. The cubicle hive was empty, so she moved the chair out from under her desk to unroll the sleeping bag there. With her head sheltered by the clumsy metal desk, she couldn't see the *blink blink* of the fire alarm light directly above her. Her brain registered some movement nearby after a while, but it passed. Greta slept longer than she meant to. Maybe she should have been sleeping here this whole time. The floor seemed to move next to her body, and Greta pushed the "Home" button on her phone. Seven thirty.

She sat up fast, slamming her forehead into the desk above her. "Fuck. Fuck fuck." Blood from her forehead bubbled under her palm. She could feel the welt there as she fell backward on her makeshift pillow.

Max stood above her. "There's a desk there."

"Fuck you too."

He moved to her desk and offered a hand. "Can you get out of there without a crowbar? Or a stretcher?"

"Maybe a concussion will give me the inspiration I need to pass prelims."

"Move over and let me have a shot."

Greta grunted. She managed to shimmy the sleeping bag out from under the desk. She grabbed his outstretched hand and clambered into a sitting position. His hands were cool against her warm ones. "It was easier to get under there than it was to get out."

"Seemed like a good idea at the time, I'm sure."

"How are the wasps?"

"As waspy as ever." While Max settled himself into his desk chair, Greta relayed her incident with the library police. Max turned his attention from the e-mail on his laptop when she finished. "Used your privilege to get out of trouble, then?"

Greta rolled her eyes. "I'm a student."

"You think everyone gets off so easy? After sleeping in the library for a week?"

"Three days."

"Okay, white girl. Okay. I get it. Just three days." Max laughed, and Greta couldn't help but smile in response. In years of friendship, she had seen many wry smiles and ironic eyebrow raises, but laughs were few and far between. He probably thought the same thing about her, though. He knelt by her on the floor. "That's going to bruise," he said as he examined her forehead. "May I?"

"May you what?" Greta asked.

Max sighed and moved her hair aside with gentle fingers. Greta felt a residue of grease that the strands left behind, reminding her she hadn't washed it in three days. If Max noticed that, he didn't give any sign.

"Will I live, Doc?" she asked, her voice mimicking Meg's earnestness. "Give me the truth."

Greta's skin tingled as he traced the area of impact. "I can diagnose a bump on the head."

"Medical school paid off," Greta said, laughing and pulling back.

His fingers hung there, over her head, as if in benediction. Then Max pulled his hand back and pursed his lips, suddenly serious. "I try not to regret any choices I make."

"I didn't mean—"

Max interrupted her. "After that first year, I knew I didn't really want to be a doctor. Not a medical one, at least. I moved back from Iowa City, and anyway, it's good to be around my parents. I don't regret it."

The admission felt so personal, it almost felt like a transaction was requested. Was this what Max meant about being reciprocal? "I just got kicked out of a hospital group therapy thing for being an asshole," she admitted. Even if that wasn't exactly what had happened, it was exactly why she felt she couldn't go back.

"Therapy for what?"

They sat cross-legged on the carpet now, a few feet from their own office chairs. Sitting on the floor of the empty cubicle corridor was such a different perspective. She noticed someone else's gum on the underside of her desk. "Caregivers. Because of Danny."

"How is he, anyway?"

"Physically, fine. He finishes PT next week. Otherwise, I don't know." Greta ran a hand through her hair, the grease rubbing off on her hands. "How are you? Is that what I'm supposed to ask?"

"I'm tired," Max said. "And you can always ask that."

She nodded. "I think I'm going to shower at the gym. Prelims make me all sweaty."

"I noticed," Max said. Even with her back turned to him, rolling up her sleeping bag, she heard the smile in his voice.

Greta left her pile of belongings at her desk, the desk she'd been absent from for so long. Overheated or not, it still felt like being a kid again and touching home base. Something about seeing the familiarity of Max's sparse desk made her relax. Her desk wore a dress of papers. Anything she had left in the "In" box on her desk had multiplied with Xerox babies and tumbled into the "Out." "I'll be back in a bit," Greta said over her shoulder, as if Max cared. As if someone would come searching for her.

What happened next she would hear from multiple accounts, the looming disaster she wouldn't feel the shockwaves of for hours. She ignored three phone calls in that time because she was showering.

As she rubbed the combination hand wash and shampoo into her short hair, Greta pondered that in a parallel universe, she would have been just finishing up the research with the eminent Dr. Lawrence Almond. He had stayed in paradise while Greta got kicked out of the library by a campus cop and a library page who appeared to be about twelve years old.

The parallel universe trap was an easy one to fall into these days. If Danny hadn't had an aneurysm, she would have been there. Her data collection would be about glasswings, not harvester ants. Her funding would be intact, and she wouldn't have to defend her oral preliminary exams until fall. She wouldn't have had to talk to her mother again or beg Brandon for a favor.

She wouldn't have this welt in the middle of her forehead. It burned as the soap hit it. She must have broken the skin.

Greta rinsed her hair and mused that if Danny hadn't survived his aneurysm, she would have gone back too. A darker parallel universe that had, by all accounts, been the more likely out-come. No rehab centers, just a funeral. No PT, just a pine box. Different decisions, all worse and all over so quickly. After Dad had died, after the funeral, Greta felt guilty at how little her grief debilitated her. It didn't chain her down or force her into bed. If anything, grief followed her around. It shadowed her while she worked and covered her eyes with its hands, occasionally, to remind her that things couldn't ever be like they were. It would have been that way with Danny too. Two shadows following her, holding hands as they trailed her on the plane to Costa Rica after a few weeks' absence.

Guilt. A rush of it as she toweled off her body. She didn't wish her brother was dead. That was the last thing she wanted. She hated herself the entire bus ride to her office. She hadn't brought her phone with her to the gym, or she might have called Danny then and there, as she rode, and told him that she loved him, that she was glad he was alive, that it didn't matter if he had a relationship with their mother as long as he included her too.

Danny had always put up with her. Always. No one else, not even Brandon, could claim that distinction.

Max was gone when she got to the office, but he had left a note in his messy scrawl on her desk. She recognized the "y's" and "l's" across the room. He used to copy her notes from lecture when he was absent—it happened a lot—and always had returned the notes with sarcastic commentary along the side, and doodles, as if he had been sitting through the lecture alongside her. "Call your brother," the note said.

She paused for a second, wondering if he were psychic, but then she saw her phone sitting on the desk alongside the note. The phone she had all but ignored for the last twenty-four hours registered six missed calls. Two were from "Don't Answer." The most recent was from Danny, ten minutes ago.

When she called him back, Danny's voice sounded weird, like he was speaking through a gag. "Are you being held hostage?" she asked.

"I had a few drinks."

Greta turned abruptly and changed course for the bus stop, performing mental calculations. The commuter parking lot was at least a five-minute bus ride away, and then she needed ten minutes to drive to Danny's place. "Danny, don't drink anything else. Your meds." The spring air blew through her wet hair. Handheld dryers weren't the most effective at getting hair dry, but the wind did a better job of it. "What's going on?"

"I crashed the car."

"What? What car?"

"And we broke up, Greta. Last night." His

voice cracked, like the imaginary cloth gag over his mouth had torn. She hadn't seen him cry since their father's funeral, and pictured the way his eyes filled and overflowed. He never cried aloud, not even when he had fallen off his bike and broken his arm in two places.

"I'll be there in fifteen. I swear. Don't move."

On the bus ride, an early-season mosquito blew in through the open window and taunted her with its buzzing. The department had assigned her to study up on its kin and their ability to reproduce and spread harm, but the harm was already here. She would pass her prelims; after three solid days of work, her confidence had increased. She had always known how to get by in school, but Danny faced a challenge that she couldn't study for and didn't know how to help with. Danny didn't respond to her further texts, and she dug her fingernails into her palms until she could get to his apartment. Her nails made half-moon dents, so deep that one of them bled.

# CHAPTER EIGHTEEN

When Greta arrived, a horror movie was playing while Danny curled into a fetal position on the couch in front of it. He seemed to be sleeping, but she grabbed his wrist and felt for a pulse to make sure. It thrummed slowly under her fingertips, and she released her breath. "Danny," Greta said, giving his shoulder a gentle shake.

He roused briefly and mumbled.

She lowered herself onto the floor and leaned against the couch. Over the next few hours, she watched him and the movie. It was *The Exorcist*. Go figure.

Danny always liked horror, but never liked the monster movies—which Greta preferred. Instead, he liked ordinary things doing damage. Deranged kids, haunted movie tapes, the serial killer next door—he loved it. Once he told her that his original interest came from the movie scores, specifically for *The Exorcist*, which he'd watched at a friend's house when he was about the same age as the possessed girl in the movie. Danny always heard music differently than Greta did, and so when he told her that he saw the movie score in slashes of red and goldenrod, and a sickening puce during the main theme, she had to believe him. When she closed her eyes now, she tried to picture the notes landing on an empty music scale in blots of sunrise.

The priest on the screen mumbled some sort of prayer, and Danny finally stirred, rolling over and pulling himself up on his elbows. "Has the head spun yet?"

"No."

They watched in silence for a while. Greta stared straight ahead, more afraid to look at his expression than at the horror on the screen. "How much did you drink?"

"A few shots of whiskey. Most of it came up."

The head spun. Pea soup. Demonic garbling.

"You freaked me out, Danny. What were you thinking?"

"She's gone."

"Then she's gone, and we'll figure it out." Greta's head hurt. "You're doing better every day."

He grunted at that, his words slurring a little. "Is it normal to feel like your brain is against you?"

"Your brain *is* you," Greta said, finally turning to him. "What else do you think 'you' are?"

"And that's supposed to make me feel better?"

"You think you're possessed or something?" She was joking, and she could see from his raised eyebrows that he got it. Joking as a defense mechanism. Dad didn't leave money, but he sure left behind a legacy of joking avoidance.

She raised herself to the couch, shoving his feet aside to make a space next to him. "No matter what kind of hijinks your brain is doing, you know I'm here for you, so either start talking or shut up so we can watch the movie."

He fell asleep before she could get anything else out of him—the car crash, the breakup. She could almost guess the cast of characters from the missed calls on her phone that she refused to return. Meg. Then of course, the two calls from "Don't Answer"—Martha. If she'd actually answered them, would something have gone better? The ending credits rolled, leaving Greta nothing to watch but the steady rise and fall of Danny's chest.

Over a bribe of cinnamon toast later, he gave up the information. After Greta had left the cafeteria, Martha said she would take him home. By the time they reached her car, Martha offered him the keys since it was such a short drive. "A short little drive," she had said. Dad had taught them both to drive; Martha had been gone for two years by the time Greta received her school permit. Greta wondered, during that time, if Martha would have white-knuckled the center console even when Greta drove under fifteen miles an hour.

Supposedly, Danny's drive was going fine until Martha turned on the radio.

"Just a mailbox," he mumbled when Greta asked what he had hit.

The first missed call on her phone lined up with the time of the accident and came from "Don't Answer." When Greta told Danny Martha had called her, he crumpled. "Well, that's probably how Meg found out."

Greta swallowed. "So you didn't tell your girlfriend you got in a car accident?"

Danny glanced away. He mumbled, mouth full of toast, "It was just a mailbox."

When Meg had gotten home last night, she knew about the crash, and she also knew that Danny hadn't told her. She didn't say a word to him as she walked into the apartment, just started making spaghetti on the stove. Danny had heard her in the kitchen, filling the pasta pot. Then the pop of a jar of sauce unsealing, but he hadn't gone in. He'd let her and the sauce simmer, and then at dinner she had asked him how his day was. She'd put the bait out there, had begged him to take it, and he hadn't.

Of course, that wasn't how Danny saw it.

"She was waiting to catch me out. The look on her face," he said, unable to finish what that look was.

Greta could imagine it was something like that blank doll's face of shock she'd seen the day of the birthday party. She filled in the rest of the details herself. A call from Meg around nine. A call from Danny at ten. And then the string of Danny calls that morning. She pictured Danny sitting on the couch from nine to ten last night, waiting for Meg to come back in the door. Waiting for whatever fight they had to retract itself, but you couldn't un-pop a balloon. Once that air was out, you could never contain it all again.

Meg planned to collect her things during his final physical therapy appointment on Friday. Greta mentally divided that which had been Meg's and that which was Danny's. While mentally calculating, she saw the grimace on Danny's face. She suddenly had a terrible premonition of a late-night phone call she might miss, and didn't stop herself this time. "Do you want me to move in?" she asked him.

He swallowed his last bite of toast. "Do you need a place to stay?"

She thought about the money she had saved for her apartment, for those sparse and beautiful eight hundred square feet all to herself, and then she met her brother's gaze. "Yeah."

Greta submitted the written portion of her preliminary examination early—at least twenty minutes before the requested midnight deadline on Thursday. All that remained was the oral portion before her full committee. Too nervous to sleep, she packed.

It was surprisingly mind clearing to pack someone else's shit, especially if that someone was Meg. Before Danny's bedtime, she had moved an old dresser from his room into the sitting area, whose couch she would reside on for the duration. From the closet, she carried armfuls of Meg's things, lumping them into a pile. Meg had a closet full of dresses and pressed skirts, some still in dry cleaning bags. It had taken Greta until last year to realize what those little hooks were for in the back seats of cars.

With Danny in bed hours ago and her prelims turned in, Greta started with the dresser. For the first few hours, Franz kept Greta company as she pieced through Meg's things, drawer by drawer. He nudged at the boxes and whined. Greta scratched his ears, and he settled onto his haunches. Named by Danny or not, Franz was really Meg's. Even if they kept him for a while, when Meg got settled, this dog would be just another stranger's dog, and the thought made Greta sadder than she wanted to admit.

The piles grew larger. Size small T-shirts. Size four pants. It felt like doing laundry that had shrunk in the wash. When she got to the underwear drawer, she picked up the items with a T-shirt on her hand as a makeshift glove. The underwear dropped into the box, some lacy and some frilly and others ordinary, but all small and clean and previously folded. She found the bra that she'd baked months ago and noted it was no worse for wear. The rest of the underwear drawer baffled her. Who folded their underwear? Who folded their T-shirts, in fact? None of it was folded by the time it landed in the box. By the time the clothes were sorted, the novelty of the exercise wore off for Franz, and he curled up on the couch.

On top of one of the less full boxes, she tucked the photographs she knew were Meg's. They featured a smiling, short man in a tacky T-shirt and three women who looked nearly identical to her—a mother and two sisters, Greta assumed. Meg herself had Mickey Mouse ears and was about ten years younger. Greta moved on to the bookshelves and tried to separate his books from hers. Who would have read *Freakonomics*? Meg, probably. The fantasy books were Danny's, she was sure. She thumbed through a few and noticed they had been hers originally, her name crossed off with a thin line to be replaced by her brother's. *Ass.* She continued her assessment. The wedding planning notebooks, Meg's.

The whole activity felt like a question of how well she knew her twin. Something like a metal detector pinged in her. She felt confident about her piles by two in the morning. After this initial sorting, only the *Calvin and Hobbes* comics remained on the shelf, and Greta bit her lip. She flipped the cover of one of the anthologies and noticed handwriting on the title page.

*To my boy: you make me real.*

The looping script practically begged for hearts over "i's" and "j's," if there had been any of those letters. Underneath, a second note in jagged, familiar handwriting.

*To my tiger: I'd fly off a cliff in a wagon with you any day.*

*Gag,* thought Greta, flipping the book closed. She couldn't help herself at opening one of the other volumes, however. She skipped the title page, turning to the strips themselves. Beside every fifth or sixth one was a penciled comment in the margin, or a smiley carefully circled and embellished into a full stick figure in varying thicknesses of lead. Obviously passed back and forth like a note in a classroom.

Leaving these shared comics here felt like a self-pity time bomb set to explode whenever some unfathomable date creeped up on Danny: Meg's birthday or the anniversary of some silly milestone like the first time he complimented her pierced ears.

One thing that kept her coming back to *Star Trek* was the idea of the Prime Directive, the purity of it. Don't interfere. Observe. Study. Better to help prevent the problem before it came up. She took the stack of books and put them in Meg's pile, then thought better of it. She slid the comics between the futon and the frame, feeling the same relief one might in disarming a bomb. As for the rest, she boxed it all up with the authoritative scritch of tape torn off a roll.

"So, how's Danny?" After an hour of drilling on entomology, with her dissertation in progress and her sudden shift of focus, this question unsettled her. This question, asked so many times by so many people, sounded different from Larry's mouth. Pointed somehow. She'd only seen him in passing since he got back to the States.

What was she supposed to say: bad? Good? *Geez, Lar,* she imagined herself saying with a wide-eyed smile. *It is a good thing I came home because, you know what? Turns out it wasn't an aneurysm, but a radioactive spider bite and what he really needed was a sister who knew a little something about arachnids and had seen most of the superhero movie canon.* She bit her tongue, literally, and tasted iron. "He's getting better every day."

Larry nodded seriously. "Good."

Both assembled professors filed through paperwork, pausing every few seconds to mark something in damning red ink. Tom Plank, the bigger guy, and deep red in the overheated conference room. Larry Almond, shorter and deeply tan, probably from the Costa Rican sun. Even that intensification of melanin, which could signal early risk for skin cancer, made Greta's stomach churn with jealousy. Lucky bastard.

Larry passed a piece of paper to Tom, who glanced at it and nodded.

Tom cleared his throat. "Your entomological knowledge is extensive. We did get a status report from Brandon, and he thinks your design will work well for research and hopefully for practical applications as well."

Greta nodded, unsure if they expected her to say anything.

"I move that we approve the candidate's preliminary examinations," Tom said, glancing up the table.

It took a moment for Larry to chime in his affirmative, but when he did, Greta felt a genuine smile curl her lips. The hard part was over—well, all but the dissertation. All but defended. ABD. She claimed the title proudly.

She texted Max from the hallway. "ABD. You?"

He sent a dancing hippo gif and the message, "ABD."

"I was going to eat a whole cake by myself, but I'll give you a slice," she texted back, and included Danny's address.

Half an hour later, she sat down at Danny's table with a small sheet cake in front of her. The HyVee bakery had at least half a dozen to pick from, but this was the only chocolate cake with chocolate frosting. Who cared if it was decorated with race cars? Who cared if the name Joseph was misspelled "Joeseph" across the bottom in blue icing? She had just grabbed two forks when she heard a knock at the door.

She opened it in a quick motion, a smile already on her lips. It melted when she saw Meg waiting on the other side.

Meg's eyes took in the apartment as if she hadn't left it days ago, scanning left to right until her gaze fell on the stack of boxes. Her voice was hard. "You touched my things?"

"I thought you wouldn't want to linger."

Meg stepped inside the apartment, pushing past Greta and walking over to the bookshelves. Franz yipped along behind her, but Meg didn't seem to notice. Dazed, she touched their blank spaces with such a deep frown on her face that Greta thought she might be a dentist looking at a mouth half empty of teeth. Meg and Franz disappeared into the bedroom and then came back out again after a few minutes, a piece of paper in Meg's hand. The small neat swirls and swoops were familiar to Greta when Meg put the paper on the table. "You actually got a lot of it, but I wrote down some of the furniture I need. Ginger said she can pick it up later in her truck—I mean, some of it we bought together, and I don't . . . She swallowed, her attention on the table itself now. "Did you get a cake?"

"No, it actually just appeared. Didn't cake materialize when you lived here?"

Meg's voice rose. "That is so like you, Greta. To celebrate him breaking up with me. To be so happy when I'm upset."

Greta stopped her. "*He* broke it off?"

"He said he couldn't see how all this could work. All this, meaning everything, I guess. When I asked him—"

Greta waved a hand in front of her face. "I don't need the details." The less she knew, the more she could disconnect from the situation. To know was to become part. Danny's choice? That was hard to believe from the look on Danny's face that morning, the whiskey, the mourning tone in everything he said. When even "pass the cornflakes" sounded like a eulogy, she wouldn't have guessed he was the one who'd broken it off.

"And this cake. Race cars?" Meg lowered herself into a chair at the table, a table she had probably helped assemble from some box kit years ago. She had purple rings underneath her eyes like bruises. Her voice shook when she continued, "Cars? Is that because of the crash?"

"You think I'm celebrating your breakup with some kind of voodoo cake? That I've renamed your relationship 'Joseph'? Not everything is about you guys," Greta said. A laugh bubbled up inside of her, which she stifled when she saw

Meg's face. She flicked the second fork in Meg's direction. "It's just a cheap chocolate cake. Jesus, have some if you want."

The fork landed inches from Meg's head, which she had just laid on the tabletop, cheek against faux wood. "I don't even have a place for Franz right now," Meg said, her voice muffled. She turned her head to let more sound escape. "But I will. I mean, along with everything else—"

Greta cleared her throat. "I can take care of him until—"

A rap at the door signaled Max's appearance. Greta called him in, and the surprise on his face at seeing someone else in the apartment was almost worth having a pitiful Meg around.

"Meg, Max," Greta said, pointing with her fork from man to woman. "Max, Meg."

Max's eyebrows raised. He knew Meg from Greta's stories. He seated himself across from them. Meg silently bit an empty fork, staring toward the bookshelves.

"So, who's Joe and why are we eating his cake?" Max asked after a quiet minute. His eyes asked several more questions, but Greta liked holding him in suspense.

"It's Joe because I already ate the 'seph.'" Greta said, standing. "Lemme get you a fork."

In the end, the three of them ate until only a smear of brown frosting and the inedible car decals remained. Max helped Meg load boxes when it was time for Greta to pick up Danny, the choreography working so all parties exited the stage at once to clear it for the next act.

When Greta picked Danny up, he had the nerve to slide into the passenger seat and ask, "So, pass me the keys?" His face had the slimmest smile on it, that agonizing slice of charm that had gotten him out of sticky places when they were younger.

Greta chose not to dignify that with a response. She started the car and floored it for a few meters before stopping abruptly at a stop sign. "God damn, I forgot how many stop signs this neighborhood has."

"They should move the pesky hospital. Maybe that would fix it."

"Ha. Good session?"

"Good or not, it's the last one," Danny said. "Insurance says I'm healed, so I should be happy about that. Actually it was okay. And your exam thing?"

"Passed," Greta said. She pulled forward again and turned onto the backroad she usually took to avoid campus traffic. She cruised for a few blocks, only to have to stop when a line of orange cones appeared in the middle of the road. "Damn, did they start summer construction already?"

A line of cars were stopped in front of them, six or seven. An ominous one-lane-will-disappear-into-oblivion sign stood in the median a few cars away. A construction worker waved traffic from the opposite side past the obstruction. Taking turns had always been a weakness for Greta. She didn't have much choice. The cones blocked the way from the intersection to the next possible turn.

As they stalled, the car at the front of the line laid on the horn.

"Oh, that's helpful," Greta said. She beeped her own horn twice. Still, the horn continued, a droning bagpipe of a honk. "I'm not going to be stuck in traffic with that going on, I can tell you that."

At least four cars had stopped behind her now, and she put the car in park. After casting a sidelong glance at her brother, she shut the engine off and pocketed the keys before locking him in the car. He gave her a "what?" face through the window.

The day was warm, and the red bud blossom canopy above her belied the jarring noise. Even birds rose from their nests to get away from the honking. When she reached the car at the front of the line, a blue Elantra with spoilers, she rapped on the window with both fists.

A startled face stared at her, young and framed by her fists on the window. The guy was younger than twenty, with a baby face, and looked legitimately afraid of the six-foot-tall woman peering in his window. The honking stopped. She motioned for him to roll the window down, and he shook his head. Before she got a chance to rap again, traffic started moving. She had to jog to get back to her car, but by the time she settled in the driver's seat, her car was forced to yield for opposite traffic again, even though she was at the front of the line.

Greta swore under her breath. She, too, felt like laying on the horn now.

Danny chewed his lip in the silence of the car. "I should have told you that I talked to her when she got in touch last year."

Greta turned to her brother. "Who are you talking about?"

"Mom."

Greta bristled. "You really think this is the time?"

"What else are we doing?" Danny asked. When Greta didn't respond, he rolled down the window and angled an arm across the lowered arc of glass. "She sent an e-mail to the school, an invitation for Thanksgiving, an apology, an attachment of photographs from our childhood I'd never seen. Shit, Greta, you were a cute kid. Who would have guessed?"

"I grew into such an ogre. Kind of a *Shrek* thing."

"Want to know what's twisted? I liked not telling you. Not telling anyone. It was my thing."

Like the affair with Meg, before she was fiancée Meg. *Now ex-fiancée Meg,* Greta's brain corrected. Greta contemplated the horn again. Maybe the dumbass teen had been having an uncomfortable conversation, too, and was trying to drown it out.

"I was going to tell you when you got home from Costa Rica," Danny said. "I wanted to let it settle, give myself a chance to work through the knots before you came home."

"If our situation was someone else's—a friend's, maybe—would you tell that friend to get back in touch? If this friend, an adult, lived without a mother for years and didn't miss her. Didn't need her. And when she did need her, this mother wasn't there."

"But when I need her now, she's there."

"To get you in a car accident." Greta's breathing pained her. She gripped the steering wheel harder. What she really wanted to say was *Why can't you need me? Why can't I be enough?* Greta felt like she would bend herself for him, learn to be his parachute and landing pad or whatever he needed. They were supposed to be enough. They could be enough.

Finally, the line of cars moved again, and the construction worker waved them past. For a second, the sound of jackhammers coming through the open window drowned out his words, but she finally caught them and immediately responded with as many rejections as she could find. "No. Way. Nope, Danny. No."

"I invited her before this. It's just a dinner."

"Mother's Day? Really?" Greta turned onto his—their—street and parked.

"Gret, come on."

She got out of the car without another word. She knew, even with his PT, he couldn't catch up to her if she jogged. Her legs were longer. On the solo ride up the elevator, she realized that she hadn't even locked her car, but she would rather have her puny stereo stolen than finish that conversation.

The table still bore the marks of cake crumbs, but Meg's things were gone. Lighter—the room felt unanchored somehow with half its weight gone. Greta would have to move in her things that weekend just to keep it from floating away. One weakness of the place was that it didn't offer many spots to hide. Greta stashed herself in the bathroom, sitting on the toilet with her head in her hands.

It was the shortest hide-and-seek game on record. Greta used to purposely prolong their games as kids, walking past Danny's spot again and again to hear the giggle he couldn't suppress. She heard a knock on the door, one-fisted and lighter than the one she'd imposed on the teen honking his car horn. Danny's voice matched the level of care. "Gret?"

As if it could be someone else.

"Look, give me a dinner's-worth of pity for the ending of the only meaningful romantic relationship I've ever had."

Greta opened the door a half inch. "Fine. One dinner. Your pity coupon is cashed at that point."

Now she had to figure out what kind of Sunday dinner took the least amount of time to eat. The sooner Martha got in and out, the better.

# CHAPTER NINETEEN

Saturday night, Greta took Max out. It had been a long time since they watched *Voyager* together, and it almost felt like their time away had paused a real starship crew somewhere in the Delta Quadrant. It felt natural to be sitting with him again in the musky bar, chatting between episodes.

"To being almost out of this shithole," Greta said, holding up her mug to Max.

He clinked it against hers and then noticed the bartender's stern glare. "Not this one, Bruce. We're almost done with our PhDs."

Not "almost," but it felt that way. No more teachers, no more books, only the existential dread of producing the most thorough research of your professional life.

Bruce went back to polishing mugs with a dirty rag, which, in Greta's opinion, seemed like a metaphor for something. Neither Mikey's clientele nor decoration had changed much from the last time they'd had a beer together months ago, with one exception. The bar now boasted an additional three hundred channels of bad television. Even the country music had been silenced to make way for this new arrangement. Greta, who had grown up without cable TV, was always amazed at the wide variety of stupidity on at the same time. Bruce seemed amazed too, but in a more positive way, flipping to a new station every time a commercial threatened. Mud wrestling flipped to bull riding, but eventually televised skeet shooting won out. Greta had to guess some sports were just hard to find advertisers for in the first place.

Max rested his mug back on the counter. His raised eyebrow matched the angle of his collar. Greta had always hated the idea of short-sleeved dress shirts on adults, and denim shirts for that matter, but somehow the combination of both made Max look like a print-ad model of himself. "Now that it's summer, we could probably safely find a different place to drink and watch TV," he said under his breath.

"Where's the fun in that?" Greta asked.

"Where's the fun in *this?*" was his response.

"One"—she ticked the number off on her fingers, taking his question seriously—"no one talks to us. Two, cheap drinks. Three, world-broadening perspectives." She made a gesture to the television, which was displaying a score for a sport she didn't know existed.

"Just seems like Iowa to me," he said.

To Greta too, to be honest. She didn't want to admit to Max that the men in this bar reminded her a little of her father, the smell of sweat and wood chips and smoke that came off them. Ames had plenty of polished-top bars, but this one was rough in a way that made her ache. "Yeah, well," she said, settling on the easy answer. "We're Iowans, right?"

He just laughed into his beer. "Have you even had a conversation with my parents?"

She examined her beer so he wouldn't see her blush. "Why?"

He smiled and shook his head. "Well, my mom is originally from California. She was kind of a hippie before I was born, but I think Iowa knocks that out of you. You've seen how she dresses now. Dad's from Xi'an, China. He's only been here for—" He paused, doing mental calculation. "Thirty-three years?"

"Only," Greta said. "Was that your age plus a year?"

"Plus two years, thank you very much." Max smiled again, a different light in his eyes talking about his family. Greta liked that light, which dispersed the dustiness of Mikey's instantly. "Believe it or not, though, he wanted to name me Bruno. My mom overruled him, thank God."

Greta spit out a mouthful of beer, then wiped her lips. "No," she gasped, laughing. "Bruno?"

"My mom lived in San Bruno and worked at the airport when he came over. She's fourth-generation Chinese—her family had been settled in the area forever. Anyway, she worked at the lost-and-found counter. He lost a bag, and she found it," he said simply. "My dad made me take Mandarin growing up, even though he doesn't speak it at home. Just when we go visit family or I call my grandparents. I was sure the only reason was in case I ever met a girl in an airport that needed help."

"But if she was German, she'd be out of luck," Greta said.

"Maybe I'm not meant to fall for a German girl," Max said, directing the full weight of his smile at Greta now. It disarmed her.

"Or maybe German girls just don't need help."

"I'm sure that's why I didn't learn German instead," he said, his voice stoic. Back on solid ground. Back to the tone where she could get a foothold. "Anyway, tell me about that Meg thing."

And she did, relieved at the change of topic. Relieved at the dark room and the receding blood from her face.

Uncle Ritz had landed, and Danny couldn't hide his grimace. Franz was likewise intensely creeped out by the immense stuffed goose their dad had taxidermied years ago. The thing had been named after its favorite snack crackers, but Greta always thought of the beast as a monster that chased her and Danny as kids. Franz leapt to the hypothetical rescue, yipping at the thing on the way in the apartment. Despite both Danny's and Fritz's protests, Greta perched the goose on top of the sprawling IKEA bookshelf that divided the dining space from the living space. The bookshelf itself now contained Greta's textbooks and fantasy novels. Some duplicates between Danny and herself, Greta realized as she stacked her collection, but that just showed the distance that had grown between them in the past few years with Meg in the picture. They hadn't even known what books the other was reading.

Danny napped on Sunday afternoon while Greta settled the things from her storage unit. Even when he was awake, Danny sat for hours on the couch, sometimes with the television on, but sometimes not. The mornings that weekend, she watched the closed door to his bedroom, wondering what time he might emerge and what mood he might be in. Saturday, the time was ten and the mood was sunny. Sunday, the time was eight and the mood was grim. The inconsistency made Greta wish she could throw on a disguise and waltz into the caregiver meeting. *Hey guys,* she might say. *I wasn't really caregiving before. I was care-watching, but now . . .*

When she tried to return to the group, she noticed Meg's car parked in Greta's usual spot, and drove away immediately. The unfairness struck her. Why should Meg get to stay in the caregivers' group even though she left him? She went so far as to search for another local group to join, but discarded the idea as just as unlikely as an animal adapting well to an entirely new habitat. Whale, meet desert. She had barely transplanted successfully once—if she could call that relative comfort with strangers a success.

Strangers were better than Martha, though. She would rather go to a million "get to know you" sessions, play a zillion ice-breaker games (oh God, the humanity) than eat dinner with the woman who had birthed her. Greta decided dinner would be gazpacho. Worst situation: she could suck up her bowl with a straw and disappear into the backrooms of the apartment— a closet, if necessary. Then Martha and Danny could talk about whatever in the world Martha and Danny actually had in common besides genetic code.

She hadn't thought about their Hansel and Gretel costumes since the month after Danny's aneurysm, but as she chopped apples for salad, her brain replayed past memories. Hansel and Gretel, kicked out, left to wander. That was Danny and her in a nutshell. She didn't know if Martha was the neglectful mom in the story or the big bad witch, ready to eat them up.

The first thing Greta noticed was how nice Martha looked when she arrived. Nice in a fake sort of way. Martha had combed her hair in a bouffant. She wrangled the rest of her dark hair into a messy bun, and her mole had been concealed under pancake makeup. She seemed to be trying to appear younger and to impress, and it made Greta anxious. Danny gave a one-armed hug as he ushered Martha inside.

Greta opened the windows of the apartment to let the May air seep in. "I hear you passed your prelims," Martha said. "So this is a celebration?"

"I can fill you in on anything malarial."

"Fabulous," Martha said. "A medical pursuit after all, huh, Gret?"

"More about the mosquitoes than the disease. If you'd like to know, it's actually the anatomy of a mosquito that makes them such a good vector for transfer." The bowls of gazpacho were already set on the table. "Let's eat."

Danny stood next to Greta. He tried to keep Martha across the bookcase divide in the living space. "We don't have to rush."

Greta had already taken a seat at the dining room table. "Well, the soup's getting warm, so I think we should." Greta unfolded her cloth napkin with a flap.

Martha didn't raise an eyebrow as she took the seat next to Danny. She scanned the apartment with wide eyes. "Looks different. I see the goose came home to roost."

"I hate that thing," Danny said, his voice flat.

"It bit me at least once," Martha agreed.

Greta swallowed a spoonful of soup and began

to feel more charitable toward the goose. She passed the bowl of apple slices to Danny.

Martha cleared her throat. "Tell me more about your research."

"Okay. Some types of mosquitoes actually require a blood meal in order to produce their eggs," Greta said. She rested her spoon across the bowl like a bridge and picked up a slice of apple. "Others can produce a first litter, if you will, on sugar alone."

Danny's spoon lowered. He looked a little green. Maybe Greta did understand how he used to see colors that weren't there. "Do we have to talk about mosquitoes?"

Greta continued, gaining momentum. "And actually, the antennae on female mosquitoes detect all sorts of odors, not just of humans as feeding targets but also for egg-laying spots. You know, does this smell enough like home for them to plop their young into."

Martha refused to waver. She tore off a hunk of bread and dipped it in the soup. "This is good. Garlic? A little balsamic vinegar?"

"You'll have to ask the chefs at the co-op," Greta said. "Anyway, a mosquito, once it lays its eggs, will have to recoup for a while, feed again, before it gets to mate and lay another whole set of eggs. Somewhere else, by sniffing out a spot again. Crazy, isn't it?" Greta slurped her soup. "I mean, shit, if I know why mosquitoes can't stick around long enough to find out if their eggs hatched okay, help them figure out what to do when no one asks them to prom—"

"You got asked to prom," Danny said.

"By Jacob Alwitz. I wasn't going with Jacob Alwitz."

Martha swallowed her mouthful of bread. She folded her hands in front of her and stared Greta squarely in the eyes. "Alright, Greta. Let me have it."

Danny cut in. "Can't we have our first dinner without someone wanting to call the cops on us for disturbing the peace?"

"No," Greta said, pulling herself together again. She mimicked Martha's posture, leaning forward and staring at her. "It's a good point. Danny, did you ever tell her how things were after she left, or were you so grateful for the crumbs of her attention that you didn't bother?"

Danny's eyes narrowed. She couldn't tell if he was angry or thinking, but she knew he wasn't happy.

"We'll never get past it if we don't have it out," Martha said. "So out with it."

"You left us. You chose Kurt. Why do you think you can dictate terms to get back into our lives?"

"I don't."

"Then why are you here?"

"Maybe I'm here for whatever . . . crumbs

you can give me. After your father's death—"

Greta shook her head. "You don't get to talk about Dad."

"No," Martha said, her voice and eyes both ice, "I do. I had been with your father since we were both seventeen, but when he came home from the Gulf, he was different and I wasn't. I didn't know how to help him."

"Help him with what?" Danny spoke for the first time, channeling Greta's question.

"He didn't show it to you kids. I think he would have hid the moon from you if he thought it shined too bright through your window. Stress. Bad memories." Martha ran a hand over her hair, and the strands that came loose flipped backward. "I don't know."

A memory, different from her mother's, pinged in Greta. The doctor reviewing the coroner's report with them. Hypertension, aggravated by smoking. Unusual, the doctor said, in someone as young as he was, as fit. Before his death, their father stood a solid one hundred eighty-five pounds, with a chest like a metal door.

Greta swallowed the memory back. "I don't think it was just Dad."

Martha pulled on the edge of her blouse. "I got us into a lot of trouble financially. Debt."

"What are you talking about?" Greta's tone pulled Martha's chin up. She caught Martha's eyes. "I saw you leave with a man. That day.

Remember? That day—don't try to lie. You were running away with Kurt."

"Kurt. My bookie. It wasn't love, but it wasn't not love. Does that make sense? I wasn't thinking clearly then."

"But you are now? That's a newsflash from the woman who let her son with a brain injury drive a car—"

"I asked—" Danny cut in.

"This is not about that," Martha said. "Leave Danny out of this."

"You don't get to dictate what 'this' is about. 'This' is about my life and Danny's and the royal fuckup you made of our lives by running out of them when we were fourteen."

"You can't blame me for everything that has ever happened to you, Greta," Martha said. "I'm sorry, but I'm not actually that powerful. I don't control everything."

"You can't even control yourself, obviously, so how could you?" Greta shouted.

"I had a problem. I—I couldn't think most days. I mean, I haven't gambled in years now—but when it was bad, it was bad. All I thought about. I racked up a lot of debt." Martha's eyes had crow's-feet around the corners, which she had tried to dab concealer over. It didn't work. As if answering a question nobody asked, Martha continued. "Blackjack. Dog racing. I tried to quit, but I wasn't in a good place. The time I took

Danny after piano lessons. Do you remember that, Danny?"

Danny hadn't said anything, and, unlike Greta's, his gaze searched his bowl like it was a Magic 8-Ball. "Yeah."

"What time?" Greta asked. "What do you mean?"

"We drove to Jefferson and I left him in the car. Hours. It was hours. You were old enough to sit in the car, I thought. I knew you'd be fine. I kept thinking about that time when I finally got help, the look on your face when I got back to the van and there you were, curled on the back seat."

"I didn't know about this," Greta said.

"I thought that you would be better if I left. I thought . . . well, I thought a lot of things. I'd been thinking about them a long time before I met Kurt, before I started gambling. I know that doesn't excuse anything. I got help, and now I'm trying to rebuild—"

"If Danny hadn't gotten sick—"

"We probably wouldn't have seen each other, Gret, but Danny and I were already talking again."

"But you didn't tell him about the debt, did you?" Greta asked. It only took a glance sideways to get confirmation. She remembered those first days after Dad's death, buried in bills and letters from creditors. Debt didn't die, and it couldn't just pack up and leave either. Unlike mothers. Danny had to drop out of Oberlin because of that debt. Greta had negotiated with creditors to make time lines for paying it off, which it finally was. In the aftermath, Danny had to give up his dream.

Danny's face purpled, like those thoughts ricocheted in his head too.

"You okay, Danny?" Martha asked.

"I thought you were in the hotel. That night in Jefferson. After you left, I thought that you were meeting that man, you know that?" Danny said, his voice quiet. "And I never told Dad. I never told him."

Martha's face softened, gaze lowered. "I left because I was afraid of what having me around would do. To you. To both of you. I wanted to come back a winner. For such a long time, I thought it was coming, just around the bend. Next hand. Next race. Something."

No further response from Danny except to put his spoon on the lip of the bowl and look down at his lap. It churned in Greta's stomach. "That's dinner. Bye," Greta said.

Martha put her spoon beside her half-empty bowl. "What?"

"We're through here."

Danny pushed his chair back from the table and, a second later, slammed his door closed behind him.

# PART THREE

## Summer

"What makes things baffling is their degree
of complexity, not their sheer size . . . A star
is simpler than an insect."

—Martin Rees,
"Exploring Our Universe and Others,"
*Scientific American*, December 1999

# CHAPTER TWENTY

I'm staying in the car," Greta said.

"All day?" Danny stared at her from the passenger seat. "Because this is a lesbian thing?"

"I don't have a thing against lesbians."

"Sure." He sounded one-fifth convinced.

"I don't. I just don't like weddings. Any weddings. Plus, it's pouring." A freak June rainstorm, heavy and wearing dark clouds, didn't seem all that celebratory to Greta. She stared out the windshield at the pocks in the parking lot, filled with rainwater, the blacktop a terrain of isthmuses and islands.

"There's a tent. Want me to carry you across the puddles?"

"Sure—your doctor would love that." Greta sighed. "If I come, it's only so I can see Franz with a bow tie."

"I knew you loved him," Danny said.

"I just love bow ties."

Five minutes later they hoisted equipment on their backs, dodging raindrops on their way under the canopy. The tent was the largest one Greta had ever seen, and the inside was strung with hundreds of strings of pale green lights. Rows and rows of folding chairs stood in strict formation facing a raised platform, and to the side of the platform was a folding table with a folded card on top: Danny Oto, DJ.

The only other occupants of the tent jerry-rigged speakers and installed changing tents in the back. Even with a tarp underneath her flip-flops, the ground felt swampy and uneven. Greta was afraid of dropping the equipment, but she made it to the table without breaking anything. "You could have dressed nicer," Danny murmured, kneeling to plug in an amp. "Sweatpants?"

"It's not *my* wedding," Greta replied. She connected male to female ports and felt a little dirty about it.

"You'll probably find really dressy sweatpants for yours someday. Versace sweatpants."

Greta rolled her eyes so hard she worried she might fall over.

Danny always used to DJ when school wasn't in session, even during college. The equipment had paid for itself twelve times over, but Greta still didn't understand why Danny accepted this gig. She saw the drag in his body, the way he still couldn't listen to music for more than a few minutes without complaining of a headache. When she pushed him on the question, he gave her a look. "Friendship," he said, but Greta had a suspicion he was anticipating seeing someone and that it wasn't his dog.

The huge tent filled with guests and soon every chair had an occupant. Though the rain had let up a bit, attendees closest to the tent edge kept their umbrellas up, their laps getting soaked in the rainy cross-breeze.

A tall man in a blue vest approached Danny. Everything was about to begin. As soon as the blue-vested man scampered out of sight, the green lights strung above flashed on. An audible "ooh" came from the guests. The music started, something jazzy and sweet, but unplaceable.

First down the aisle was Franz, bow tie neatly in place. From what Greta could glean, Meg had moved in with Ginger and Leanne for a while, and they'd fallen in love with the mutt. *How could you not?* Greta thought bitterly. She missed the messy scruff of hair around his muzzle when he woke her up to go on their early morning walks.

After Franz completed his part, he pranced to the side of the platform and sat. Greta wanted to fetch him, but the rest of the wedding party was coming down the aisle. Meg and the man in the vest linked arms, synchronized and stepping carefully. The tarp shifted under them and sunk a quarter inch with each step. When Meg's heel caught in a dip, Greta surprised herself by feeling relief when Meg didn't fall on her face.

Ginger and Leanne came next, arm in arm. Leanne wore a pale green dress, like first spring leaves. The color accented her dark, shaved head and long bare arms. By her side, Ginger wore a long forest-green gown. The only matching feature were the garlands of white flowers wound around both of their heads. Unlike Meg with her stilted walk, these women glided. Greta assessed their footwear smugly. Flats, of course. Not that Greta herself had ever worn anything besides flats. Even if Greta were to marry, she would wear flats.

There was an unlikely thought. She breezed right past it.

Martha had worn spikey heels like ivory daggers the day she married. On her anniversary every year, Martha pulled the box out of her closet to marvel at them. Greta remembered comparing her feet to the shoes, the way the ratio of their size narrowed each year until finally Greta knew she could never fit into them. The family would gather around the dining room table, and Dad and Martha would open the huge album and point out details of their wedding day. Martha's wedding dress had been a white blooming monstrosity with bubbled cap sleeves and pearl beading. Though Greta had never favored anything "girly" as a kid, she still had been in awe of that dress. When she touched it, she thought of Glinda. Dad, with his neatly pressed brown suit, wore his sideburns longer then. The differences in her parents, the little additions of hair or reductions of weight, always made Greta feel like she was looking at someone else in the old pictures. It was the unfamiliar expression more than anything, the dazed smile on Martha's face as she leaned on Dad's chest, that Greta had recognized the least.

Danny wore his poncho throughout this ceremony, with a tarp draped protectively over his equipment. But by the time Leanne and Ginger took their vows, the rain had stopped, and the wind blew the clouds into wavy wisps. Men packed up the chairs and tables while the guests mingled in the wet grass by the lake. The sun peeked out for the reception, and when Leanne and Ginger cut the cake, Greta's stomach rumbled in the late afternoon sun that knifed across their tent corner.

"Do we get dinner?" Greta murmured to Danny. When she didn't receive a response, she elbowed him, and he took out an earplug.

"What?"

She'd forgotten about those damn earplugs, but they were probably the only thing keeping him here. Already his eyes were drooping. His doctor had been lukewarm on the idea of a six-hour outing. So had Greta, in all honesty, but for more selfish reasons. They were here now, though. She weighed the embarrassment of talking to other humans with the possibilities of low blood sugar. "I'm getting food."

Danny nodded and held up a number two on his fingers before replacing the earplug.

Reconnaissance went smoothly. She cut in front of a table of poky older relatives and eyed the buffet for something palatable. Labels described the food: one dish was "tempeh" something, and some had phrases like "a play on," which always put Greta on guard. If she wanted "a play on" something, she would add barbecue sauce to a hamburger. She managed to find rice pilaf with some cherry tomatoes and fresh mozzarella chunks. She grabbed some crusty rolls of bread with butter rosettes. She assumed it was real butter, but maybe it was a play on butter.

On her way back to the DJ table, Greta felt eyes on the back of her head and turned around too quickly. A cherry tomato bailed over the side of the plate, which Greta decided was Danny's. Caught in the act, Meg's face turned downward from her seat at the head table. With its position on the podium, the DJ table and the head table were within shouting distance of each other. Greta wondered as she plopped down Danny's plate whether Meg had requested to be on the side farthest from them or if that had been the couple's decision.

Danny gave a nod of thanks. He speared a mozzarella ball and returned his attention to the screen. His selection of dinner music was overly sentimental, Greta thought. Acoustic versions of love ballads. Greta hoped his strength wasn't failing him now, with kryptonite just fifteen feet away. Physically, he seemed almost his pre-aneurysm self. He no longer needed a cane, his hair had grown back, and he had even put back some of the weight he had lost. In other ways, he was likely never to be the same. It was hard to quantify things that set him off—noise, exhaustion, too much activity. Greta wasn't too good with the unquantifiable.

She weighed words that she could use to get him to take a break. Sometimes she felt like she walked the fine line between commandant and conspirator. She just wanted him to be the more responsible one again, the one who had things figured out. More often lately, he was chafing under her help, and she hated that. She just wanted to cocoon him until he was perfectly healed.

*"He will never be perfectly healed,"* she imagined Dr. Traeger saying. *"And that's the truth."*

*"He'll never be the same Danny,"* an imaginary Pam said. *"And that's life."*

*"He will always be your brother,"* a ghost Dad said. *"And that's luck."*

"Can I give it a shot?" she said, pointing to the computer. "I swear I won't break anything."

He agreed, pushing back for a moment from the table and rubbing a hand over his eyes.

As the sun disappeared under the crust of the lake, the dinner tables were spirited away. Danny resumed the next set.

A bark made Greta look up from the novel in her lap. Franz nestled his muzzle on Greta's pants. Panting, he leaned his head to the side as if she couldn't find the right place to scratch his ears otherwise. Greta scratched. Meg appeared, decidedly shorter, having left her heels somewhere. "Could you take him for a walk?" she asked.

Greta glanced at Danny, who stared at the computer. He hadn't been drinking, but his face suddenly flushed. In the background "Sweet Caroline" rang out, as cheesy as a Wisconsin farm, but nobody seemed to mind. The group on the floor danced with sloshing solo cups and intoning the "Bah-bah-bahs." Ginger spun with the man in the vest. When the song ended, Danny picked up the mic. "The help is taking five."

"Take ten," Leanne shouted from somewhere in the group.

Danny took one of the wax earplugs out of his ear, but not the other. "Hi," he said.

Meg handed the leash to Greta. "Thanks for doing this."

Greta took a few steps away, realizing she hadn't agreed to anything. Franz didn't seem to mind nosing around in the grass near the edge of the tent.

"How could you hear the music with earplugs?" Meg asked. "I just noticed."

He shrugged. "Well enough."

Franz nosed at the tent stakes and rope, shaking free some collected rainwater on a lower corner of the tent's roof. Greta covered her head.

Oblivious to the drips, Danny asked Meg, "Having a good summer break?"

She gave some noncommittal nothing about new textbooks and added, "So, are you coming back? To the school?"

Greta led Franz, newly mud-spattered, to a different shadowed corner to get a better look. Danny nodded slowly, fingers tapping the computer keyboard soundlessly. "I'm going to try. I haven't been able to . . ." He stopped. "I guess brain injury only gets you so much time off."

His eyes were back on the screen. Was he queuing up music while she stood there? Greta shouldn't have worried so much. He sounded as dispassionate as a kid in the dentist's chair. Meg must have heard something too, or the lack of something, because she blushed suddenly. The blush spread down to her collarbones; a stretch of bare skin highlighted in pink. She touched the necklace that hung there. When she didn't say anything more, Danny replaced his earplug. The music started again, twangy opening chords of the next song. Greta saw her cue.

She handed the leash back to Meg. "I don't actually know if he pooped or not," she said honestly. "So watch for land mines out there."

Meg took the leash, not looking back over her shoulder as she meandered back into the swarm of dancing bodies.

"Want some cake?" Greta asked. When Danny didn't answer, she didn't bother to ask again. She snagged two pieces of cake ("A play on strawberry rhubarb pie" the label read) and a beer from the cash bar to wash it down.

Greta ate one slice of cake, then the second. By the time she'd finished, she caught Danny's gaze. It wasn't directed at her, of course, but the fairy-lit dance floor. In the darker night, the green lights glimmered brighter and turned Meg's hair a kiwi color. She twisted. She turned. Danny cued up another song, and Greta felt him looking closely at the playlist. After the next song, Meg's hair fell loose from her bun and tangled around her face in curls and waves.

At ten, Danny rested his head on his elbows.

"Time to go," Greta said. Not a question. At the signs of him packing up, Ginger rushed over and gave him a tight hug, and Leanne plugged in her iPhone. The dancing bodies barely paused their twirling, turning, twisting.

# CHAPTER TWENTY-ONE

The third of July began bright and, as her grandfather would mumble, as hot as the devil's tit. The heat certainly warmed Greta's breasts. When she woke on her futon Saturday morning sweat had pooled between them. Broken air-conditioning. She dragged Danny out of bed so they could find refuge downtown. Between the board game store and the farmer's market booths and everything else, she was sure he could find some distraction on Main Street while she wrote for a few hours in air-conditioned sanctity.

Café Diem offered the best coffee in Ames, and Greta found herself writing her dissertation there that morning. Long descriptive passages of ant behavior made up the initial section. Ants used scent and also sunlight to navigate, a trend backed up not only by research (see endnotes 12, 15, and 16) but also by observation. The glass dome of the butterfly house had no artificial light. On clear days, the refraction of the light blinded. On foggy days, the air inside held its humidity so that she was inside a cloud.

Blah blah blah. She felt sick of her own voice, except she wasn't saying anything. Instead, she was sick of the Times New Roman font and her brain. And citations. And ants. Oh God, was she sick of ants.

Besides five-year-olds with warty knees, and entomologists like herself, Greta didn't know how many people examined ants. Butterflies had many fans. They were a pretty insect, easy to want to protect. People wanted to save Monarchs like they wanted to save elephants. They were majestic in a way that made you feel unimportant to be around them and important to protect them. It was like standing up for the pretty girl in class when she got a pimple, while the nerd cowered in the corner.

She didn't pity ants, and she didn't pity herself as the former nerd in the corner. Or current nerd in the corner, but research necessitated that. She could take care of herself, thank you very much. And so could the harvester ants; that's what made trapping them somewhat difficult.

Even ninth-graders knew the scientific method, but it was odd to see it in action for research where she had no concept of the outcome. Most of her career, up to this point, she'd been replicating other people's theories, but now she and Brandon walked on untrodden ground.

Make observations and form a hypothesis.

The ants hadn't been there before the planting of the new palms last winter, and they'd arrived shortly afterward. They showed many hallmarks of an invasive species, including dominating food sources and reproducing quickly.

It had all started in March. Greta and Brandon

on their knees, catching ants in Dixie cups, to look at under the microscope. She still remembered the way his hand hit hers on the concrete, the way the rubble left an imprint on the soft skin of her knees.

Develop testable questions and scenarios.

He brought his prototype, and she hers. One Sunday morning, two months ago, they set them up equidistant from the central action of the ants and their most serious nesting grounds. He opened a carafe of coffee he'd brought and poured her a cup, and they sat on the rocky center of the butterfly house near the waterfall. The butterflies looped around her, and he made a comment that she must have switched her perfume. The butterflies noticed. He did too. They watched ants make lazy trails below them for a few hours after dawn, talking like they used to.

Gather data and analyze.

After a day of activity, they corked and removed their prototypes, anesthetizing the tubes of ants with smoke, like is done to calm a hive of bees. She installed hinges in her bamboo version so she could open the door and peer inside. The whole contraption came up to her thigh and weighed about ten pounds. After a day, that weight had doubled. Insects only added weight in bulk, and as she guessed from trying to heft it, the inside teemed with ants. They crawled over each other in a red-brown mass so tight it looked like human hair. Brandon peered over her shoulder. "The hinge was smart," he commented as he cut into his cube prototype with a saw. Hers was reusable and caught more ants. Another plus.

Replicate. Ad nauseum.

Science was repetition. She thought about Danny's endless piano scales as a kid. Up, down, up, down, change keys, up, down. She used to needle him, "When are you going to play something real?" She understood now. The scales were real, they were the blocks, the data gathering.

After several rounds of removal, raw data showed a ninety-nine percent decrease of the population.

A ninety-nine percent increase in joking with Brandon. Some troublesome constants, like the gathering pictures of Eden on his desk. Like the gathering knot in her stomach as she realized that she might still have feelings for him.

And now she had to present her findings. Science couldn't exist in a vacuum unless she worked with a Hadron Collider, and she had long ago ruled out physics. She liked things she could hold in her hand, manipulate. Now she knew more about harvester ants than anyone in the state.

She chewed over the best way to present the prototype visually, to explain how it worked, and ate a few bites of sandwich. The hum of the coffee shop played like music behind her, interrupted every few minutes by the squeak of a chair or a child's cough. She was adding a caption to her 3D image when someone tapped her on the shoulder. In the tap, the quick press and release, she knew it was her twin behind her. Her shoulder as an oboe, her shoulder as a viola string. Plus, who else would touch her in public? "You can sit for twenty minutes, but I can't afford more distraction than that."

"So generous," Danny said. He sounded joyful, and she couldn't resist pushing the issue.

"What? What are you so happy about?"

"I went into the music store," Danny said.

The music store, the same one that twenty-some years ago they'd wandered in together and had been inspired to adopt a piano. "Did they recognize you?"

He nodded, then turned suddenly solemn. "I think I've lost my colors for good."

"You never know," Greta cut in. She didn't want to waste their twenty minutes with self-pity. She suddenly felt guilty for rushing him. "I mean, why do you say that?"

"I thought maybe the store would trigger my synesthesia. Stupid, I guess." He ate a potato chip off her plate, and she congratulated herself for not batting him away. "But nothing. I mean, the owner and I improvised a little, like we used to. He has this . . ."

And Danny descended into a stream of nonsense words about brands of piano and composers she had never heard of. Last year she would have cut him off. Now, she was grateful to see him there, hear him talking about things she didn't care about. She thought about Max's advice to be interested in other people and nodded at Danny, who took it as a cue to keep talking. Maybe she was developing some kind of patience and maturity.

*Probably not.*

"You take one more goddamn chip," she muttered as he took a breath, "and I'm sending you an itemized bill."

He swallowed and laughed at her.

The bell to the café tinkled. She saw the change in his face as he turned toward the door. She had the seat facing the back of the café and the restrooms, while he could look over at patrons ordering their frothy drinks. Something had changed. "What?"

"Meg," he said, his voice quiet. He put an arm up to shade his face, curling his hand in a mask to cover his eyes. "Can you switch spots with me?"

Greta slid out of the booth and moved to the other side, do-si-doing with him in the narrow walkway between the coffee bar and the table. She saw the reason for expediency. Soon, very soon, she would be close enough to the counter to see his old seat very clearly, but the spot facing away would be far less visible. "She's not alone," Danny murmured, which Greta saw too. Saw very clearly, in fact, as the couple approached the counter to pay.

"That's my office mate," Greta said. "Oh God. She's with Max."

It was noon and the lunch crowd stood in an orderly line, waiting. Meg held a pint of strawberries from the farmer's market and stood with Max. The two chatted, leaning their heads together in the rising tide of lunchtime conversation.

As if Meg could feel Danny's eyes on her, she turned slowly. Her mouth became a little "o" of surprise, but she adjusted it into a smile before she reached their table. "Hi, Danny."

Danny seemed ready to respond, but Greta couldn't imagine what he would say. After a second, he cleared his throat and left, pushing past Max's shoulder and spilling iced tea over the rim of his glass. Max stepped backward to avoid the splash. A second later, the chime of the door sounded. Danny moved so quickly that the chime came long after him, like a movie with a frame cut out.

"Is he okay?" Meg asked. Her gaze tracked the door after Danny left through it.

"He was," Greta said. She sharpened her tone enough to make Meg look at her. She did, finally.

Max didn't, his glance on the spilled iced tea spots on the floor.

Was it her own fault? That day over chocolate cake, him loading her into the car. Jesus, had she set all this in motion? She gestured to the pair of them, matched in their preppy clothes, standing there like salt and pepper shakers. "How long has this been going on?"

Max stammered, "This isn't anything."

"Looks like something."

He wasn't used to her sharp edges, her hate, like Meg was. He'd only seen her in a lab or the bar. New variables in the wild. "We're friends," Meg said. Greta didn't believe her. Meg's word was garbage, a growing pile of garbage that included Max's word too.

"I could not care less."

"Greta—"

Before either of them could say anything else, Greta packed her bag and left.

The Fourth of July dawned even hotter than the day before, and Greta's temper matched it blow for blow. She chewed her breakfast so hard that she nearly bit her bottom lip along with the toast. Danny didn't eat at all, pressing his head against the table as though he hadn't slept all night. "Okay," Greta said, "we need some fireworks therapy."

Greta saw the inflatable gorilla before she saw

the tent itself. The twenty-foot-tall ape always graced the mall parking lot during fireworks season, its arms stretched above its head like an angry ballerina's. The tent was just opening for the day. It wasn't until Greta locked the car door behind them that she realized how stupid this idea was. They could have gotten their usual choices at any gas station. Danny, just like when he was ten, chose a box of snakes instead of black cats. It comforted her that he always hated the Fourth of July and that this year was no different. Greta grabbed some sparklers, even though she was unsure if Danny would be awake late enough to use them. And where would they? On the lawn in front of the apartment building, stealing space from the neighbor kids?

On the way home, Greta rolled down the window and felt the inrush of oven air, barely cooler than the inside of the car. In fireworks selections and pretty much everything else, Greta mused that people never change from their childhood selves. Sure, she was taller, broader, and smarter than herself at age ten or twelve, but she still sensed that kernel of adolescent insecurity as keenly as a hangnail. Hangnails are easier to clip off; insecurities gestate.

Danny had always been the favorite child. Greta accepted that. He was a latte, and she was day-old coffee. Supposedly, their differences started at birth. Though he had never slept much, he didn't cry much either. Greta had been a screamer, in love with her own loud voice. Maybe, Greta thought, he knew colors from birth and could see them drifting above him like shadows on the wall. Maybe he could hear colors in the voices that spoke and sang to him. He cooed, he watched, he sang.

Though he was half of her, Greta had hated him.

At five, Greta had decided to pack up and run away. Danny had taken her things again, and Dad had done nothing to stop him. Danny had made Martha laugh again, and Greta didn't know how to compare. Her suitcase, as she remembered it now, was an old grocery bag. Inside she put her Rainbow Brite doll, her Beatrix Potter collection, two pairs of clean underwear, and a fresh pair of suspender pants. She had told Martha, "I'm running away," and Martha, who hadn't known that Greta didn't have much of an imagination, took it for a game. If she'd told her Dad, he would have stopped her. Her Dad was like Greta—he knew she meant what she said.

She'd only gotten as far as the neighbor's house down the block. One of the neighbor kids was a year younger than Greta, a frequent playmate, and she'd welcomed her. Greta liked this house—they had a dog and a cat. Martha was allergic, so they'd never had pets.

The neighbor kid ushered Greta inside like she

had been expecting her and offered her a home behind the couch in their den. Greta unpacked. The dog nosed open her book of stories, and Greta paged through a few while her neighbor friend ate lunch in the kitchen. The house smelled like hot dog water, and Greta's stomach growled. She tried to read to make the time go faster. She liked Beatrix Potter because the pictures looked like real animals, not wide-eyed cartoony imitations. Although she couldn't read most of the stories by herself, she could sound out "The Story of the Bad Rabbit." It was shorter than the rest. The good rabbit got a carrot from his mother, and the bad rabbit scratched him. In the end, the bad rabbit loses its tail and whiskers to a man with a gun. The good rabbit, Greta noticed, didn't get the carrot back, though, and she thought about hitting Danny to see what happened, but never did.

Good rabbits wouldn't think about that.

Good rabbits wouldn't have run away.

Sitting in their apartment, which still didn't have working air-conditioning, Greta set up the dominos along the table. She watched Danny take some for himself. Decades later and he was still the good rabbit. Did there always have to be an evil twin and did she always have to be it? "You can go first," she said.

He clicked a tile in formation.

"You're quiet today," she said.

He grunted, then rose to get a glass of water. When he returned, he didn't notice the way she'd cheated in his absence.

"Earth to Danny." She waved a hand. "Anyone home? Too many people home?"

"Sorry. Money."

She believed and didn't believe him all at once. She, too, had seen the hospital bill that had arrived the day before. He'd torn it from its envelope and returned it back, like putting it to bed would prolong the inevitable. "Money's overrated."

"My last disability check came, and now I should be prepping for the fall, but . . ." He shook his head, his hair flopping.

"I thought the noise was gone."

He sighed and placed another domino. Snake eyes. "I'm so tired, Gret. So tired. I get up, try to play a little music, and it takes all my effort not to want to go lie down again. My head hurts by the end of the day. I mean, I got headaches before everything happened—you can't be around a middle school band and not—but now? And medication doesn't touch it."

The shelves of medication, he meant. Some, blood thinners. Some, antidepressants. Some, pain. Their apartment was a regular Walgreens these days.

The summer after their freshman year of college, she had gone home to find everything in the trailer moved to a different but better place.

Danny had been home for a week before her, and things were tidied up, put away. He could always see where things belonged. If only he could hold up a mirror to himself to see where he belonged now. "Maybe you'll find something else you love to do."

He laughed, but it was bitter. "I'm starting to worry that things that I love change on me, so why love anything?"

"I love you," Greta said, but she knew she didn't say it right. In the movies, a touching family moment would have hugs, voices dripping with sentiment. The revelation should be heavy, but her voice sounded like she checked things off a grocery list. More Cheerios. More milk. We've got plenty of eggs.

"I'm glad," he said. A grin tweaked his lips, and his voice echoed some of that heartfelt moment they were supposed to be having. Leave it to Danny to pick up the slack.

"I'm sorry I was a bitch to Meg when there was a Meg," Greta said.

"There's still a Meg."

"You know what I mean. She has a habit of breaking it off with fiances. You deserve better. You're Danny, for shit's sake." *You're supposed to be the favorite,* she thought. *You're the good twin.*

"When you meet someone, just someone so perfect—"

Greta's tiles were gone. The dominoes made a

road of white dots across the tabletop. As kids, they used to line them up like this and drive matchbox cars over the top. "There's a song in that," Greta said.

Danny laughed, a real laugh now. "Sure there is, but I can't hear it."

"Do you need help with the bills?"

"You don't have any money," Danny said.

"I know, but I figured I'd at least act like a sister and ask," Greta said, grabbing the envelope from the hospital on the counter. Her eyes moved up and down the list of charges, balances paid out by insurance, remaining funds due. "The hospital must think an awful lot of your life to charge that much for saving it."

"I'm honored. Truly." Danny's voice mirrored Greta's then. Twinned it. It hurt her to hear sarcasm in his voice.

She'd always been bad at being a sister. After Martha left, Greta should have taken better care of him. Better care of *them,* but she hadn't seen what they needed. Maybe if she'd forced him into the bathtub, the social worker wouldn't have visited. Maybe that little bit of stress built the clot that ended their father's life eventually. Parallel universe. But she had a chance now to try, at least. "We'll figure it out," she said. "Whatever it is."

"Maybe lightning will strike twice," Danny said, tapping a finger to his head.

"Don't."

"Or I guess it's a third time?"

"Danny." He scared her now, this dark hint behind his voice. "It's going to be okay."

He ran a hand across the tabletop and shoved the dominoes back into their box.

Things didn't get better or worse after Greta had run away and come back; they only got different. Danny became more imperfect as he got older, and Greta did quiet things that delighted her parents. She would always be first in birth order. Ten minutes. She strived to be first at home whether in reading or learning to play soccer. He still laughed louder, joked more, picked up music like a first language. She would never be the outgoing one, the popular one, so she made sure, at least, she was the one whose ant farm didn't break. She made sure she got perfect grades to compare to Danny's failure in handwriting and consistent "C's" in English. She collected his failures quietly and glued them together into a shell over her insecurity.

The time when Greta had run away, she'd kept waiting for someone to come knocking. She'd waited so long—through lunch and most of the afternoon—that by the time her friend remembered she was there, Greta had fallen asleep on the open book of Beatrix Potter. Even as a runaway, she was easy to forget. Finally, after a few hours, some action. A phone call woke her up, and the friend's mother, still unaware of Greta taking up residence behind her couch, made surprised noises and offers to help. Jackets were grabbed from the front closet, and Greta's friend was tugged out by the hand and loaded into a minivan, which pulled down the driveway.

Alone in the house, Greta decided to requisition some supplies. A gallon of milk and a cup. A box of cereal. A pint of fancy ice cream, the kind Greta's family usually only bought for birthdays. Two spoons—one for cereal and one for ice cream.

Greta's friend must have spilled the secret, because forty minutes later the minivan parked, and several sets of heavy footsteps thumped into Greta's new residence.

"Greta," her Dad's voice boomed from the front hallway. From behind the couch, she could picture his expression. He was not happy, and when Dad was not happy, the face behind his beard turned red so that his yellow facial hair looked like threads on a crimson sheet. "Greta Ann Oto, you get out here this instant."

Her stomach, full of ice cream and Captain Crunch, emptied itself onto the hall carpet before he had a chance to finish his tirade, and her mother swooped in with her hands open, as if to catch it, to save it from the floor. Her mother had just graduated from nursing school, freshly trained and so proud of her unflappability. Mess or not, nothing deflated anger more than vomit. Tears could be ignored, but vomit required team-work and action. Apologies from Martha, sudden concern from her father.

"Why?" her Dad had asked later, when she was home and clean in the tub.

"Because of Danny," she had said, as if it didn't need any more explanation than that.

"Don't you like him?"

"There can only be one good rabbit, and it's not me." This logic made sense to five-year-old Greta.

She went to bed without dinner, without a story, but her father appeared as she tucked herself in, and he kissed her on the forehead. "It's always better to be with family and a little sad than alone and happy," he had told her. That thought burrowed inside and hibernated.

Greta put the lid on the dominos box. "You going to talk to Meg?"

"You going to talk to your office mate?"

"Fair question. You first."

"No."

"That goes for me too." But she knew she would have to, and soon. She had classes to teach in the fall—thank the registrar gods for that—and Max did too. Just like on a starship, there wasn't enough room to ignore each other at the university. Their online lives, the lives that had intersected so much before, ran in two parallel tracks. She didn't "like" his posts on Facebook anymore. He stopped e-mailing her stupid cartoons and jokes. Her work e-mail today only contained work-related things now; she missed the small amount of junk that Max had imposed on her life.

If Dad had been caretaking, he would have sucked it up like he did every other slight and injury, hidden it under his layers of practical jokes and things he never told them. Carrying the woes around on his back, guarding them. She had never seen that Dad had always been a little sad—maybe more than that—with them. Maybe she should have. Maybe, all things considered, Danny's demeanor seemed familiar. A way of focusing on nothing, at least nothing that Greta could see. A way of clenching his hands on the tabletop.

She wasn't the bad rabbit; she understood that as she got older. She was an ordinary one.

Danny was never good at being ordinary, but he'd never minded it until now.

By dinner, his eyes drooped and he kept checking the time. Still, she made him stand on their narrow balcony and light the snakes. The tablets unrolled, tarry and wiggly. "They look like shit," she said.

He laughed, but she knew he was humoring her. He went to bed at eight, and she sat on the living room couch, with her knees pulled up to her chest, watching the sun set outside Danny's window.

Two years ago, she might have made out with Brandon in the back seat of his car and pretended he wasn't leaving, pretended there was something there. A few months ago, she would have drunk a wordless beer with Max and pretended that they were real friends. Pretended that he wouldn't be the type to want Meg.

It wasn't quite dark yet. It wasn't the end of the Fourth just yet.

Greta pulled out her phone and sent a text to Brandon. "You watching the fireworks anywhere?"

# CHAPTER TWENTY-TWO

The flask had something sharp in it that smelled of nail polish remover. Greta passed it back to Eden after faking a pull and leaned back in the lawn chair. She, Eden, and Brandon sat with the other hundred people on the lawn by the middle school, staring into the empty, dark sky. It was like waiting for a curtain to come up. The other bodies near hers emitted smoke and sweat, and memories of summer camp bonfires rushed back to her. She had always hated camp. Girls squealing over spiders in the tents, girls making stories and friendship bracelets, girls everywhere and no solitude anywhere. Brandon's body in the chair next to her didn't remind her of camp, though, unless it was of the horses. Wide shoulders, long legs. She stopped herself from thinking about riding and accepted the flask from Eden on the next pass. The sip stung all the way down.

She sat between Eden and Brandon as though they were sharing her. The placement seemed purposeful, the lawn chair empty when she arrived. Both had gazed at their phones, faces lit up from beneath. Eden had looked her way first, shooed her into the chair and started talking to her immediately about a leggings company she patronized. Greta found, strangely, that she missed Meg at that moment. Meg's conversation was always a give-and-take. She pried pieces of you out in it, forced you to reveal your interests. She was curious. Eden spoke in an excited avalanche of give-give-give. The minutes ticked by, and the crowd hushed together as the start of the fireworks show approached. When the start time came and went, the conversation started again until the sudden flower of light appeared above them with a pop.

Greta couldn't stop the grin that hit her face. Before, when Danny saw colors with music, Greta always pictured his synesthesia like this. A rosette, a sudden shock of pink and gold against a black background. The idea had made her jealous. While Danny always hated the Fourth of July, it was her favorite holiday. If she ever got married, she wanted it to be on the Fourth so that she could have fireworks, endless fireworks, without having to pay for them.

This part, the end, was her favorite. Rockets shot up ten at a time, overlapped and bled into one another. She knew it was designed, but the end of a fireworks show had the feeling of a going-out-of-business sale, the carelessness of a toddler throwing everything into one toy bin. Sudden silence, and the sky was all smoke. The assembled crowd packed up their chairs, and soon only the three of them were left on the dark hill by the school. Brandon turned to Greta. "It'll take us forever to get out of the parking lot with this crowd."

Greta dug around in her purse and held out the box of sparklers. "I brought supplies." She paused and corrected herself. "Shit, but no lighter."

"I think I've got one. Just a sec." Eden opened her purse with a manicured hand and pulled out a dainty pink lighter. She gave a mischievous smile and tugged a plastic baggie out as well. A single white joint hung in the bag—or that was what Greta assumed it was. Greta felt, suddenly, years of DARE training spin uselessly in her mind.

None of them noticed the disappearance of headlights from the parking lot. In the shade of the trees near the baseball field, no one would see them, even with their sparklers. Eden took a puff of the joint and handed it off to Brandon before lighting a sparkler. It fizzed in her hand and she traced her name in cursive in the dark sky. The afterimage of Eden's name written backward printed itself on the inside of Greta's eyelids.

The sparkler had nearly burnt down to the handle when Greta saw a flame leap from the metal to the tip of Eden's long hair. A strand, coated with hairspray, caught the spark like a kid with a firefly. Greta turned to Brandon first, but his mouth went slack-jawed in surprise, and his hands were full of lighters and drugs. Without pausing, Greta grabbed the water bottle sticking out of Eden's purse and poured it all over her burning blonde skull. The elapsed time from flame to smolder was just seconds, but still a lock of Eden's hair had burnt like a wick from its original past-shoulder length to near her ear. "Holy shit," Eden gasped, dropping the used sparkler on the ground. "Thank you."

It was then, and only then, that Greta began to laugh so hard her stomach hurt. "Jesus Christ. I wish I'd gotten that on video."

A few minutes passed before Eden said anything. She sat in the grass, holding the strand of burned hair like it had nerves. Brandon settled where he had been standing and motioned for Greta to join him. He passed the joint to her.

She held it between her thumb and forefinger and looked at it before passing it back. "I don't smoke. Sorry."

Brandon chuckled as he took in another breath. "It's funny. That kind of video used to earn you money. Remember the old shows? Ten thousand dollars for a kid falling on a birthday cake. Now they're all over YouTube for free."

"They want to be watched," Greta said. "Just to be seen."

"Maybe that's harder now than when we were kids, huh?" His voice was soft, directed toward her as if through a cone.

She knew he was looking at her, even in the dark. She could still barely see the backward "Eden" in cursive, swirled in light on her inner eyelids, so Greta stared at him through the name. "Maybe," she said.

Eden slunk over to them and sat next to Brandon, practically falling into his lap. She draped a lazy arm onto Greta's leg. "I owe you my life, Greta Oto. I swear I do."

Greta inched her leg away. "Don't mention it," she said, hoping that if Eden wouldn't, Greta could pretend Eden didn't exist at all.

The thought of ending her time at Reiman in a few weeks almost made Greta mournful. The routine of the lab felt like a time table to her, and even on her days off she felt herself checking the clock to see when the next task needed to be completed. Brandon even let her fill out a request form for the next shipment from a pupa distributor, though they both knew she wouldn't be there to unpack it when it arrived. One day, in early August, Greta saw something in the butterfly wing that she scarcely believed. She ran back to the lab to get a capture box that they had been using for their ant experiments and put the thing inside. When Brandon got back from his lunch break, she presented it to him with a trumpet noise: "Ta-dah!"

He narrowed his eyes at the little plastic cube,

then widened them when he saw. "Really?"

She nodded. "So what do we do?"

The lab was empty except for the three of them: Brandon, Greta, and this illicit caterpillar. It was bristly and squirming against the side of the box. "I think it's a morpho. You know we can't keep it," Brandon said.

"But I'd take it for walks and everything," Greta said, her voice falsely earnest. She took a breath. "Why can't we just let it pupate?"

"Our license doesn't allow for breeding, Gret. You know that. We don't want to get revoked over a free morpho."

Cost wasn't even a consideration in Greta's mind, but simply the wonder of a caterpillar hatching in the strict conditions of the butterfly house. The likelihood of it was preposterous— the controls in place, the lack of patches of host plants for egg laying, the limited numbers of the right species, and yet here was this lone caterpillar. "I guess I just thought it was cool."

Brandon ran a hand through his hair and sighed. "No one else saw it?"

With the glass fronts to the lab, she couldn't say for sure. Still, she had tried to be as careful as she could in retrieving it. She didn't feel like she was lying when she shook her head. "If you get caught, you can blame it on me anyway. I'm leaving in a month."

"Fine," he said. "But don't name it, and don't

let the assistants get attached. They're too young to know not to think of lab specimen as pets."

Despite the warnings, by the end of the day, Maura had named the caterpillar Morpheus and had constructed a variety of fake pieces of furniture taped to the outside of its box, complete with television set and a replica of the Mona Lisa.

Greta realized the irony of anthropomorphizing a caterpillar. After all, caterpillars were just larvae, in the same way that maggots were. When she was ten or eleven, her father used to take her to his friend's taxidermy shop on weekends while her brother shuffled from one music lesson to another. One Saturday, a man with a beard and a sleeve of tattoos had brought in the biggest specimen she had ever seen. The client had been on a hunting expedition to Northern Minnesota and come back with a bull moose. It was clear that the animal hadn't been shot, but been hit by some sort of vehicle. The client said he'd hunted it, but even Greta didn't believe him. In her memory now, she believed him even less.

By the time the specimen found had its way to the shop, time, heat, and flies had all taken their turns at it. The biggest wound in the beast was along its right side, near the front leg. It was obviously the spot of impact. In the curdled flesh was a mass of maggots, writhing.

That sight nearly turned Greta from a future in entomology to law. Greta's father, though, didn't even blanch. He and his friend salted the wound and put the moose in the industrial-sized freezer that he had for just such occasions. When the client picked it up a few months later, they had expertly patched the missing hide. What he couldn't fix with material, he fixed in the setting of the beast—curling the leg up in mid-stomp to minimize the wound's visibility.

Those wriggling white larvae had just been hatched fly eggs. They shouldn't be more or less adorable than Morpheus, but such was the way of the world that, even in her supposedly rigid scientific view, she couldn't stop herself from showing Danny a picture of the caterpillar that night.

"Sounds like you and Brandon are getting pretty close again," Danny said. His tone was unreadable; ditto his expression.

"It's just work."

He clucked his tongue. "Whatever."

"And don't tell anyone," she warned, putting a finger up in librarian-esque caution. "About the caterpillar."

"Greta, literally, who would I tell?" he asked. His eyes flicked over the picture on her screen and back to the book he was reading called *Guitar Repair: A Manual*.

"The guys down at the shop. Seems like they

take up all your time lately. Shouldn't you be—I don't know—prepping your classroom?"

He rolled his eyes. "I've got a few weeks. It'll be fine."

As much as he said that—and he repeated this script each time she brought the topic up—time started to contract upon itself. On her way to work, he had her drop him off at the music store instead of the middle school. Meanwhile, Morpheus went through his larval instars, shedding his skin each time and changing his appearance. Greta gave up using gender-neutral language the second day and sexed the caterpillar to give a true pronoun. Morpheus neared the end of his fifth instar and stopped eating as much. His frass became less solid as he moved to pre-pupa stage. Finally, he began to construct his chrysalis.

After transferring him to the emergence cage, she felt the weight of the secret lifted from her. She and Brandon wouldn't shut down the Gardens after all. She washed out Morpheus's box and unstuck the ever-growing collection of paper furniture from its walls. Inside the cage, Morpheus's chrysalis looked like all morphos' did. When Brandon walked into the lab, she pointed to the line of hung moth cocoons and chrysalises. "The Eagle has landed."

Brandon nodded and set down a folder. When he turned back to her, he held out a few pieces of paper toward her. "Here."

She stared at the proffered papers. "What's this?"

"Concert tickets."

She raised her eyebrows. "Really?"

"For you and your brother. Eden bought them as a thank-you . . ." Brandon's words came out quickly, begging her to interrupt, which she did after examining the tickets more closely.

"Liszt? Did she know that's what he studied?" After a third read-through, Greta found an even better detail. She knew she had a stupid grin on her face but couldn't dampen it for Brandon's benefit. "It's his friend. Oh man. His friend Henry is the pianist."

"So you're free?" Brandon asked, relief evident in his voice.

"Duh," Greta mumbled, folding the tickets in half.

"We can pick you up at five on Saturday, then. Carpool down to Des Moines."

Brandon's wide grin made Greta realize that he had no idea of the wriggling unease in her stomach when he stood like this, hand on the desk, leaning casually toward her. "Sure," she said. "Why not?"

And in her head, like a true scientist, she came up with three dozen possible answers to her own question.

# CHAPTER TWENTY-THREE

Greta's keys were in her hand, held out to the lock, when she heard it—that opening cascade of notes, Danny's fingers hopping over each other. It was that song, the opening song from that old show about astronomy on public television. "Keep looking up," the astronomer would intone at the end of the program. That was her real introduction to space, between squinting up at stars in the backyard and hopping aboard the *Enterprise*. It had been *Stargazer* and those too-late Saturday nights by the TV.

She put her ear against the apartment door, and just as certainly as she had heard the cresting waves, the waves faltered and skidded to a halt. A jarring pound on the keys and then silence inside the apartment.

Greta began to rethink her strategy.

Should she have told him about the concert earlier in the week? *Maybe.*

Should she wait in the hall long enough to pretend she hadn't heard him playing? *Probably.*

After a few heartbeats, she unlocked the door and surveyed the scene. Five o'clock on a Saturday night and ten thousand pieces of sheet music littered the floor of Greta's apartment. Danny sat in the middle of a pile of music, the notes of a hundred black eyes staring up from an open score. Other piles of music stood in corners of the room, precariously tilting against table legs.

After setting down her backpack, Greta picked up the closest sheet of music. It bore pencil marks of indiscernible gibberish on the front. "What the hell are you doing?"

"School starts next week and my old system of music organization . . ." Danny raised himself to his knees. "I just can't use it anymore. It was by color. By the color I heard it as. So, a new system. Two rooms—the living room and the bedroom. One for choral and one for orchestral."

Greta turned to face the bedroom. "You mean there's more in there? Seriously? Did my taxes pay for all this music?"

Danny ignored her and continued, "And then in the bedroom, four quadrants: unison, two-part, soprano-alto-baritone, and more than three-part. Within those, I'm making alphabetical and seasonal piles. Plus pop, jazz, and classical piles."

She surveyed the piles and thought about the slam on the piano keys. The evening's plans felt all wrong somehow, but she knew that Brandon would be at the apartment in fifteen minutes. "That sounds boring."

"Seriously, Greta, you are the one that—"

"I've got a surprise for you."

A suspicious grimace came over Danny's face. "What is it?"

"Franz Liszt," she said, as if that explained everything. "And not the dog. Put on a real shirt and a pair of shoes, and let's get going." She turned to the dresser in the middle of the living room and removed a wrinkled skirt from the back of a drawer. She shook it out and held it against her waist.

"Is that the skirt you wore to Dad's funeral?" Danny asked. "Is that your only skirt?"

"You can't wear skirts in a lab," Greta said. She slipped it over her jeans, unbuttoned the pants at the waist, and slid them down. Greta assessed her shirt. It was clean enough. "Well, chop chop. Their car will be here soon."

"Who's 'they'?"

"Me, Brandon,"—she sighed—"and Eden. Brandon's girlfriend. They had extra tickets for tonight."

Danny nodded. "Five minutes."

Her phone buzzed with a text from Brandon. "I'll be in the car. And don't tell them this is my only skirt," she hissed.

"You don't think Brandon already knows?"

She didn't have anything to say to that, only tapped her wrist and closed the apartment door behind her.

The windows of Brandon's truck were open, and Danny climbed next to Greta in the rear seat. "All comfy back there?" Brandon asked.

"Yeah," Danny said. "Thanks for inviting me."

"It is the *biggest* pleasure to meet you, Danny," Eden said.

Greta's eyes rolled so hard that the car shook. It might have been a pothole, though. Greta could only see the top of Eden's head from her spot, but she could smell her—vanilla and almond, like a scone.

"I can't believe I didn't know something Liszt was coming to Iowa," Danny muttered.

"You could have missed Liszt?" Greta said with mock surprise. "How terrible!"

"People used to be obsessed with Liszt," Danny defended. "Treasure his cigar butts, faint during his concerts."

"I don't think it'll go that far tonight, but the guy—the pianist—is supposed to be pretty good. Henry Prasad, I think. Is that it?" Brandon passed the tickets from the beverage console to him.

Danny laughed as he turned to Greta. His eyes showed honest surprise tinged with something else. That something colored his voice, too, and made him sound hesitant. A kid waiting to step into the street. "Yeah. Henry. He was actually a college friend."

Greta tried to right the ship, distract that note of worry from his voice. "When it's an elite private music school, I feel like you're supposed to refer to them as chums."

"Like fish," Brandon said. "College fish."

"School of fish," Greta said, grateful for someone playing along. Even more grateful it was
Brandon.

"Did you think of going into music?" Eden
asked.

"He *is* in music," Greta said, the humor iced.

Danny cut in. "You mean performance? No.
No, I always wanted to teach."

Greta knew the lie, but she also assumed he
didn't want to derail the evening with sob stories
of losing Dad, debts, and settling for a life he
didn't want. Meg had been the one thing he had
chosen for himself, damn the consequences. And
he had been happy then, with Meg. She had been
like music after all.

On the highway now, nearing the interstate, the
air from the open window blew in earnest now.
Danny didn't seem to notice. He watched the
fields go by. Greta realized it had been months
since he'd been anywhere farther than a few
blocks from home.

The wind blew around Greta's face, drying out
her eyes. "Can you close the window?"

Brandon apologized, and the air-conditioning in
the truck hummed on. Brandon peppered Danny
with questions about composers, pleased to have
an expert in the car. Greta watched the back of
Brandon's head as he drove. When he moved the
steering wheel, the muscles in his neck shifted
gently left and right.

Halfway into the drive, an ambulance passed them, sirens blaring and lights spiraling. Greta couldn't stop the thought that this was the way Danny had last traveled. In the back of an ambulance, on his back, and heading somewhere he couldn't see. Danny caught Greta staring at him. He said, "There's a name for that siren interval—did you know that? It's called a tri-tone. Liszt used them in his *Dante* sonata. Tri-tones up and down the chromatic scale for the whole first movement. When I used to play it, my fingers would ache from how loud it was, but I guess hell isn't subtle."

"I wonder if it's on the program," Eden mused, her voice mild and unburdened with thoughts of death.

"I wonder," Danny echoed, his voice aimed at the windowpane.

The seats were center and about halfway up. The *Dante* sonata was not part of the program, but even without hellfire evoked, Greta caught herself studying Danny, watching for signs of life. Pleasure, pain—anything, but his face was blank as Henry's fingers hit the keys. At intermission, Greta caved, finally asking Danny how he liked the performance.

"It's a little like eating food with a cold," he said.

Greta didn't know why she thought a real concert might awaken something in him, something old and forgotten. "So it's not in technicolor."

"Wizard of Oz, Kansas location only." After a second, he caught her gaze, and he must have seen something there. He cleared his throat. "But that's where she sings 'Somewhere over the Rainbow,' so you never know."

"Right, it's not like you want to be welcomed to Munchkin land, anyway."

"School doesn't start for a week," Danny said. "Can I buy you a pack of Twizzlers?"

They shared the licorice during the second half of the program. One of the songs reminded Greta of the song Danny had been playing in the apartment. A bit, but not quite. She checked the program. "Liebesträume: Nocturne Number Three." She elbowed Danny and whispered, "Was this what you were playing?"

His eyes widened when he realized what she was talking about. Somehow in the dark of the auditorium, she felt like she could bring it up. "No," he whispered. "Debussy. 'Arabesque Number One.' "

"Keep looking up," she whispered back, but his eyebrow quirked in a question mark. Did he really not remember watching *Stargazers* with her and Jack Horkheimer's famous closing line? She remembered those nights seeing the universe in her living room, the television volume on low to keep from waking Dad. At a backward glance from a couple in the row in front of her, she didn't say anything else. She tried to enjoy the concert. Greta could appreciate the technical excellence, the exactitude. Music and science had that in common—when something was right, it resonated. Purposeful placement of notes, of accents, of data.

At the end of the performance, Eden insisted everyone wait by the stage door. Danny flipped the program against his thigh. The area by the loading dock was dark. Greta checked her nonexistent wristwatch for the fifth time before finally the stage door creaked open. People came out in pairs and trios, and then came Henry, alone, with a black leather suitcase slung between his shoulders. "Henry," Danny called out before he could get too far away. He probably hadn't spoken that loudly in months, and the air pressure in Greta's own diaphragm changed in response.

Henry turned around and his face broke into a smile. His dark hair was longer than the last time she'd seen him, and his teeth were whiter by at least three shades. "Daniel? Daniel Oto?"

"Danny most days."

Henry pulled Danny in for a hug, hitting him twice on the back like he was burping him. "We missed you. The whole gang of us. We had a little thing out in Portland. Did you get the e-mail?"

"No," Danny said.

"The alumni . . ." Henry's face froze. "Shit, I forgot. I'm sorry. The alumni listserv."

Danny waved a hand in front of his face. "Don't worry about it, man. I just wanted to say congrats."

"Congrats for touring in Podunk, Nowhere?" Henry laughed.

"Seeing as I live a little north of Nowhere . . ."

"I'm sorry. I'm not getting any of this right." Henry's mouth twisted. "You know what? Come out with us for a drink."

"I can't drink and I'm with some people." Danny gestured behind to where the rest of them stood.

Greta waved. "Hey, Henry."

"No way. Greta? The famous twin?" She obviously was memorable from Danny's stories, which wasn't a good thing. His smile didn't darken, though. "Please. Greta, your friends— you can all come."

The bars in downtown Des Moines had a bigger mix of characters than Ames bars. Right away, Brandon and Eden ran into some friends they knew from a young professional group, and stranded Greta.

The bar bled pretension, exposed brick, and a purposeful mishmash of furniture. In Ames, there were college kid bars—fratty and loud, starting at happy hour—and townie bars like Mikey's. The thought of Mikey's pinged her now, pricked at her. Max wasn't hers to miss, though. Meg had always been good at swooping up people that didn't belong to her and claiming them.

"Hey!" Henry clapped Greta on the back, interrupting her thoughts as she nearly fell off her stool. She stood up and pointed to it with an offering gesture. He nodded his head. "Thanks for saving me a place. This place is packed."

"Not much to do in Podunk, Nowhere, but drink," Greta said.

"Ha-ha," Henry said, each sound accented. "You know I didn't mean it."

"Yeah, well, you two have fun," Greta said, excusing herself.

"No, no, sit," Henry said. "I'm just glad to talk to people from the old days."

Danny tapped a finger against the bar top, unsure. "It's probably easier to ask what isn't new than what is, big shot," he said.

"Your words, not mine, and certainly not my agent's."

"There you go," Danny said, letting out his breath. "Isn't that what we always talked about? And you're touring solo?"

"I paid my dues."

"At the Los Angeles Philharmonic."

Henry appeared pleased. "You heard about that?"

"It might not be in my subscription of *Nowhere Monthly*, but I read it somewhere."

Henry waved down a bartender and ordered a

drink. "So," Henry said after the bartender had moved on, "I heard some rumors about your health."

"Some minor brain surgery. That's all."

"Oh, that's all," Henry scoffed. The bartender put a beer in front of him, its head foaming over the rim of the glass. "But you're okay now?"

"Depends on who you ask. My doctors think the prognosis is pretty good. My ex-fiancée didn't, I guess."

"Ouch. Sorry. That's cold."

"I pushed her and pushed her. I haven't been myself." The pain in Danny's voice made Greta turn red. It wasn't that she thought she had been enough for him. She wasn't a replacement for Meg, but she honestly hadn't had any idea he still missed her so much. The writing in the comic books came back to her.

*"My boy." "My tiger."*

Henry attempted to comfort, to excuse. "God, you had brain surgery."

"But not a lobotomy. It was probably my fault."

"It's not," Greta broke in.

Danny rolled his eyes. "Oh boy, my sister thinks it's not my fault, so it must be true."

Greta felt a stab. "Well, I'm going to find Eden and Brandon,"

"No, sorry, it's just"—Danny paused, taking a sip of water—"I'm kind of depressed, I guess. I have meds—for my condition and for my depression—but they bring me to normal. It's not like what you have."

"Fuck, I'm on them too, Dan. Half the universe is. I have been for years—since before Oberlin."

Danny toyed with his soda straw. "They bring me to a middle place. They don't fix the problems that made me feel this way."

"Shit, Danny, talk to her if you miss her is what I'm saying. This is free good advice. Take it. And you can name your first kid after me."

"Maybe," Danny said. "But I'm naming my first kid Prodigy and my second Unrealized Potential. You can have dibs on the third."

"Well, the third kid is going to be a genius. And shit, Danny, you like teaching, right? You don't want to be on the road."

"No, I mean I love teaching. It sucks to have your health make all the decisions in your life."

Henry took a sip of his beer. "It's a race to death, and music sets the tempo."

"I don't think that's going to catch on, but if I see it on T-shirts, I'll make sure to give you credit."

On the truck ride home, Eden fell asleep against the passenger seat window. Greta could hear her snoring, snuffling in her sleep. "She had a few tequilas," Brandon murmured to Danny.

"And Greta?"

Greta's eyes were closed, too, but she wasn't sleeping.

"I think people tire her out," Danny said.

"They're so sweet when they're sleeping," Brandon said.

"You're so condescending when we're sleeping," Greta muttered, her eyes opening to catch Brandon's eyes in the rearview mirror.

The rest of the ride was quiet. Greta watched the scenery, though she couldn't see anything. In the dark landscape, there were acres of tall corn, like fingers pointing up. Above the highway, lit only by scattered headlights, she couldn't see the corn, but she could see the stars they pointed at. The constellations.

*"Keep looking up."*

She was almost home when she realized she never had watched that star show with Danny. Never. It had been Martha, those secret late Saturday nights. That had been Martha.

# PART FOUR

## Autumn

"That we imagine the butterfly effect would explain things in everyday life, however, reveals more than an overeager impulse to validate ideas through science. It speaks to our larger expectation that the world should be comprehensible—that everything happens for a reason, and that we can pinpoint all those reasons, however small they may be. But nature itself defies this expectation."

—Peter Dizikes, "The Meaning of the Butterfly," *The Boston Globe*, June 2008

# CHAPTER TWENTY-FOUR

Another month, another birth control shot. If Martha had been around for Greta's teen years, maybe she would have found out earlier that the debilitating pain she got with her menstrual cycles wasn't normal, but as the only woman in a house of men, she assumed it was. After three missed classes her sophomore year, a TA teaching the intro bio lab had pulled Greta aside and asked if she was okay. Greta said she hurt, and after describing the intensity of the pain, the TA suggested she go to Student Health. Since starting the shots all those years ago, Greta's pain had become manageable, as did her understanding that sometimes she had to tell people when things felt wrong.

Things felt wrong a lot lately, but those things involved the only people she would have talked to. In fact, as Greta adjusted the side mirror in the hospital parking lot after a birth control shot, she recognized the car parked next to her.

It was Max's hatchback. She was absolutely positive. Why Max's car was parked in front of the hospital, though, Greta had no idea. Greta had been congratulating herself at somehow avoiding contact with him in the lab. She was not going to wait around to run into him in the hospital parking lot.

Danny had not been so lucky. If Ames was a small town, then the middle school was a smaller town. Small towns have gossip; smaller towns have telepathic gossip, so well-known that no one needs to whisper it. No ring on Meg's finger, separate rides to school—Danny said he knew the conversations must be happening about them, but couldn't tell when they were.

On Friday of the first week back, he ran into Meg in the hallway. Literally ran into her. At Sunday supper he lowered the collar of his shirt to show the bruise on his shoulder.

"So what happened after?" Greta asked him.

Greta saw the sudden flush in his cheeks, remembered what Danny said to Henry all those weeks ago. She hadn't told him, but Greta knew where Meg lived now. It had been an accident that Greta found out Meg moved into Brandon's area. She saw Meg walking Franz Liszt over by the cemetery, and when Greta went back to visit her dad a few days later, she saw fresh flowers there. Greta half-suspected that Danny didn't mind the bruise if it meant getting close to Meg again, but Greta worried that the real pain wouldn't just bruise him this time. He was setting himself up for disappointment.

"Nothing happened," Danny said. "I mean, we apologized to each other. For the collision."

Greta assumed he meant the hallway collision, not the vehicular one that had set everything off.

"And I smiled at her, but—"

"Just move on," Greta said.

Danny dunked a piece of garlic bread in the leftover alfredo sauce on his plate. "That would be the smart thing to do. But I love her."

"We saw her with someone else." She didn't mention that someone else was her friend, her once-friend who she now went out of her way to avoid.

"Could be nothing." Danny began to clear the dishes. "Could be innocent."

Greta made a *pfft* noise. "Sure."

Innocent. If Max were innocent, she wouldn't find anything in his desk to incriminate him. With the excuse of grabbing a few things before she left on Monday for the conference, Greta headed into the cubicles Saturday morning to scope things out. In their years of sharing an office, Greta had never done anything to break the unwritten coworker code of conduct: wash your own mug, stagger office hours, and don't touch each other's stuff. He would probably notice if she did touch something. If she didn't leave physical fingerprints, something might get misplaced if she wasn't careful—and so she was careful as she worked. She thought about Saturdays watching her father work on a specimen. The dental tools he used to prepare them, the way he squinted at the animals under the light. She had "careful" genes somewhere in her body, and she hoped they would kick in right about now.

First, she examined the desk's exterior, its morphology. His desk was always neatly kept and had multiple anchors. A *Far Side* calendar with tear-away pages stood at the corner. The year and the jokes on the calendar changed, but its location on Max's desk didn't. Next, Max's computer. He dusted the keyboard weekly, using the sprayable air to clean in the crevices even though it didn't need the attention. Finally, a picture of him and his parents, which Greta had never gotten close enough to really look at before. Absurdly, now that she was close, she realized that, like the picture she had packed in Meg's stuff, Max's family was at Disney World. Behind them, Cinderella's Castle loomed over the trio. Little Max had a buzz cut and wore a red T-shirt, and his face was as round as a tomato. All three of them had the mouse ears, just like Meg's family. *Just another thing they have in common,* Greta thought bitterly.

Max's desk had a long central drawer for pens and knickknacks, then two big file drawers along the side. Their hulking metal desks were standard issue from the college, probably the same as they were in all the departments, but it was hard not to feel sentimental about her cubicle. Probably like how some shipwreck victims get attached to their lifeboats. Unlike her desk, Max's didn't have a pencil-thin scratch along the front edge of the pen drawer, but just like hers, it did require a key to open. Also like hers, the key was the same—standard issue. She clicked it in the lock and turned it.

Inside was a rainbow assortment of rubber bands, an army of paperclips, several black pens, and a single red one. *Hardly worth locking,* she thought, even though the high quality of the black pens did make them above average. She didn't move them from their compartments as she shut and locked the drawer again.

She opened the top file drawer next; she did so slowly because he kept his coffee mug in there. Breaking a handle off his Insects of North America mug would cost her more in pride than it would in dollars to replace. Behind the mug, and the collection of canned soup he sometimes warmed for lunches, were his class files—labeled and color coded. Insect Biology, Fundamentals of Entomology, and the rest of the assorted intro classes that they had shuffled through during their time at Iowa State, both as students and as teachers. She didn't think he would hide love notes from Meg in there.

Was that what she was really looking for? She didn't stop to ask herself that question. The trappings of their affair were probably all digital, as Danny and Meg's had been. Traded texts or DMs or whatever. Maybe he e-mailed his stupid forwarded jokes to her as well. That thought stung momentarily, without Greta stopping to think why.

The bottom drawer held academic papers: printed articles and notes from classes. Greta removed the stack from the drawer and started to sort through it. She recognized his notebook from their Chemical Biology and Behavior seminar, mostly because he had used a Pikachu notebook and she'd teased him ruthlessly about it, all the while battling him between classes at one of the Pokémon Go gyms on campus. She flipped idly through it and saw the scrawl of his handwriting. Up close, the "p's" looped down and curled in a "q"-ish manner that made her smile. Her own handwriting joined his on some pages, almost unreadable even to herself. During boring lectures, they had played a game at passing the notebook discretely back and forth, each adding a line to a drawing until, incrementally, it became a monster or a flower. She ran a finger over a morphologically correct grasshopper that they'd drawn, line by line, without consulting each other on the project to begin with.

She replaced the notebook in the stack and looked through the other handouts. Graduate programs don't have yearbooks to flip through, but this pile brought the same feeling that high school yearbooks were supposed to evoke (probably did evoke for non-Greta people). Here was the paper they helped collect data for during their first year. Here was the feedback she'd given on his dissertation proposal. And here, she noticed, was a paper authored by just Greta. Just a thing about cicadas that she had sent off to a regional publication. She was just mulling over the last item when she heard footsteps behind her.

*On a Saturday? Oh hell.*

She shuffled the papers into a sort of order, but hadn't gotten everything back in the drawer before Max came around the corner. Her eyes caught his. Though his eyes were dark brown—the color of weathered bronze—they seemed to darken further when he saw what she was doing. "This isn't what it looks like," she said, standing up.

"Greta, I don't even know what it could look like. What are you doing?"

She was on firmer ground with anger than disappointment, and his lack of vehemence unnerved her, sending her into honesty. "I was seeing if you had anything from Meg."

"Meg," he repeated, his voice level but threatening to seesaw into either a laugh or a shout. "We're helping each other. Meg is a friend."

The term "helping" was too suggestive to leave

alone. She repeated it back. "Friend, huh?"

"My mother is dying, Greta." The statement was so matter-of-fact, the narrowing of his eyes so pointed, that Greta felt the line as though he had repeated it a million times.

"What are you talking about?"

"Pancreatic cancer. Stage four."

Greta leaned on Max's desk, knocking the calendar sideways. The air in her lungs suddenly took up too much space. Her ribs felt tight. Her whole body felt tight, and she couldn't meet his gaze. "I didn't know."

But Max didn't stop talking, closer with each sentence so that she could feel how wrong it was to be on this side of the divider. "Meg's been going to the caregiver meetings with me. She's been sitting with my mom after school."

Greta slid off his desk and moved to the corner of his cubicle. His voice followed her.

"They've become friends," Max said. "Again, if you don't know what that term means, I can define it. A friend is someone who supports, who gives. Who doesn't suspect someone's motives and take and take."

Unwelcome tears stung Greta's eyes. "I didn't know, I swear."

Max just shook his head. He took three steps closer to her, and she had no place to retreat to from his voice. She wished he would shout, but instead his voice had gone slack. "I wanted you to. That's the thing. I don't know why, but I did. When you came by with that silverfish? You could have come in, met her. Met both of my parents. I wanted you to ask, to know. At least now you do." He stepped back from her cubicle and knelt, opening the top file drawer in his desk. Once he had drawn out the stack of folders, he tucked them under an arm and headed down the hall without another word.

For a long time after he left, Greta stood with her head in her hands.

Not for the first time, she wished to redo the entire year. Parallel universe syndrome again. How long had he had the diagnosis? Before which beer night did he find out, or did he know all the way back to that drive from the airport?

Monday she would be packing to leave for a conference that would change her life, and she was leaving him angry and leaving angry with herself.

# CHAPTER TWENTY-FIVE

It rained in Florida—a lot. Greta checked that piece of trivia off on her first day. Since she hadn't traveled much, her maroon rolling bag appreciated its second-ever trip. Unlike both Meg and Max, her family hadn't taken a picture with mouse ears in front of a castle. They had one in front of the Iowa State Capital, in front of a butter cow at the State Fair, and—on her dad's direction—even one with both herself and Danny wrist deep in a deer carcass that her father was stripping. If nothing else, the rain here was like the rain in Iowa—perhaps here it was more persistent and less polite. The rain was not Iowa Nice. She'd forgotten to pack an umbrella, and that summed up Greta's luck in a nutshell. Her clothes were soaked as she sat at a large table in front of a roomful of people, some of whom had received grants worth more than a small country's assets. If anything good had come out of the rain, at least her damp hair wasn't standing up awkwardly. Instead, the dampness made it lie flat against her scalp like an otter in a pantsuit. The wet slacks—well, at least those were hidden by the table.

Brandon prepared the presentation, checking cords and adjusting projector settings. Greta hated talking, hated the feeling of a million eyes on her. Funny how it didn't matter when bugs stared at her. It should be more unnerving to have multi-sectioned eyes staring than to have an audience full of human ones. Complex brain function on both sides, though, meant that while flies might have creepy eyes, they probably weren't judging her clothes or the pitch of her voice, or . . . Greta burped back a sudden rise of bile.

She took a deep breath. Brandon planned to handle most of this. Brandon immediately charmed everyone that he ever met . . . well, except for herself. And Max. And if whip scorpions could hold grudges, Gary. Despite their argument, Max had sent her a good luck e-mail that morning. A cat in a graduation cap at a podium, "Have a Purrfect Presentation." He said he would text Danny later to check in. How the fuck did she deserve a friend like Max? She didn't. What if there were an audience full of Maxes? Her pulse picked up again. A room full of men dressed in Starfleet uniforms, with fade haircuts, thin wrists, and dark brown eyes. Slight men with a punny sense of humor who were also mad at her but somehow able to get over it. She couldn't picture more than one of those, but maybe that was a good thing. She was realizing that he was one of the few people she actually cared to impress.

Bodies shuffled into place, landing and alighting to move next to colleagues. People scooted toward the center of the ballroom to make more room on the aisles for latecomers. This was the largest crowd that she had ever spoken in front of, and certainly the most accomplished. How many graduate degrees were there from how many countries? *Shit, it's just ants, people,* she wanted to tell them. *Go home. It's just ants.*

Brandon started before she was ready, but if his cue were to come based on her readiness, there would be a skeleton audience instead. He showed a few slides of the issue, the carefully documented infestation. He tossed in jokes. "These are the most photographed ants in history. The Real World: Ant Hill." Polite laughs.

But her part was coming. Brandon insisted that she had to say something. They had forty minutes, plus questions, and the design was hers. She needed to have fewer good ideas if it meant having to present on them. But this was science too. She knew that. It wasn't enough to learn if you didn't share your data.

To his credit, Danny had offered to help her practice. He sat on the couch, watching her. He didn't have segmented eyes, or the scary glare of the audience full of experts, but his puppy-dog expression was bad enough.

She went through it once. Damn teacher; he made her do it again. A third time.

"Slow down. Take a breath," Danny told her. He demonstrated. "Right down here. From the abdomen. Breath support."

"I'm not singing a fucking aria."

All the same, Greta took a deep breath and stood when Brandon clicked over to the slide with her ant-trap design.

And then her mind went blank.

"It wasn't that bad," Brandon told her afterward. They sat next to each other in the hotel bar. To his credit, he let Greta bitch for half an hour before cutting in. He waved a finger at the bartender, signaling two more of whatever they were gulping down to forget. At least, that was why she drank. "We are supposed to be celebrating. We got some great comments."

"After my train wreck."

"You didn't actually vomit. It only sounded like it."

"If I had eaten anything I would have vomited."

"Maybe if you had eaten, you wouldn't have almost fainted afterward."

"Fair point," Greta admitted, taking a long sip. Her drink was pink, fruity, and not what she ever would have ordered at home. She also had a full stomach now, but despite a plate of chicken nachos as buffer, the vodka had gone to her head. Her cheeks felt numb, and it made her brain feel a little numb too.

The numb brain might be from all the people she had met the past few days. The last day of a conference was always full of hand-pumping and exchanging numbers, but Greta found that even truer when she was actually presenting. Someone had asked her if she had a website or was on LinkedIn. After the presentation, even with the almost puking, a man from Boston slipped her a card and encouraged her to apply for a postdoc. A gentleman from South Africa pressed a brochure into her hand and tried to engage her in conversation about ants. She hated to tell them that she wanted to do what Brandon did. His job—half education and half research—seemed like what she wanted to do. *I might look like an ant girl,* she wanted to tell the man from Boston, *but really I love butterflies. Really.* Still. It was a habit she didn't want to unlearn.

Brandon had just called for the check, when a man from the restaurant side of the bar came over. "Hey!" His merry voice came muffled through a thick black beard. "I tried to talk to you both after your presentation, but this is destiny. Plop. Right into my lap."

Brandon shot a glance toward the man's lap, probably unconsciously or perhaps to ensure that the man didn't have other-than-academic motives in mind. It turned out the guy, Jeremy Plumber wanted to talk about butterfly house management. He was the curator of the butterfly collection at Florida State and the only other USDA-recognized facility in the country of its kind, which made Florida State and Iowa State lepidopterous cousins, or something. Suddenly there were handshakes and back slaps, memories of e-mails sent back and forth, and name-dropping of colleagues and paper co-authors. Jeremy led them deeper inside the bar. Another round. A few funny stories. She finished her third drink and Brandon, his fourth. After Jeremy finished his beer, he handed Brandon his card and checked his watch. "Promised my wife I would drive home tonight," he said. "But keep in touch."

Greta was about to ask him for a card, too, but he had disappeared, and Brandon had tucked the rectangle into his back pocket.

"I'm conferenced out," Brandon said with a sigh.

Greta nodded, and they strolled back into the hotel lobby. Scientists milled in pairs and trios, talking in a variety of romance languages. Not romantically, but Latinate. Greta sometimes wished she'd learned a different language instead of Spanish, something more useful to science. But her knowledge of Spanish still allowed her insight into snatches of conversation as she passed by. Discussions about bugs, in Spanish, caused a pang for the Costa Rican rain forest again. Maybe someday.

Brandon pressed the elevator button, extricating them from a conversation with some old hands from the USDA. The elevator door closed, the only noise from the ambient piano music bouncing off the burgundy carpet and mirrored walls of the elevator. "I'm sick of people," Greta said. "God, I'm ready to go home."

"There aren't people at home?"

"I'm a hermit. You know that."

"I think you like people more than you admit. At least when you can study them."

"I don't study people," she shot back. "They mess up the microscope lenses and don't fit into petri dishes."

"Well, I guess you can only study people when you let yourself get close enough to them."

She noticed the weight of his body on the elevator railing next to hers. They both leaned against the mirrored wall, side by side. He was at least four inches taller than her. She examined him, studied him in the mirror in her periphery until she noticed him looking at her too. The elevator dinged. His floor.

"Want to come in? We can watch TV." He put a hand in front of the door sensor. A mirror version of Brandon watched her from every angle, fingers outstretched.

She could have made an excuse. Early flight. Long day. "Yeah, okay."

His suitcase must have exploded upon entry,

because not a single speck of clothing was left inside of it. She almost made a comment, but then he would know that she noticed his dirty clothes spread around the room. Maybe he would assume that she was thinking about him naked. Which she was definitely not doing, even though some of his underwear was new—black boxers, name brand.

She rubbed a hand through her hair. "I don't get cable anymore. This is a treat, actually," she said. "More than the beach."

"Well, it's been raining all week."

"Right." He must know she wouldn't have gone to the beach anyway. Even swimsuits on catalog pages made her blush. She wore a ten-year-old tankini when Brandon took her to a lake before he left for New York. Eden probably wore a string bikini.

Brandon flipped on a home makeover show and cleared a space on the bed for her to sit. It was a bed. Just a substitution for a couch. Just a substitution for two separate chairs, really. She sat near the bottom of the bed, where his jeans used to be, and tried to follow the plot while he leaned against the headboard. The show was even more ridiculous than sci-fi. After ten minutes, they were laughing at the outlandish budget of the couple on the show. They wanted a greenhouse. The wife didn't like the first one because it was "too much glass."

• • •

Brandon put in a call to room service for dessert. "Bread pudding," he said. "Your favorite."

"Usually putting bread in front of a word makes it sound less delicious, but shit, with pudding it's magic."

"Bread spaghetti doesn't sound appetizing to you? Bread cake?"

It was like playing tennis to talk to him. The easy back and forth. Volleys across the net. "Bread sauce? Bread salad?"

"I think bread salad is a thing, actually," Brandon mused. Commercial break. A vacuum cleaner, animated and magically sucking up the rain clouds from the sky. Fine print: this vacuum will not affect the weather. She tried to point out the fine print to him, but the commercial ended before he saw it. They watched the channel for another half an hour until the commercial came on again so that she could point out the small font at the bottom of the screen.

"You're so good at noticing those little things."

She shrugged. "Noticing the ridiculous. Do you think someone would sue because a vacuum didn't literally make the sun come out?"

A knock at the door. She'd forgotten about the bread pudding. The serving was dinner-sized, with a scoop of vanilla ice cream in the center—the fancy kind with the specks of vanilla bean in it. Brandon had remembered to ask for two spoons.

He sat next to her near the foot of the bed, setting the room's phonebook as a table between them.

Cinnamon. Butter. Rum. Still, in some ways it didn't taste quite as good as she'd imagined it might. Underneath the ice cream, the dessert lost its heat and became an eggy, lukewarm sponge. She took a few bites and put the spoon down. Brandon didn't notice, scooping the bowl clean, then moved the bowl and phonebook to the TV table.

She yawned and glanced at the clock. Eleven. But it was only ten in her time zone. She waited for him to say something, to tell her to get out, but the next show started. It must have been a marathon, and she knew the personalities of the two relators now, which one played idealist and which shot straight. She went to the bathroom and splashed water on her face. The numbness fled, leaving her head less fuzzy than it had been in the bar. When she entered the main room, Brandon lay on his stomach as he watched TV, head propped in his hands. Greta mirrored his pose, flopping a foot away from him on the bed.

A bed was just a couch substitute.

A bed was just a place for sleeping.

A bed was just the only convenient furniture in the room.

The scientific method enforced rigorous questioning. Forming multiple possible hypotheses. A bed didn't allow for much space between people, and so just because she reclined close to him didn't mean that he caused her shallower breathing. Maybe the higher elevation on this floor of the hotel had increased her need for respiration. Maybe her body, as it broke down the alcohol, required more oxygen. Maybe the blood rushing to her cheeks was a response not to the smell of him, a foot away from her, but to, shit, something else. Anything else.

It had been easy to return to campus and teach and not be near him every day. It was easy because he wasn't her boyfriend. Easier, maybe, not being with him every day than having him footsteps away typing at his computer with his awkward pecking motions because he still sucked at typing.

She gasped for air—quietly, but still gasping.

"You okay?" Brandon asked.

"I think so," she said.

He pushed himself up to a seated position. His hair was messy, like it used to be in the mornings. Sex hair without the sex. "You look like you might vomit."

"It's the theme today," she said.

He glanced at the clock. "Tomorrow's theme too."

"Yeah, I should get out of here. Early flight and whatever." She said it, but she didn't move.

He didn't check the clock again. Instead, he ran a hand over her cheek and moved a strand of hair aside. "You sure you're okay? You look kind of pale."

His hand warmed her cheek. His gaze was soft. How many data points did she have to glean to confirm her guess? Someone else would know how to say something. Someone else would know the joke to make in some kind of artful, round-about way. She wasn't art. She was science. Run a test. Run a test, stupid.

She leaned toward him. In the old days, he would have leaned halfway, or more than half. He would have covered the distance and closed it. His lips were usually chapped, and he carried around a tube of Blistex. He was sensitive about it, but now his lips looked soft. All the humidity from the rain, maybe, or the magic of Florida.

But he didn't lean in. Instead, he pulled his hand from her cheek like she had burned him.

Voices in the hallway of the hotel. Female voices, giggling drunkenly together. Their high-heeled clomps covered the silence. Is this how it started with Meg and Danny? The silence, like the wait for divine intervention. A sign you were doing the right thing, wrong thing, very wrong thing. Thinking of them made her stomach ache.

Brandon wasn't looking at her anymore. "I'm confused, Greta. I don't know. Maybe I shouldn't have invited you here."

"Because of Eden?"

He nodded. "I, um . . ." He cleared his throat

and started again. "I asked her to marry me a few weeks ago, and she said yes."

Greta didn't remember standing or turning off the television, but she must have. "Well, congrats."

"She and I had been in this fight, and—"

Greta held up her hand like a crossing guard. She wanted the world to stop, her heart to stop beating so fast.

She would have settled for Brandon to stop speaking, but instead he continued. "I'm sorry."

Her stomach was steel. "Sorry? Seriously. "You're dating her. You're engaged now." She grabbed her bag in one hand, the door in the other. "What are you apologizing for? You're such a great catch that every single woman must be devastated?"

Brandon rose and crossed the room in three strides, those long legs of his. He put a hand on the door and pushed it closed. The movement was sudden, but not violent. "Greta, listen to me for one minute before you never listen to me again, okay?"

Her hand reached for the doorknob again, but his hand covered it first. "What?"

"You push people away, Greta. You sprout pins." He closed his eyes, and when they opened again his expression was softer. "When I got the job in New York, you were the one who said that meant we were breaking up. I didn't want to. I would have made it work long distance."

"Easy to say now."

"No, nothing is easy to say when it comes to you and serious conversations." His tone was flat. "We kept dating all summer before I left. I called you, made dates, made dinner. Didn't you think that was strange? I kept waiting for you to say that we should at least try. I sat in my apartment in New York for the whole first week and thought, 'So she'll call tonight and tell me she misses me.'"

Greta had missed him, but she wasn't going to tell him that now. "You could have called me."

He let go of the door. "I could have. That was probably when I knew it was over. The second week, it hurt less. The third week, less. I found distractions."

She laughed out loud, but she knew it sounded bitter. A coffee grounds laugh, dark and strangely bracing. "Distraction, huh? Cute nickname for Eden."

"You need to trust people that you love, and I loved you, the you under twenty-thousand layers of jokes and defense mechanisms. I'm still attracted to you. I admit it. But I don't love you anymore. And Eden is not you, but I love her. I do. Eden says what she means and does what she says she's going to do."

Greta could think of a million comebacks, but she didn't know what she was coming back against. Eden's entire character? Her whitened teeth, the flip of her blonde hair, her fanatic worship of a basketball team? Greta didn't say anything. She gave Brandon a steady frown. It must have been a key, because he swung the door open and moved aside to let her leave.

He leaned into the hallway to call after her, "Hey. Safe flight tomorrow."

Greta raised an arm, and then a middle finger like its extension. Her fingernail could nearly graze the ceiling as she strode down the hallway, not turning back.

She only had to ride two floors down, but the mirrored elevator showed copies of her red eyes and blotchy face from all sides, staring at the other red-eyed women. She flicked them off too. Looking at herself from so many angles, she could almost see through herself to the nugget inside, the soft caramel center. Looking at herself from so many angles she could see what everyone else saw looking at her straight on, the left, the right, above. She was everywhere, but none of those things were her, and she knew that no one else knew that. She thought of her butterflies. Her butterflies back in Costa Rica with panes of glass worn on their backs. So translucent it was their protection from predators. It felt like love in that way. A lack of protection, and true camouflage, was letting someone see straight through you.

She didn't get on her plane home the next day.

# CHAPTER TWENTY-SIX

Thank the good lord of cell phones, Danny actually picked up. "Hey, dummy. I need a favor."

His reply was more growl than speech, but she still caught the gist. "Gret. It's like five thirty."

No, it was exactly five thirty, at least in his time zone. "Is Meg there?"

"Why would Meg be here?"

"You need to talk to her. I need Max to sub for me today."

"This is a problem e-mail should take care of."

"No e-mail. I'm stuck at customs. I'm being detained. You're my fricking phone call. Just get Max to sub for me, okay?"

She felt the words steep in his brain, and his next question was more alert. "Do you need a lawyer?"

"No. I'm being deported today."

"Where are you?" She pictured him sitting up straight in bed. She also pictured a blood clot, imagined and menacing, pulsing in his brain.

"Calm down. I'm in Costa Rica. At least for the next, oh, hour and a half." Greta appraised the holding cell, the long stretch of concrete she had spent the night on. It could have been anywhere, really, but she knew it wasn't.

"What the hell?"

"Blame Brandon. He was leading me on, I think. I don't know—"

An exasperated sigh traveled through the earpiece to her. "Jesus, Greta, when a guy is worth it, there won't be any leading. Or any running away. It'll all just, I don't know, fall together."

"I really appreciate the romantic advice." Her guard held up a finger and raised his eyebrows. Her time was almost up. "Okay, listen. They're cutting me off, so get Max to sub, okay? Oh, and I need one more favor. Credit card?"

"I only have Martha's."

She swallowed hard. "Martha is letting you use her credit card?"

"It was to pay for Uber rides while you were gone. I'm sure she wouldn't mind."

The guard was gesturing again. Rapidly. Pointing to an invisible watch on his wrist.

"Okay. Okay," she said. "What's the number?"

Perhaps Greta hadn't fully realized what privilege meant until she broke an actual law, but sitting in customs as a special snowflake because she was a white American woman certainly made the process faster. "You cannot enter without a valid return ticket," the customs officer said. It was the third time he said it, and he was the fourth customs officer since she had been detained hours ago.

"Right," she told them. She'd maxed out one credit card to buy a spur-of-the-moment one-way ticket to Costa Rica. One-way because she didn't know when she'd go back. One-way because it was cheaper. Standing at the airport ticketing desk in Orlando, she felt grateful that she always traveled with her passport. She could blame the doomsday corner of her brain or having a military father. But when she landed in Costa Rica, she discovered that the passport wasn't enough. They wanted to make sure she would leave eventually too. The customs official saw hundreds of tourists a day, could categorize them as easily as Greta could her butterfly collection. In this case, Greta was a moth and didn't belong there.

They took away her luggage and put it in a large, caged closet. She spent one night in a holding cell by herself, smaller than the closet had been. In another cell across from her, also barred, two men were sleeping when she arrived. While their cell had two cement benches, hers had only one. She couldn't picture where in the anatomy of the building she was exactly, but everything smelled like the sterile airport air. Her guards spoke rapid-fire Spanish and called her a spoiled American, and she couldn't think of a retort in Spanish good enough. Maybe that's what had kept her out of trouble—her lack of knowledge of Spanish cuss words.

In the morning, a uniformed official leaned against the bars to talk to her. "So, you don't get to stay," the official said again. "You can either purchase a one-way trip on your own and skip the legal process, or you can wait to be tried in court."

"Is there a court in the airport?"

"Judges come here," the official said, shaking his head. "And you don't want that, so buy a ticket."

"Right," she said. "Fine. I've got a credit card number written here."

"Is it yours?"

She shrugged. "My mom's."

She must have looked irresponsible enough that that was expected. The customs officer switched to Spanish, turning to the other officials behind him. "An hour until the flight to Orlando. Get her bag."

The cell clinked open, and thirty minutes later she was on her way to the United States, handcuffed to the seat. The steward eyed her warily as he walked the aisle with drink carts, probably thinking she was some crazy person. Maybe she was, actually. What would she have done if she'd made it back to her research, back to the bird calls and serenity of the Cloud Forest?

She saw the holes in her plan now, from several thousand feet up. The resort—which she had no money to pay for—was booked up months in advance. Without that room, she was hardly Girl Scout enough to camp in the mud. All that malarial mosquito knowledge wouldn't repel mosquitos—she didn't even have a lousy bottle of OFF!, let alone clothes for field research. She went to a conference with a bag packed with black slacks and white dress shirts. She dressed like the waitstaff at the hotel. Someone at the conference had actually handed her a tray and pointed to glasses of water to clear from a table. She wore the same sweatpants that she'd flown out to Florida in five days ago. Was it only five days ago?

Always pushing people away, Brandon said. Always running away. It was hard to run from herself. It was more like she was trying to run back to herself, who she'd been nine months ago.

She was lucky she wasn't blacklisted from entering Costa Rica again. She was lucky she was taken about as seriously as a balloon animal. Poor young American who'd lost her mind. Pack her onto a plane and get her some peanuts and a glass of water, but don't take off the handcuffs until she's on US soil.

On the plane ride, Greta dreamed about Martha. Martha, the unknown benefactor of her flight home, the woman she had refused to talk to since the cold soup, cold shoulder dinner. In the dream they were making cookies, but the kitchen was outdoors with a full star-slung sky above them. The cookies burned, since they both forgot to set a timer. Without the stars, it could have been a memory, Greta thought when she woke up. She yawned, tried to stretch, but her handcuffed wrist caught on the armrest.

The man across the aisle eyed her, and with no more prompting than his raised eyebrow she murmured, "I thought it was legal there." His eyes widened and he turned away, and she imagined what he imagined of her.

She got a literal slap on the wrist at the airport in Orlando. The handcuffs banged against her skin as they slung off, but she managed not to swear. Airport security met her at the gate, and she spent two hours in yet another customs office. After much shrugging and excuse-making (didn't my visa say *this* year?), they let her go. After all, she had paid her way there and back and never left the airport in Costa Rica. There and back again, an awkward tale. A two-day tour of airports and no one the wiser, including herself.

Thank God for Max. What he would say about all this, why he would help her after all this, she had no idea. He didn't deserve this. She didn't deserve him—his friendship or his help.

She plugged her cell phone into a charging port at the airport and waited for her flight back to Iowa (well, back to Chicago and then back to Iowa). Her e-mail overflowed with student questions because—surprise, surprise—the sub didn't know how to explain the new assignment. Well, duh, because the sub wasn't prepared to sub because she'd put him in a terrible position.

Sometimes a lack of a thing proved more telling than its existence. There were no e-mails from her advisor and no e-mails from the department. Max must not have ratted her out. There were also no e-mails from Brandon. As far as anyone was concerned, it might as well have been last week, and she wished it were.

She should text Danny. She should text Max. Instead, she sent a text message to "Don't Answer."

At least Martha would know to expect her.

It was four thirty by the time she got to campus. The entire drive to Ames, she thought about her dream of burnt cookies, the smell of smoke and ashen sugar. She parked in front of Student Health and steeled herself in the car. Her heart thumped and her body told her to run, to just drive away, but that had been the problem all along.

At almost closing time, the chairs in the front lobby were empty. Informational posters about venereal diseases and flu shots decorated the walls—definitely more venereal diseases than flu shots. Glass canisters sat on counters in the lobby, each one filled with colorful, individually wrapped condoms—sex gumball machines, or some stupid metaphor. No one sat at the front desk, but Greta spied a bellhop's bell. She dinged it lightly, and a man appeared from behind a row of cabinets. He inquired about whether she had an appointment and she shook her head. "Martha here?" He looked puzzled, so she clarified, "I'm her daughter."

The man turned down the hallway then, calling out like everything was normal. Everything was normal because a daughter would of course come visit her mother at work. Greta used to visit her dad at work and watched him weld from five feet, with her own kid-sized safety equipment. Martha came out, glancing around like someone had played a trick on her. Maybe someone had, but they might be playing a trick on both of them. That would be dead Dad's sense of humor.

"Oh, hi, Greta. I didn't know if you were serious about coming."

Greta rubbed an arm. "Well, I am."

"Did you want to come back?"

Greta nodded, following Martha down the hallway into a small examination room. "Do you spend most of your day telling nineteen-year-olds to have safe sex?" Greta asked, eyeing the gynecologically correct illustrations on the wall.

"I have a binder full of pictures of boils to dissuade them from other options," Martha said. She closed the door behind them. "Want to sit?"

"Not when I know people have been in here with boils. No thanks." She looked around the room, and the room looked back at her from the faces of trendy teens pushing flu shots. In the enclosed space, she smelled herself for the first time. She smelled like she had been in an airport detainment cell for a day and hadn't showered in three. Accurate. "I charged your credit card for my flight home. I just wanted to say I'll pay you back next Friday."

Martha leaned against the paper-covered table. "Well, I should have guessed you wouldn't be here for small talk."

"I just didn't want you to see it on your credit card statement. I don't smell good enough for small talk," Greta said. "I'm going to go—"

Martha stood and put a hand on Greta's shoulder as Greta tried to open the door. "Oh, come on," Martha said. "I think you owe me more than that."

"I *owe* you? *I* owe *you?*" Greta's mouth gaped open as she wheeled on her. Her heart rate jumped, then jumped again as her mother's steady gaze met hers. "Oh my God, you are serious."

"Sit. I don't care about the money, Greta. Just let me have twenty minutes."

"No, let me get this straight. What do you think I owe you?" Greta asked.

"A chance—"

Greta had to sit down. She lowered herself onto

the doctor's stool and put her head between her knees. The breath wouldn't come. When she felt Martha's hand on her shoulder again, asking if she was okay, she flung it off. "Don't touch me."

Martha stepped backward, pressing her back against the door.

In the silence, Greta's breath returned. The stool swiveled under her as she steadied herself. Greta's gaze flitted around at the passive audience on the walls around her. They wouldn't judge her for coming onto Brandon, not unless she was going to have sex without protection ("Your future; your choice," read the caption underneath the teen in a jean jacket ahead of her). Her mother couldn't judge her for what she had wanted to do in that hotel room. Martha couldn't throw stones in that glass house. Meg and Danny couldn't have judged her. They started as cheaters. Maybe the problem was everyone had a glass house. Everyone she had ever loved or hated had been living in one, and Greta had been throwing stones her whole life. It didn't make putting down the rock any easier now.

When Greta turned back to her mother, she was unsurprised to see her looking back at her, waiting. "You kissed that man," Greta said. "You said it was all about gambling, but the day you left you kissed him. I saw you."

"Kurt. Yeah. I did. But—" Martha paused. "The sex is never really just about the sex."

"I don't need to hear about sex with you and Kurt." Greta couldn't hide her disgust. "Or with you and Dad, or with you and Bozo the clown."

Martha raised an eyebrow. "I didn't think you came here to talk about sex, Gret."

If she got it all out in one breath, it would be easier. Greta felt the words rush from her. "What if it's your fault I'm like this—like I am."

"What are you like?"

Greta's forehead crinkled. She thought about the words Brandon had thrown at her, the expression on Max's face when he saw her leaning over his files. "I don't know. What am I like?"

Martha took a deep breath. "Greta, you were never a cheerful child—"

"But happy doesn't always look cheerful. Just because I wasn't always smiling didn't mean I wasn't—" She swallowed back the tears that threatened to come now, but she couldn't choke them down far enough. "I broke when you left. We broke. Danny and I, and Dad. What if because you left, I don't know how to stay. With anyone."

"You've stayed with Danny," Martha pointed out.

Greta narrowed her eyes. "Somebody had to."

Martha paused. "Do you want an apology?"

"Don't you think it's not a real apology if I have to ask for it?"

When Martha she spoke again, her words were careful. "You're not destined to be me."

Greta laughed, a tearful bark.

Martha continued, undeterred. "And you're not destined to be your father, who didn't know how to say what the hell bothered him because he worried it would scare me. Love is scary. I would have been okay with being scared if it meant knowing what was actually wrong with him. With us."

"You can't blame your leaving on Dad. I won't let you."

"You shouldn't." Martha's tone was firm. "Maybe I ran because I didn't know how to make things better. If I could run, it was at least a choice. I ran away from who I was. I hated the me I was when I was home."

*The me she was with us,* Greta thought. Wasn't that what she expected? Wasn't it always what she guessed? "I'm sorry we weren't good enough."

"*I* wasn't good enough. I wasn't enough for any of you," Martha said. "That's my apology. I am sorry. I am sorry that I lost control. I know it's not logical. I know. It's not about logic, just like gambling wasn't about cards. That's what you learn in Gamblers Anonymous. For me, it was about power. I felt the wins. But at home, it was all losing, and the costs were so much higher . . ."

"How long?" Greta asked, and she didn't need to specify what because it was almost like Martha was waiting for the question.

"Two years with the gambling. Just a few nights a week at first, and then . . ." Martha turned to a drawer of instruments and began to sort. "Kurt might have been a bookie, but he gambled too. When we left, we drove all the way to Tucson—one straight shot. For a year we made it work with a trip to Vegas every few weeks. Paid the bills, but the economy went downhill and some investments went belly-up."

"And you're back?"

Martha closed the drawer and turned to Greta. Her hazel eyes were soft. "Back for three years, haven't gambled for five."

Greta stared at her mother, not sure if she was trying to read her face for the truth or for shame. It wasn't like she could ever smell casino on her breath or test for cards in her blood. "So you ran away from Kurt too?"

Martha smiled sadly at that. "Kurt met someone else. Funny how attraction faded once the line of credit disappeared. I didn't run back. Even if I had, problems don't go away when you leave, because other people aren't the problem."

"I happen to disagree," Greta said.

"No, Gret. Here I'll pull seniority on you. I'll pull out my research, documented. Twelve steps of it. Fifteen years' worth of regret of it. Want to see the photo albums we never got to make together? Me too."

Greta saw the lights in the hallway outside the

examination room flick off and stood from her stool. "I should go."

Martha took Greta full on. "Greta, I don't expect you to love me, but I do hope you'll let me love you. It won't cost you anything, I promise. And don't worry about the plane ticket."

Something like pity, like empathy, roiled inside Greta. She forced herself to reach out and pat Martha's arm. Once. Twice.

Greta frowned as her mother slipped her arms around her shoulders and pulled her in for a hug. "God, you really smell awful, though," Martha laughed, her voice thick.

"It's a long story."

# CHAPTER TWENTY-SEVEN

An e-mail pinged Greta's inbox, and Greta laughed at the irony of it all. A recommendation request for Brandon's job application at Florida State. The sender's name seemed familiar, and all at once she pictured a jovial man in a hotel restaurant. Of course. She hadn't heard from Brandon since the conference, and now this?

She chewed her lip as she read through empty form. It had places for "evaluate the scholarly work" and "evaluate the leadership skills," but it didn't have a spot for "evaluate whether or not you were actually led on by this person or it was all in your head."

Brandon obviously chose her to write a recommendation for him despite the drama of the last few months. He trusted her to be fair, but she didn't know if she wanted to be. She flagged the e-mail and set it aside. She had enough damage control to do today as it was.

Danny made it through the day, but she couldn't call it "unscathed." Fridays were hard enough. In the month or so with school in session, Danny on a Friday looked like his battery had completely run down. His face was drawn by the time she picked him up from school. Nothing over the counter touched his headaches, and he usually went to bed by seven. But this Friday was worse than the others combined, because this Friday was October 5.

October 5, the day that had marked the save-the-dates cards ordered too many months in advance. October 5, the day that Greta had had to repeat thirty times while making phone calls to cancel vendors and locations, only to find out that Meg had already done so. October 5, the anti-anniversary.

Greta had planned a horror-movie marathon when Danny got home, complete with pizza and sour gummy worms, but Danny shut off the TV before the first murder and shoved away his plate. "I just want to go to bed," he said.

"It's five thirty," Greta responded.

He pulled his head into his knees. "God, Greta. She was right there today. Two rows away at an assembly. And you know what I said? Nothing. Nothing at all."

The light in the living room shifted as she watched him, head down. Outside, the sunset bruised purple and red and sent shadows across the floor. "What did you want to say?"

Half a face turned toward her, the other half still buried in denim. "I wish we'd gotten married tonight."

If love were a game, the moves here would be simple. Greta had told him weeks ago about

Max, even if she hadn't been able to meet his eyes when she confessed. She broke the Prime Directive to let slip that piece of information that Max and Meg really were just friends, but he didn't seem interested. She didn't get it. No other players on the board, so why no checkmate?

If it is love, no one's leading and no one's running, Danny had said. Well, neither Danny nor Meg was running away, but they weren't exactly being drawn together either. They were frozen somehow, caught between the halves of a microscope slide.

After Danny went to bed, Greta sat in the living room, alone except for the stuffed goose looming above her. No harm, no foul. They used to purposely mix up the phrase after Uncle Ritz arrived in their house as kids. No fowl would be harmed. No farm, no howl.

No harm, no foul. She could do something, or try. If it didn't work, she never had to tell Danny, and she wouldn't. Ever.

After putting an ear to Danny's bedroom door and hearing the reassuring sound of snoring, Greta felt between the futon and the frame until she hit upon the Calvin and Hobbes books. Four of them, four books that she had admittedly read through when she had trouble sleeping. She did her best to ignore the romantic back and forths in the margins, but occasionally one had caught her eye. Usually it was a sentence that started with "I can't wait to . . ." in Meg's curly handwriting, or a blocky "I remember when . . ." in Danny's. The alternating past and future alongside the strips had made even Greta miss Meg. Almost.

It was October 5, though, and she could try to help her brother. Some of the most interesting episodes in *Star Trek* happened once the Prime Directive had been broken. Once, Picard accidentally convinced a civilization that he was a god, and he only undid the whole thing by almost dying in front of them. Well, if Picard could take an arrow, Greta could take a drive. The setting sun made Greta miss the turn into Meg's apartment lot, so she doubled back past Brandon's. His car was parked in its usual spot, and the recommendation request threatened to derail her thoughts, but she mentally shoved it aside. It was October 5, dammit. If she stopped to think about something else, or to think at all, she wouldn't do what she was going to do. Meg's car was missing, but Greta had a suspicion she knew where Meg might be.

Max's neighborhood tucked itself in at dusk. Greta's was the only car moving on the street, like she had driven onto a movie set. The houses blurred into a sameness of late-eighties construction. Meg had parked in front of one of the same-looking houses. The houseplants on the porch were just empty pots now. As she knocked, she realized with a shock that she was about

386

to talk to Max's parents for the first time. She carried the comic books in one hand and jingled her keys nervously with the other.

Max's father answered the door. He eyed Greta up and down and gave a gruff, "What do you want?"

Greta had two inches on the man, but his tone insisted she was shorter. "Meg. Is she here?"

"Not a good time," the man said.

"Remember me? I'm Max's . . ." She paused and chewed over options. Classmate? Office mate? "Friend Greta." She hoped it was true.

Max's father turned back into the house, and she heard movement. Max appeared a minute later, alone.

"Greta, leave her alone." Max's arms crossed in front of his chest.

"I need to talk to her."

"Tomorrow."

"Tonight," Greta said, as if this were coming to terms of an agreement. "She and Danny were supposed to get married today."

"You think she doesn't know that? You're letting in flies." Max grimaced but took a step backward to allow Greta into the front hallway. It was narrow and hung with cedar-framed pictures. "It's not a good time. She's with my mom."

Greta nodded and looked down at her shoes. Noticing that Max had bare feet, she slipped her tennis shoes off. A scent wafted down the hall to her, something like lilies. "Right. How is she?"

She could hear the clench in his jaw. "Not good. Any day now."

"Are you okay?"

His face softened. "I feel like we've been mourning for months. Preparing. Loving her so hard. I don't think there's anything else we can do."

Greta wouldn't get to see Meg. That was clear now. It was a mistake to come and barge into this peaceful house. "Just tell Meg I came, okay? And give her these." She thrust the stack toward him without looking up. She slipped her feet over the back of her shoes, flattening them. One of her shoelaces was untied, and the white threads had crinkled leaf particles sticking to it. "And Max?"

He grunted, and Greta watched his bare toes shift side to side. She didn't know how to speak this language, the language of comforting, but she tried. "I'm here if you need anything. Not here, but at my house. Or here, if you need me to be."

Max didn't say anything, and if his face said something in return, she wouldn't see it with her eyes cast toward her dirty shoes. A few seconds later, she opened the screen door and stepped onto the front porch. She stood dazed for a few seconds, like she'd been temporarily abducted and brainwashed. Max's back disappeared from the hallway, too late to say anything else now. What would she have said? What could she have offered? She stood there, trying to get her bearings, trying to understand how she got from the apartment to here. How she got from January to here.

She had just stepped off the front porch when the door opened again. Meg stepped outside. Her feet were bare, and Greta saw her toes turn up at the concrete. It must feel like ice, a sure sign she wasn't here for long. Now that she saw her, Greta didn't know what to say.

"I came to say I'm sorry, Meg."

"For what." Her voice was a lake: flat, wet, and murky.

"That you didn't get married today."

Meg took a ragged breath. "I don't want to get into this right now, Greta. I just can't."

"Why did you come out here, then?" Greta's cheeks burned. "He's still in love with you, Meg. He's miserable. He's coming up for air after the worst months of his life and looking around to find you gone. He needs you."

"I was there, Greta." She sounded tired, as tired as Danny had, his face peeking at her from his jeans. "I was there. I was there to help, and he pushed me away. *You* pushed me away."

"And now you're pushing me away," Greta pointed out.

"Can you blame me?" Meg said, her voice suddenly sharp. "Can you?"

Greta wanted to scream yes at her, or to tell her no and go to hell, but Meg was already inside. The fight curled into her veins and pumped through Greta's skull like a back beat as she drove home.

Back home, her blood settled into an even rhythm, but she had trouble going to sleep that night. She opened her laptop and stared at her inbox. Finally, under the watchful eye of Uncle Ritz, Greta opened the recommendation form and filled it out for Brandon. Her assessment was honest and complementary and professional. As it should be. As she should be.

# CHAPTER TWENTY-EIGHT

Three days later, the department sent around an e-mail. Max's mother had died. In the mail room sat a card scrawled with condolences. With Max gone the whole week, Greta offered to cover his sections. It was literally the least she could do after his help with the Florida debacle. The students in his classes were like her students. They wore red and yellow sweatshirts, the freshmen distinguishing themselves with lanyards around their necks and too much makeup. She reminded herself that they weren't her students despite their similarities. Different sample size, different constants. They were used to looking at Max in the front of the lab, listening to his jokes, reading his neat handwriting. While the students examined specimens, she read through his syllabus. A *Far Side* comic graced the front page, and inside the thick language of the course policies, Max had a single line: "If you've read this sentence, e-mail me a picture of a kitten, and I will give you ten bonus points."

Greta watched the heads bowed over their microscopes, the pairs and trios whispering and looking at their cell phones without trying to make it seem like they were. Greta took out her own phone, sneaking it under the desk.

She e-mailed Max a picture of a kitten peeking out of a box of cereal. She didn't know what to put in the message, so she didn't write one. In the subject line of the e-mail, she typed, "No catastrophes yet."

Twenty minutes later, as the students cleaned off their lab spaces, her phone buzzed. A picture of a kitten stuck inside a Kleenex box, the tissues poking around its too-large-for-its-body head. The title of the e-mail was "Catharsis." Below the picture of the cat was the funeral time and location.

If there was a limit on the number of times that she could draft her brother into service as a stand-in for a friend or date, she hoped she hadn't hit her quota. She especially hoped that five-AM deportation-related calls didn't count in that tally. Danny wasn't pleased about the funeral invitation—that much was clear. He rubbed a palm across his closed eyes and moaned about getting a sub, about only having so many sick days. In the end, Greta promised a family dinner with Martha.

"This gives me the right to insist on a public dinner out."

Without him mentioning the name, she knew this meant Hickory Park, the sprawling home-style family restaurant, whose placemat featured twenty types of sundaes and brought up memories of every family birthday when she was young. Sundaes were free on your birthday. "You're going to make me eat barbecue with Martha, aren't you?"

"I'd be missing my opportunity if I said no. November sixth."

"Martha's birthday?"

"I'm providing you accompaniment to a funeral and reminding you of the woman who ensured we were born. Two-for-one deal."

She grudgingly agreed. Nothing would have made her feel more alone than going to a funeral by herself.

On the morning of the funeral, Greta tugged on her skirt and found her least-ripped pair of pantyhose. If men had named pantyhose, they would have thought of something badass like "future socks." Maybe that was also lame, but nothing sounded as granny-ish as pantyhose, which was one of the things that barred Greta from purchasing a new pair. The other thing was that she didn't own many clothes that required future socks.

Luckily for the occasion, she had a funeral skirt, which could double as a concert skirt when needed. Five years ago, she'd gone into Yonkers with the single mission of buying clothes for her father's funeral. She told the bewildered salesclerk she needed something sturdy and black. The fact that she couldn't specify whether she wanted a skirt or a dress was the woman's first clue that Greta wasn't used to shopping. Actually, Greta's green sweatpants and Homestar Runner T-shirt probably tipped the woman off first. The woman found a skirt that only deserved two adjectives: black and straight. It wasn't long or short. It wasn't flashy or lined with tulle. It was just a skirt. "Perfect," Greta had said, and bought it without trying it on.

She pulled on the skirt, adjusting the zipper first to the side, then the back. Who had come to her father's funeral? She tried to remember, but a mental fog remained that allowed her to study her own hands and see them shaking, but she could not see past herself, not even in memory. Other people must have lived through that year too, but it was hard to imagine. She'd resided on an island of grief, staring back at the mainland.

It was a beautiful day, at least. As if that counted for anything. The leaves in front of the Methodist church were a trapped sunrise— all pinks and oranges. A line of people snaked down the church steps, waiting to find a seat, chattering. Greta and Danny shifted, not talking and not admitting to listening. Max's mother had worked at a bank in downtown Ames for twenty years. She had volunteered at the church during the evenings, made bags of supplies for women saved from sex trafficking. More than the story of the woman, the tone of the voice of the mourners told Greta what she needed to know.

The woman on the front of the program smiled up at Greta, like she had always smiled. Even though she was dressed in severe black and white, her eyes were warm. How odd that Greta and Max grew up thirty miles apart but in such different worlds. In some other universe, they would have gone to the same high school. Maybe they would have found each other in some AP bio class. Maybe Greta would have grown up going to Max's house for dinner, adopting his parents as secondary to her own. After Greta's mother left, maybe Max's mother would have gone prom dress shopping with her, insisted that Max and Greta go together. As friends.

Or as something else, if she were being honest. If she had ever been honest enough to deserve him.

Inside the door of the church, seats were hard to come by. An usher waved her and Danny over to a side stairway, and they went up to the choir loft. "Box seats," Greta said. Joking was armor. Joking was a reaction, not a solution.

From the first row of the balcony, Greta saw the wall of flower arrangements in the front of the church and a set of empty metal brackets, stage center. Behind her, an organ thrummed with a dirge, bone-shakingly loud in its closeness. Danny's whole body tensed beside her. "We can leave if you need to."

He shook his head mutely.

The organ stopped when the minister came out. The casket proceeded, its front right corner supported by Max. After placing the casket in its brace, Max and his father sat in the front pew. From above, Greta saw identical sunken shoulders on Max and his father. Two points on a line that used to have three. They'd lost a dimension; no wonder they looked flatter. Greta thought about Martha's card tower months ago. Triangles. Things were stronger built in triangles.

As far as funeral services went, Greta had limited experience. Compared with her father's service, there was less staid patriotism. Compared to her father's service, there was more of everything else—more music, more crying, more remarks from friends and family. "We sucked at planning Dad's funeral," Greta said out of the corner of her mouth.

Danny refused to acknowledge the remark. He squinted down at the casket like he was trying to find someone he knew in the crowd, and a second later he turned back to Greta. "Did you ever call the florist?"

"What?"

"For the wedding."

"No," Greta said, honestly flustered. "I called a dozen other venders, and Meg had already . . ."

"Never mind." Danny just shook his head and rested his chin on the bannister that ran the length of the choir loft.

Greta followed the path of his eyes and saw a blonde bob in the third row, center, on the church floor. Meg wore a cap-sleeved black dress and lace crisscrossed her collarbones. From above the lace could have been a net to catch fish in. Greta shook Danny's leg with her hand, and he finally looked over at her. She mouthed the word *Sorry*. Of course Meg would be here.

Between the organ and the ex, Greta was amazed Danny sat through the whole service. Afterward they walked together across the street to the parish hall. Greta put her bag down at a table occupied by some other people from her department. Tom Plank, Larry Almond, and a few graduate students sat with Styrofoam cups of dark black coffee. Greta saw Danny's head swivel away from the table of scientists to take in the crowd. "We don't have to stay long," Greta said. "I need to pay my respects." The phrase tasted cold and formal in her mouth, borrowed from some Victorian manner's guide.

"Sure. Sure," Danny said. He still searched the crowd.

Greta tugged on his sleeve until he made eye contact. "Stay here," she warned, urging manacles into her voice. She hadn't told him about her nighttime drive, that last chance. Would it break him if he knew that she'd tried and Meg had said no? Probably. God, if she could only have kept the Costa Rican handcuffs as souvenirs, she might have chained him to a chair. "Seriously, stay here, Danny."

He nodded but didn't say anything.

Max stood with his father near the door of the hall, leaning against stacks of folding chairs. "Hey," she said. She cleared her throat and tugged at her skirt. It was too small.

Max nodded. "Thanks for coming."

"Your classes are going fine," she said. "No one has started any fires yet or staged a riot."

"Thanks for covering them."

"I wasn't fishing for compliments. I didn't know else what to say." Admitting that froze the conversation. She rubbed an arm. "Thanks for covering while I was in Florida."

"And Costa Rica."

"Right. And thanks for not telling the department about that."

She felt Max considering her, sensed the line of people behind her waiting to pay their respects too, which probably cost them more and were worth more too. "So, anyone send you cat pictures? From your syllabus line?"

"Not many."

"They probably thought you were just kitten around."

His mouth twerked up in one corner, then resettled. "Thanks for coming, Greta."

"Stop thanking me, and I'll, um, see you on campus soon." Later, she didn't know who moved forward first, but either way, their bodies pressed together for an armless hug. Then, his arm wrapped around her shoulder so that she could feel his heartbeat against her shirt. He was too skinny, but his arm squeezed her firmly, and released. Max smelled sharp. Sharp and clean. Old Spice, like always. Her face burned as she walked back to her table.

Danny had disappeared because of course he had. Greta's eyes tracked through the crowd, looking for his shape, but couldn't make him out anywhere. No one from the department had seen where her brother went, at least not with any level of surety.

"I think he went into the kitchen? Or out the door?" one of the other grad students said, as if offering multiple leads helped.

Maybe he lined up to get some lunch. Maybe he went to confront his ex in some sort of embarrassing encounter.

Greta cut sideways into a conversation Max was having with a middle-aged woman. It wasn't until she had interposed herself that she realized it was Pam from the support group. "Oh, hey," Greta muttered.

Pam raised an eyebrow, but Max's annoyed glance changed when he saw the look on Greta's face. "What? What's wrong?"

"Where's Meg?" Greta whispered.

Max raised his eyebrows and whispered something to his dad. When he turned back to Greta, he grabbed her hand. "Come on," he urged, tugging her behind him through the clumps of people and past the tables laden with food. He did have doctor's hands, she mused as she fell in step. What a waste. Long fingers, thin and nimble as they moved to wrap around hers. She didn't need to be led, but she didn't disentangle herself either.

The hush deepened as they got further from the luncheon crowd. They passed beyond a set of double doors. Greta cast her gaze to the left, then right, hoping for signs of her brother. "Listen, I'm sorry for coming to the house, but . . . I just screwed it up for them. I pushed her and pushed her, and . . . Are they back here?"

"No. She's in the kitchen."

"Then where is the kitchen?" Greta didn't know why she cared so much, until she did know. Getting close to someone, allowing herself to want Meg to be a part of the family, that felt dangerous. That felt like a bigger decision than the one to change her research, to run off to Costa Rica, because it meant tying a knot, a bond that someone else had control over. Letting Meg in meant letting in the sweet patience, pure perseverance. They had started the relationship in a lie, but their relationship wasn't a lie. Meg was good for Danny—and good for Greta. Just like Danny had forced Martha back into

400

Greta's life—helped them repair what had been broken—Greta wanted to fix this relationship too.

Max sighed. "Greta, if they are going to end it forever or start it again, they need to do it themselves. They need to love each other enough to have the argument, to air it all out."

"But I fucked it up for them. Damn, is it wrong to say 'fuck' in a church?" Greta covered her mouth. "Sorry. Sorry again."

"It is their love story, and the course of true love never did run smooth."

"Is Shakespeare part of the graduation requirement now?"

Greta suddenly realized they were still holding hands, and the thought heated her cheeks. After a second, she squeezed his palm. He didn't say anything in response, his eyes tracked on the doors and the moving bodies behind the small windows. She squeezed his hand again, and he looked over at her. "What?"

"I know your mother died, and I'm so sorry. I'm sorry for your family and for you. I'm sorry to drag you away from your father at the funeral, and I hate that this is the first time we've gotten to talk in ages." She took a breath, "And I know that I'm a shitty person."

She paused for a second, waiting for an argument that didn't come. Instead, the hint of a smile appeared on Max's lips. She qualified her own statement: "Or I can be. I will try to be less shitty. And you're a good person, a better friend than I'll ever deserve. I just miss talking to you or being with you, not talking to you."

"Greta—"

"The biggest thing I worry is that I'm not really human enough. Like that Borg. Like the one they take on the crew of the *Voyager*."

"Seven of Nine."

"Right, and I'm afraid you won't notice that I'm trying to get better. It's slow. I'm going to be slow."

"My desk—" Max started.

Greta cut him off again. "I'm an idiot. I shouldn't have gone through your stuff—"

Max looked impatient, "Greta, just let me talk." He waited for her to nod her assent, and then continued. "My desk. Do you know how many times I've sorted through the stuff in there and culled the junk? You are not the junk. I chose to keep you every time."

There wasn't a single parallel universe that Greta would choose to live in that didn't include knowing that.

Greta stayed until the end of the funeral luncheon, partly to help move the half a zillion floral arrangements and partly because Danny still hadn't reappeared. Meg wasn't in the kitchen, and neither were reachable. His phone was turned off. Max tried Meg's phone and found a similar response, or lack thereof.

"Trust him. Trust them," Max said after the guests had left.

Greta found that she did. She passed the time by helping Max's father. While they packed, Max's father shared stories of his wife that made Greta feel like crying and laughing all at once. Stories that made her wish that she knew her own mother better, that she knew Max better. When Max and his father left, Max hugged her tightly before he got into the car. "Thank you," he said.

Danny and Meg still weren't back, so she helped the church women wash chaffing dishes in the kitchen. If the newcomer surprised them, they didn't mention it. It felt good to work. She pushed hard with the sponge on the baked-on cheese and washed marshmallow crème out of the small glass bowls.

Finally, three hours after they had left, Danny and Meg reappeared. Meg carried her heels in her hands, her stocking feet padding lightly on the tile floor. Danny's suit coat was wrapped around her shoulders. "We went for a walk," Danny said as explanation. "Sorry we took so long."

Greta dried her soapy hands on her skirt. "It's okay."

Meg smiled at her. "It is, isn't it?"

On a cold November day, a hostess led a party of five to a corner booth in the back of a crowded restaurant. Greta eyed the cowboy-themed advertisements like they were going to strip and dance. "If the waiters sing 'Happy birthday,' I am out of here."

"Even if we get sundaes?" Danny pointed at the placemat, tapping the options with a finger. "Caramel and whipped cream? This one has crushed nuts."

"Goody." Greta sighed so loudly the table behind them glanced over.

Max's thigh pressed against hers, and she caught his glance. He smiled at her, and after a deep breath, she returned it.

At five thirty on a Thursday, Hickory Park buzzed. High school–age waitresses sashayed past with families in tow, and children fought over coloring sheets and crayons. The smell of fried food made the air feel celebratory, like the state fair.

Tomorrow began a new adventure. Tomorrow Danny started his shift in the store in downtown Ames, where he first crawled onto a piano bench and started banging the keys. The principal had accepted his resignation, and the store offered him flexible hours. "Those who can't do, teach. Those who can't teach, sell," Danny had said. Still, Greta thought someday a kid would come into the shop and he could whisper to the kid about how to adopt a barn piano. Danny knew a guy. Maybe someday Danny would *be* that guy.

The food arrived, and a few minutes later, a circle of off-pitch servers sang 'Happy Birthday' to Martha. Greta saw Meg clasp Danny's hand on the tabletop, and he whispered, after the servers left the candle-topped sundae in front of the group. "Don't worry, I'm not going to palm this one," he said to Greta.

Martha refused to blow the candle out. "You do it, Greta."

"You need twenty-nine candles, Mom?" Max asked.

Martha laughed. He could get away with more than the rest of them. "Come on, Greta," she said. "I can't see how this is more embarrassing than being detained by customs."

Greta blew out the candle and handed the ice cream dish back to her mother. "And I can't believe that you keep bringing it up."

Meg turned to Danny. "I guess you're the kind of family to hold a grudge."

"The fact that we're any kind of anything is a miracle," Greta said.

"I'm just here for the onion rings," Danny said.

"Me too," Meg said.

"The ice cream's not bad either," Greta said, and she let Max taste two bites of hers before telling him to order his own.

# AFTERWARD

## *Spring*

Always better to ask for forgiveness than permission, Greta told the wedding party. Even better than that was to do the thing so no one would notice. She unlocked the front doors at five AM. Leanne and Ginger were late, so nothing kicked off until five thirty. Despite the delay, on a Sunday no one should notice four cars outside of a small building on a busy college campus, at least that was what Greta hoped. If nothing else, Greta could pull rank. She would be running the place in a few months, with Brandon leaving for Florida.

"Is it weird taking over from him?" Meg had asked her as they walked into the next department store.

Greta shrugged. "Why would it be? It's temporary." Instead of teaching, she was working at Reiman this spring and summer, at least until a replacement could be found. Some finagling of budgets and schedules had kept her on track to finish almost on time, but still a year behind Max.

The two of them were shopping for an outfit for Greta to wear and coming to an impasse. She wanted something to wear to commencement and the wedding, something as useful as her funeral skirt. Meg disapproved of Greta's clothes-buying strategy of holding things against her without trying them on. Meg had called her a paper doll.

They passed through the lingerie section, and Meg paused at a bra display. She touched Greta's arm and said, "I can't believe it."

Greta turned. "What?"

Meg pointed at the tiny icons along the white bra strap. "I guess it doesn't say 'don't bake.' Sure shows me."

Greta laughed.

In the women's section, Meg handed her an outfit. "Try this on."

Greta held the clothes at arms' length by the top curve of the hanger.

"It's not radioactive." Meg laughed.

Greta shot her a glance, but allowed herself to be shut in a dressing room. Inside the dressing room, Greta stepped into the outfit, felt the clothes cover the newly naked parts of herself. The navy pantsuit hugged her hippy frame and lengthened her already-long legs. Even her tousled short hair seemed more purposeful when paired with a flowy, pink button-down. She stared at the tri-mirrors reflected her body in a mise en abyme. Greta, almost smiling. Greta, repeated to eternity. Greta, hitting her head against the wall hook. "Ow. Damn," she swore.

"Everything okay in there?"

Greta responded with a grunt, but after a second, the door clicked open again, and Greta faced Meg. "You look great," she said, a huge smile on her face. "Melon is your color."

"Melon is a fruit."

"Well you should wear fruit more often."

"Call me Carmen Miranda." She flattened the pleats of the pants across her thighs, then spoke quickly, but louder, avoiding Meg's eyes. "Can you take a picture? I want to text it to Max."

Meg whistled. "Taking pics for him to hang in his apartment in Chicago?"

"Shut up," she said, feeling her face color to match her shirt. "He just didn't believe that I was allowed in the mall. That's it. That's the only reason."

"And the hickey on your neck? That's an accident?"

She slapped her neck like a mosquito had landed there. "There is not."

"No," Meg said. "But sisters like to tease. Trust me, I have two."

"Jesus," Greta said, turning back into the dressing room to hide the barest grin on her face. "You're already intolerable, and it's not even official yet."

• • •

Most weddings in Reiman were scheduled a year ahead of time and happened late in the evening. The parking lot was usually full, and the guests meandered from the front lobby past the emergence cages and through to the conference hall. After dark, who could see the flowers? For weddings at the Gardens, a clause in the contract stated brides and grooms stayed out of the butterfly wing. Most brides wore princess gowns that could trap the butterflies. Because of this, guests were in a place, but apart from it somehow. Not this wedding.

Greta swiped her card key and opened the wing. The group was only ten people, but they barely fit into the narrow passage at the entrance. Greta had to press her body against the door to avoid touching Meg's dad. Meg's sisters tittered. They both wore mid-thigh blue dresses. Greta gestured to the long list of rules on the wall. "I need to go over some guidelines before we enter," Greta said, taking on a professional tone. "First, no touching the butterflies."

"I don't even see any butterflies, Gret," Danny said.

Greta ignored him and adjusted her blouse. "Next, do not remove anything from the butterfly house. Stay on the path. Don't piss me off."

"I don't think the last one is on the list," Max said.

Greta glanced at the typed rules. "It's being added. Okay, ready?"

The door clicked open, and the dome inside was still and quiet. Ginger checked the light balance with a test shot, squinting at her preview box on her camera. "It's all glass in here, but with the sunrise we might have some issues . . ."

"Trust me," Greta said. "You need to be here in the morning."

Martha and Danny walked in front, leading the group forward into the sherbet light. They didn't miss the sunrise, even with the delays. No, there were no bouquets—who needed it with a thousand tropical flowers? No, there was no organ, but the waterfall beat against the rocks in the quiet air. Meg's gown wasn't long, but the mid-calf wrap dress was white and intricately laced. The sweat on Danny's forehead probably came as much from the humidity as it did from the nerves. No, it wasn't a traditional wedding, but why replay tradition when what Danny and Meg made was new?

Max stood on a bench near the center of the butterfly house. He wore his best suit. The fact that she was dating a man and knew him well enough to guess his best suit felt like a good sign. The fact that he was taking a year in another state and she hadn't jumped ship felt like a better one. He glanced down at Greta from atop the bench. The rest of the group gathered along the path around him, with Meg and Danny squeezing through to the center spots. Max cleared his throat. "Right. Okay, so we'll begin."

Max read from the sheet that came with his minister's license, freshly e-mailed to him last week. When it came time for the main event, the couple repeated their vows. Greta noticed Meg's voice shook, but Danny's hands shook in hers and Greta had to figure somehow their combined unsteadiness balanced out.

Greta liked a wedding with this few people. Danny had been nervous about a crowded wedding. They would have a brunch later with a few more friends, but he asked Meg for a simple ceremony. Instead of clambering guests, plants lined the paths like sentinels, and the dome rose above them in giant hexagonal tiles of glass. But it wasn't perfect—not just yet.

It wasn't fireworks, no, but what it was made Leanne and Ginger gasp. The sudden awakening of three hundred butterflies as the sun began to warm the dome of the butterfly wing. They rose from the crevices—the rocks, the floor, the greenery, and started swooping, drinking in the sunlight. Greta could picture what Danny meant about colors and music, about colors living. Maybe it was because it was her brother's wedding day, and maybe it was because she finally felt at home, but tears pricked her eyes. "Told you," Greta said. "I told you. You need to be there for the morning."

# ACKNOWLEDGMENTS

I am so grateful and relieved to have this book out into the world, and first thank-yous to the people who helped deliver it. Thank you to Veronica Park, agent extraordinaire, for believing in the book and in me. I am lucky to have you on my side. Thanks also to Jenny Chen, my wonderful editor for polishing Greta's words, though not her personality. Thank you to the whole team at Alcove Press for their wonderful work, especially Madeline Rathle and Melissa Rechter for their patience and skill. Much appreciation to Laura Blake Peterson and Megan Tripp for early shaping of this novel, and for my critique partners, especially Rebecca Schier-Akamelu, Julia Weigers, and Kathy Pestotnik. You are angels. And you, whoever you are, thank *you* for reading.

Entomology completely absorbed me once I started research for this novel, and I found the following books most useful while learning about bugs, insects, and arthropods: *The Practical Entomologist* by Rick Imes; *The Biology of Butterflies* edited by P. R. Ackery; *Lepidopterist's Handbook* by Richard Dickson; and *The Butterflies of Costa Rica and Their Natural History*, by Philip DeVries. In addition,

I loved more narrative takes on insects, whose stories and personal connections to insects gave me insight into people who love bugs: *Mariposa Road: The First Butterfly Big Year* by Robert Michael Pyle; *Sex on Six Legs: Lessons on Life, Love, and Language from the Insect World* by Marlene Zuk; *Buzz, Sting, Bite: Why We Need Insects* by Anne Sverdrup-Thygeson; and Thomas Eisler's *For Love of Insects*, where this book got its epigraph and the anecdote about using cockroaches in place of pithed frogs in lab. Eternal gratitude to the living people who I bugged (ha) for this book, especially Nathan Brockman, the director of the butterfly house at Reiman Gardens for his 'backstage' tour and patience with my thousand and one questions. If you are in Ames, Iowa, make sure to visit Reiman Gardens, or even get married there (but don't expect to be let into the butterfly house to do so. Narrative license!). Thank you to Abigail Kropf and Kelsey Fisher, entomology PhD students at Iowa State who enlightened me more about coursework, funding, butterfly-tracker transmitters, and why having a whipscorpion as a pet is a major flex. Thanks to bug Twitter (perhaps the best Twitter?), especially Megan Asche and Nancy Miorelli for their openness and knowledge. Many thanks as well to Dr. Tamara Horton Mans for her once-over to double check "the science stuff." Any mistakes in entomology, lab etiquette, or the like is entirely my mistake.

In researching brain injury, I found *Successfully Surviving a Brain Injury: A Family Guidebook* by Garry Prowe a useful guide for caretakers, and *Musicophilia: Tales of Music and the Brain* by Oliver Sacks helped provide some inspiration for Danny's synesthesia and loss thereof. The Brian Injury Association of America, including the website of the Iowa branch, had wonderful resources for support and information. For one of the most common types of injury experienced in the country, brain injury is still incredibly misunderstood in its range of experiences. Thank you to those impacted by brain injury who spoke with me. I am grateful that you took the time.

Thank you to Ames for being the amazingly weird and wonderful place you are. Some places in this book are amalgamations and imagination, but I am so proud to call Iowa home. Thanks to my local bookstore, The Book Shoppe, and staff and librarians at the Ericson Public Library for the cheerleading and support. Thank you to my coworkers in the departments of English and Speech Communications at Iowa State, and to ISU's current president, Wendy Winterstein (an entomologist by trade!) who very patiently discussed Monarch migration with me for fifteen minutes at a dinner party one time.

Finally, thank you to my support system. My friends have been my island in all of this. Thank you for wine and book club nights and just being there. A big shout out to Tiffany Morgan: you saved me with your dining room table, Wi-Fi, and endless long walks. Online friends: thank you for helping me through the next circle of pub hell. 2020 Debuts, we've been through some shit; thank you and congrats to us all. WFWA Write-In fam, thank you for inspiring me to put butt in chair and get to work with a smile on my face. To my day care providers, babysitters, and children's teachers: thank you a zillion-times over. Nothing makes you appreciate the people who help you raise your kids more than a worldwide disaster. Pre-pandemic, your work and love of my children gave me space to write and work at the same time.

Thank you to my family: in-laws, outlaws, and all. Jeremy, thank you for being my big brother and introducing me to sci-fi. Janine, thank you for loving me in all of my brattiest stages and letting me aspire to be as cool as you. Alysa, I used to read you bad short stories on the phone and you helped me have confidence to write better ones. Thank you to my parents, who have always encouraged my writing. Mom, thank you for passing on a love of books, writing, and learning (and the homemade face masks!); and Dad, thank you for reading comics to me, getting me into gardening, and for dissuading me from pursing a PhD. My kids P, A, and J (all still too

416

young to read this) are the colors in my music. Thanks for hunting for bugs with me, and thank you for not bringing them inside the house. Last, but not least, thank you to Mark, my husband and partner in puns, in *Great British Bake-Off* marathons, and in life. You may not really read fiction, but you helped this exist. Thank you for extreme my-wife-has-to-edit-and-debut-during-a-pandemic-level spouse support. So much.

# READING GROUP
# DISCUSSION QUESTIONS

1. The epigraph of this novel asks if a love of insects can make a difference in the world. Did reading about someone who studied and loved bugs change any of your impressions of them? Is there anything that other people might find strange or unusual that is central to your worldview?

2. Greta and Danny are twins but see the world—literally and figuratively—in very different ways. Who are you more like? Why?

3. Greta's independence and passion for her work define her as a character. Do Greta's priorities change as she becomes one of Danny's caretakers? If so, how?

4. Meg and Danny start their relationship while Meg is still engaged to someone else. Martha leaves partly because of her relationship with another man. Greta finds herself still attracted to her ex-boyfriend Brandon. One of the book's major themes is faithfulness—or the lack thereof. Do you think any of the characters are redeemable considering their actions? What's the line with cheating? Is it black and white or shades of gray?

5. Throughout the novel, many characters look for help in formal support groups. In what ways can formal support groups be different from support from friends? How do you think Greta benefitted from these relationships in the novel, if at all?

6. Greta and Meg butt heads throughout the book, most obviously because Greta distrusts Meg for her infidelity. By the end, Greta accepts Meg back into her life for the sake of her twin brother, Danny, but they never speak again about how Danny was the other guy in Meg's first engagement. How do you think Greta's attitude toward Meg has changed and/or stayed the same?

7. Greta and Max's relationship changes over the course of the novel. If Greta hadn't been forced to return home from Costa Rica, do you think this change would have happened? Why or why not?

8. Despite Greta's protestations, she does bear similar tangible and intangible traits to Martha. In what ways are Greta and Martha similar? Have you ever butted heads with your own parents? In what ways have you been able to find common ground with them?

9. The butterfly effect states that small actions can have outsized consequences. What are some actions that radically change the

courses of characters' lives in this novel? Do you believe in the butterfly effect? Why or why not?

10. From whose perspective would you want to see this story retold: Danny, Meg, Max, Martha, or someone else? What do you think that version of events might have added to the narrative?

**Center Point Large Print**
600 Brooks Road / PO Box 1
Thorndike, ME 04986-0001 USA

(207) 568-3717

**US & Canada:**
**1 800 929-9108**
www.centerpointlargeprint.com